ABOUT TI

CW00541712

Rachael Lucas writes novels for adults and teenagers, including the Carnegie nominated *The State of Grace*, which was selected as an Outstanding Book for Young People with Disabilities by IBBY. She lives on a beautiful stretch of coastline in the north west of England with her family and two very enthusiastic spaniels. When she's not writing at the kitchen table with a cup of coffee by her side, she's out walking the dogs on the beach or in the nearby pinewoods.

Keep up with Rachael - follow her on Facebook @rachaellucaswriter where you can join her VIP reader group and hear the latest book news and behind the scenes updates.

ALSO BY RACHAEL LUCAS

CHRISTMAS AT APPLEMORE

RACHAEL LUCAS

PRAISE FOR RACHAEL LUCAS

Absolutely delightful - The Winter Cottage is ROMANTIC and FUN and like a big, squishy hug.

— MARIAN KEYES

Rachael Lucas has created an irresistible world to disappear into once again

— LOUISE O'NEILL

A gift to anyone in need of comfort, calm, and a deep breath of Scottish fresh air. Charming, tender and funny. (Also: nice dogs, hot men, and big houses!)

— ELLA RISBRIDGER

The most deliciously wintry, sizzlingly romantic hug of a book - the perfect Christmas comfort read

— CRESSIDA MCLAUGHLIN

Cover design by Diane Meacham

For Alice, Hayley and Keris.

CHAPTER ONE

'LOOK AT THAT.'

Polly Fraser gave a dreamy sigh.

With a gentle thud, a deliciously scented cardboard box landed on the pages of her gossip magazine, obscuring the photographs Polly was swooning over. She looked up into the eyes of her friend Anna, who had arrived with a delivery, and was standing on the other side of the counter of Applemore Farm Shop with hands on her hips and an amused expression on her pale, freckled face.

'I don't know why you read that stuff.' Anna made a little *ta-dah* gesture. 'One delivery of cinnamon raisin cookies and double chocolate brownies - with gold leaf for extra Christmas sparkle.' She lifted the lid, so the scent of sweet wintry spices and chocolate floated through the air.

'Yum,' said Polly, still distracted. She glanced up, giving Anna a quick smile of thanks and raised a finger. 'Two secs.' Then she turned the page, sliding the box to the side of the counter so she could examine the glamorous red-carpet photographs from a film premiere in London.

'Polly! You nearly knocked these off!' Anna reached

out to grab a pile of delicate, hand-painted wooden Christmas tree ornaments which were balancing precariously on the edge of the counter. 'If you don't get your head out of that magazine you're going to have wrecked half your Christmas stock before it's even on the shelves.' She raised a disapproving eyebrow.

'I know, I know,' said Polly, as she turned the magazine around to show Anna, who was carefully placing the ornaments safely away from the edge. 'But wouldn't you love to be there?'

Anna shook her head. She was standing with one protective hand on the box of cakes, as if to guard them from the same fate as the decorations.

'No, I can categorically state that I would not. Don't know why you read this stuff.' Anna tucked an unruly curl of hair behind her ear as she looked down at the open spread of the page. An assortment of glamorous women with beautifully done hair and make-up were standing on the red carpet of a premiere. The dresses were a riot of bright coloured silks and satins - like an assortment of jewels, Polly thought, or a tin of Christmas chocolates.

'Because it's a million miles from life in a tiny village in the Highlands, and living vicariously is the only excitement I get.'

Polly lifted the wrapping on the top of the box to reveal an array of delights. Taking out one of the new cinnamon and raisin cookies, she looked at it reverently for a moment before nibbling the edge with a groan of delight.

'These are amazing,' she said, as the biscuit melted in her mouth. Anna was a genius.

'Thanks. Anyway, what's with the itchy feet? I thought you loved being here.' Anna glanced up at her, eyebrows drawn together slightly, an expression of concern on her face. 'You're not planning on upping sticks and leaving Applemore for the bright lights of Hollywood?'

'Of course I love being here.' Polly snapped off another piece of cookie and popped it in her mouth. She looked across the shop, taking in the white-painted walls of the converted farm building and the wooden shelves which were hung with greenery and glowing with tiny sparkles of light. The archway led through to the cosy, busy coffee shop which was full of customers. A tiny pink Christmas tree dressed with coloured lights twinkled on the counter next to the till. It was as lovely as ever, all of it. The word but hung silently in the air. She wondered if Anna could sense it and almost confided how she was feeling. A moment later a grey-haired woman walked into through the door, the little bell tinkling a welcome, and the moment was lost. She picked up one of the wicker baskets by the door, popping it over her arm and smiling a hello in their direction.

'Let me know if you need any help,' Polly said, brushing crumbs from the side of her mouth and closing the magazine, putting it back under the counter. Never mind red carpet glamour, she had a shop to run, and the Christmas preparations to organise.

Anna glanced at the clock which hung on the wall above Polly's head.

'I'd better get back. There's a Christmas show at the nursery school and I promised I'd be there to bump up the numbers. I swear Christmas gets earlier every year.'

Polly, who'd been playing Christmas tunes on the Farm Shop speakers for the last few weeks, gave a rueful smile as she looked at the wooden tree ornaments. 'Guilty as charged. I've always been the same. The moment Halloween is done, I can't help getting excited. Who doesn't like hot chocolate with candy canes, and cinnamon-scented everything, and covering the place in fairy lights, and…'

Anna raised an amused eyebrow. 'This place is always covered in fairy lights.'

'Alright, so I have fairy lights up all year round. It's not a cardinal sin, is it?' Polly shrugged, laughing. Her little cottage glowed with tiny lights as well, hanging round the front door and decorating the wooden mantel over the fire all months of the year. Christmas, however, was her time to go to town. She'd ordered another four vast boxes of solar-powered lights to decorate outside, and her brother Lachlan had promised her a freshly cut tree from his wood, which he was planning to deliver later in the week. Ever since she'd been a little girl, she'd wanted to make every-where look as homely and cosy as possible… which hadn't always been easy, growing up in the chilly, dilapidated Applemore House.

'I'd better get off,' Anna said, leaning over to rap Polly on the knuckles with a finger. 'Don't eat all the merchandise.'

Polly widened her eyes in mock-horror. 'As if I would.'

It was typical of Applemore, she thought, serving a customer a few moments later, that even when she was busy, Anna was going to help her friend. Here in the village everyone looked out for each other. There were no secrets in a tiny place like this. Yes, that might mean that everyone knew everyone's business and you couldn't sneeze without hearing half an hour later on the grapevine that you'd caught a terrible flu and should be at home in bed. But, if you really were sick, the villagers would rally together to help. It was that sort of place.

Since she'd opened the Farm Shop in a collection of old outbuildings in the grounds of Applemore House, it had become a central hub for news and gossip, so she always knew what was going on, despite being outside the village itself. The village was busy in summer with tourists, but numbers were dropping at the village school as more and more of the houses in the village were bought up by second home owners. If they weren't careful, the place was going to be taken over by people who didn't come from Applemore, and who didn't have the same tie to the place as they did. Sales were noticeably down at the shop compared to the summer season, although the new baking courses that Matt, who'd taken on one of the other outbuildings, was offering seemed to be a tremendous hit. There was a little gallery, now, too, where local artists worked together to sell their work – taking it in turns to work from the studio which looked across the fields and be on call for any visitors that popped in looking for a piece of artwork to take home as a souvenir from their visit to the Highlands.

Polly sighed again. Despite the sparkles that surrounded her, she was feeling distinctly un-shiny. She needed to get herself out of this slump – she knew what was wrong, but it was hard to admit it to herself. She loved living here, catching up on village gossip, being part of a little close-knit community. There was only one problem, and there was absolutely nothing she could do about it.

'Penny for them?' Gavin, who ran the coffee shop through the little stone archway at the far side of the shop, strode towards her, lean and immaculately attired as always, in a close-fitting black polo shirt and matching black jeans. 'What's up with your grumpy face?'

'Nothing.' Polly shook herself into a better frame of mind. 'Just having one of those days.'

'We all have them, lovey,' he said, in his warm, deep Welsh accent. 'Leave Jen in charge of the till and come over and tell your Uncle Gavin all your troubles.'

Jenny, who worked part-time for Polly, was re-organising a display of Christmas-scented candles at the far side of the shop. She looked up, glancing from Polly to Gavin and giving a brief nod. 'I'll man the decks,' she said, putting one more candle at the front of the display and dusting herself down as she stood up.

'Right then,' said Gavin, taking her by the hand and towing her across the shop, making her laugh, 'Sit yourself down there, and I'm going to feed you coffee and you're going to tell me why my little Polly Sunshine is so gloomy today. You've been like this for days now.'

She sat down as instructed, and watched as Gavin ducked behind the counter of the coffee shop, squeezing behind his boyfriend Tom to make a couple of coffees. Meanwhile, Tom prepared pots of tea and set out slices of cake on plates for a group of damp customers in walking gear.

'As if by magic,' said Gavin a moment later, brandishing two cups on China saucers, each with a biscuit perched neatly on the side. 'This is a new roast. You can tell me what you think.' He sat back expectantly as she took a sip.

'Lovely,' said Polly, who couldn't really tell the difference between one coffee bean and another. She unwrapped the biscuit and nibbled the edge.

'Liar,' said Gavin, with a grin. 'They all taste the same to you, don't they?'

'Busted!' she laughed. 'But if it helps they all taste really good.'

Gavin took a sip, closing his eyes in blissful appreciation. 'No finesse, that's your trouble,' he said a moment later. 'You might come from a big posh castle, but your taste buds are definitely more Heinz beans on toast and Pot Noodles.'

'Nothing wrong with a Pot Noodle.' It was a standing joke amongst her three siblings that she was the worst cook of the lot.

'Well, you've got Harry to make you delicious gourmet meals on tap. You two are thick as thieves.'

'Hardly.' Polly looked down into the depths of her cup, hoping desperately that her face wasn't giving anything away. Something twisted in her stomach. Harry Robertson ran the Applemore Hotel, which he'd taken over when his parents retired. Despite vague protestations from stick-in-the-mud locals who weren't fans of change, he was about to drag the place into this century with the help of investment from Rob Jones, who'd recently moved to the village, and was in a relationship with Polly's oldest sister, Charlotte.

When she'd come back to Applemore after a few years away, first studying at university and then working for a well-off family as their nanny, it had coincided with Harry's return from almost a decade away living and working in Sydney. The relationship between them was so easy, and they'd quickly become closer – but as friends, nothing more. Harry saw her as a buddy, someone he could run ideas by, and chat about the difficulties of bringing a business into the present when it'd been stuck in the past forever. The trouble was, spending time with Harry made her heart thud in her chest and filled her with a fizz of excitement she'd never felt before. That – not that she could ever admit it to Anna, or to Gavin, or God forbid to her siblings – was why she was so down in the dumps. Why would Harry see her as anything other than his friend's kid sister? Never mind the fact she was almost 30 - her brother and sisters still had a habit of treating her as the baby of the family. She sighed. Maybe it was time for a change, even if escaping to Hollywood to dress up in slinky satin outfits and pose at movie premieres was unlikely.

'That's a big sigh,' said Gavin, breaking into her thoughts. 'What's the gossip, then? Have you got the latest on what's happening with the hotel renovations?'

She brightened, reaching across and helping herself to his cookie. Gavin gave a tiny nod to say that yes, she could eat it, as she knew he would. He watched his figure like a hawk and eschewed all refined sugars.

'I think it's all systems go as soon as the last guests are gone, which should be... end of the week, maybe?'

'And then?'

'Kenny the builder's coming in to do a load of work, and Harry's got this amazing interior design person who has done all these sketches. New carpets – they're finally getting rid of those awful tartan things – and it's going to be really bright and modern looking.'

'About time too,' said Gavin with feeling. 'He's got a brilliant chef in Conor, and the place has so much potential. Imagine how much money he'll make when it doesn't look like something from fifty years ago?'

'I know.' Polly felt a swell of pride at how hard Harry had worked to pull it all together. 'And they're looking for an old vintage Airstream caravan to make into a seafood shack as well. Next summer is going to be amazing.'

'There's the smile I've been looking for,' said Gavin, reaching over and chucking her under the chin as if she was a truculent child. 'That's more like it.'

Polly shook her head, laughing. 'Don't you start treating me like a baby. I have enough trouble with that from the others.'

'It's only because you're adorable and sweet, my love.'

'I'll have you know I'm a hard-nosed business woman,' she protested, raising a teasing eyebrow.

'Oh, I don't deny that. You've made a massive success out of a dilapidated old stable building and now you've got the bakery and the gallery as well.'

'Next summer we're going to have art classes, too. And Beth's going to be doing Christmas wreath making workshops here in the evenings.' That reminded her, she must get the flyers Beth had printed off and put some beside the till.

'You're brilliant. So what is with the glum mood? You haven't been yourself for the last couple of weeks.'

Polly shrugged. 'Itchy feet, maybe? I've got this place up and running, and there's not much more I can do to make it grow unless I add on extra buildings or convert the big barn out the back, and that would take loads of work.'

'You need a bit of excitement. I think you're stuck in a bit of a rut.' Gavin rubbed his chin thoughtfully.

'What kind of excitement?'

He fixed her with a look and waggled his eyebrows. 'You know what kind I'm talking about, Polly Fraser. You're gorgeous, funny, clever, and still bloody single. You need to get yourself out there and meet someone. Everyone else in the family has paired up. What are you waiting for?'

Harry Robertson, she thought, but that's never going to happen.

She pulled a face and made an open-handed gesture. 'Come on, Gav, I know you and Tom are all loved up and happy, but it doesn't take a genius to work out that the dating pool in Applemore is pretty much non-existent.'

'You might be surprised. Tom's got a cousin who's moved back to the area. Why don't I have a quiet word, see if I can set you up on a hot date?'

Across the other side of the room, as if aware he was

being talked about, Tom looked across at them and gave a little wave.

'Absolutely no way.' Polly pushed her chair back and made to get up. The metal squealed against the polished wooden floor and the group of walkers looked briefly across at them with surprised expressions before they turned away, polite and British, to drink their tea. 'I've been on set up dates before. They're always a disaster.'

'This one might not be. You've got to kiss a few frogs, and all that. What's the alternative?' Gavin clattered his mug down onto the table and rubbed his nose thoughtfully. Polly looked around the little coffee shop, where the half the tables were full of locals she recognised, and the other half populated by out-of-season tourists clad in sensible all-weather gear. If she wasn't careful, she'd be sitting here in fifteen years looking at the same thing, and nothing in her life would have changed.

'Fine,' she said, crossing her arms and giving a resigned sigh. 'I will go on a blind date with Tom's weird cousin. If that's what it takes to get you off my back.'

CHAPTER TWO

'ONE MORE WEEK,' Harry Robertson intoned under his breath. He signed the delivery slip and waved off the brewery truck from outside the Applemore Hotel. The sky was grey, and icy cold rain was trickling down his neck. He gave a wave of farewell to the driver as he headed out of the village, and on to his next stop. A gull stood on the metal rail of the bay opposite, looking at him beadily.

The tide was out, and in the distance he could see a couple of the local fishermen checking over their lobster pots, which were stacked up now the season was over. It had been a long summer and he was very much looking forward to not having to greet hotel guests with a smile, or to stand behind the bar listening to Old Jimmy the farmer giving a detailed analysis of the problems of farming today as he supped the same pint of beer for an hour and a half. Normally he kept the hotel ticking over all through the year. His parents always had, despite the fact that in winter they did little more than break even.

It had caused a minor village scandal when he'd put up signs by the bar and a note in the Applemore Newsletter telling locals that he'd be closing for renovations, ready to open in January with an all-new, revamped, modern Applemore Hotel.

'I dinnae see what's wrong with the place the way it is,' Old Jimmy had grumbled, shaking out his copy of The Scottish Farmer and putting it down on the bar.

'It hasn't been redecorated for twenty odd years,' Harry had pointed out, for the umpteenth time, drying glasses and placing them on the shelf above the beer pumps.

'Aye, and it's fine the way it is.' Jimmy harrumphed.

'It'll be even nicer.'

Old Jimmy had given a sorrowful shake of his head and returned to reading the cattle prices.

Despite constant grumbling, the villagers had come to terms with the fact that Harry was shutting up shop for a month, helped by the fact that he'd compromised with a weekend beer pickup service. Each Friday and Saturday night, when most right-minded people would be taking advantage of the time off, he was going to open the doors for villagers to pop in and collect growlers of their favourite ale, which he'd ordered in especially. It would bring in a tiny bit of money – if he was honest, not enough to make it worthwhile – but most importantly he'd keep their goodwill. Not, as his financial backer and new friend Rob Jones had pointed out, that they had anywhere else to go, in the meantime. Applemore was a one-bar town, and competition was non-existent. He dumped the barrel down in the cellar and headed back upstairs.

'I've had a couple call about a last minute booking,' said Phoebe, who worked behind the bar. She shook back her rainbow-coloured hair and lifted an eyebrow, fixing him with a rueful expression.

'I said no more,' Harry began, but Phoebe lifted a finger to stop him.

'I know, I know…' she widened her eyes. 'But we're not closing until next week. Think of the money.' As she spoke one of the long strings of tinsel she'd stuck above the bar flopped down onto the ground. The Christmas decorations were as tired as he was. He picked it up, squashing it back into the Blu Tack so it stayed in place. He was well and truly Christmassed-out, and they hadn't even got started. Behind the bar Phoebe had propped up all the cards they'd received from villagers, and they balanced precariously amongst the colourful fruit-flavoured gins along the top shelf.

'I'm thinking of the money we're about to spend on Kenny's building work. And the renovations. And the fixtures and fittings, and all the rest.'

He'd thought that having an investor come in would make things easier, but instead – despite Rob's easy-going nature – Harry had found himself counting the pennies, conscious that he didn't want to look as if he was taking advantage of his partner's vast wealth.

'So do you want me to tell them no?'

Harry gazed out of the window for a moment, watching as a fishing boat chugged off towards the skyline. The sky was still leaden, and the distant purple hills of the islands could barely be seen through the low clouds.

It had been a weird feeling to finally have the money to make the changes he'd dreamed of. He'd always thought that if someone handed him a blank cheque and told him to do what he wanted he'd go wild, but the reality had been quite different. It felt like a huge responsibility – he had to get the place right to justify Rob's investment – and while he believed without doubt that a new, renovated

Applemore Hotel would bring in a whole new wave of guests, he still felt edgy.

'I was hoping we could get the place stripped out and ready for the work,' he said, picking up a cloth and absent-mindedly wiping the surface of the already spotless bar. Phoebe watched him with a beady expression.

'He said they'd always wanted to visit. Something about it being a surprise and some family connection, and – oh, I can't remember exactly what it was, but he was pretty determined. Said he didn't mind paying over the odds if that helped.'

'Weird.' They did get a lot of guests who'd visited years before on family holidays, it was true, but none of them were in the habit of waving wads of cash around to make sure they got their way. 'Alright, what harm can it do. But that is it, okay? Absolutely no more surprise bookings. This place is closing on Monday next week and will not be opening the doors until the new year.'

'Aye aye, cap'n.' Phoebe flashed him a grin and clicked her heels together as she raised a hand in a salute.

'Very funny,' Harry said, shaking his head. He looked across the bar, where two men were sitting drinking pints and playing a game of chess at the table by the fire, enjoying the peace of the mid-afternoon lull. 'Right, I'm going to sort out the cellar as we're quiet. Give me a shout if we have a sudden influx of customers.'

Phoebe gave him a doubtful look. 'Will do.'

He busied himself sorting the ice machine, which was temperamental on a good day. He swept and washed down the floor, stacked all the bottles of fruit juices and mixers on the shelves, and as he cleared away the boxes and wrapping he thought, not for the first time, how they seemed to pile up in corners as soon as he turned his back. Phoebe was brilliant with the customers but apparently oblivious to mess. He shook his head as he stuffed the cardboard into the recycling bin outside.

'Hello stranger,' said a familiar Welsh voice from over his shoulder. Harry turned to see Gavin standing at the end of the little alleyway which divided the hotel from the row of white-painted cottages.

'How's it going?' Harry strode across to say hello, marvelling at Gavin's choice of rainwear. 'Nice…mackintosh.'

'You think?' Gavin beamed and did a little twirl.

'Well, you're not going to get hit by traffic, that's for certain.'

Gavin adjusted the bright yellow collar of his raincoat. 'I happen to think there's nothing wrong with a bit of colour, that's all. All you Highlanders spend all your time looking like you're trying to blend in with the scenery.'

'So you've decided to bring a bit of fabulousness to Applemore?'

'Exactly.' Gavin nodded. 'Anyway, what's happening in your world? Haven't seen you for ages, now you're hanging out with Charlotte's hot totty and planning world domination.'

Harry couldn't help laughing. Gavin was a breath of fresh air. He'd settled into village life having arrived with his boyfriend Tom, who'd left Applemore years before. Together they'd made a success of the coffee shop inside Polly's farm shop, and the villagers had taken the couple to their hearts. It was lovely to see.

'I'm not *hanging around with Charlotte's hot totty*, I'm hanging out with Rob and sorting out how we're going to make this place amazing.'

'You've got to admit that Rob's easy on the eye, though.' Gavin waggled his eyebrows.

'I have not,' Harry shook his head. 'He's not my type.'

'Talking of which,' said Gavin, with a sly grin, 'I was just chatting to Polly about the dire state of her love life. I'm trying to fix her up on a date with Tom's hunky cousin who's come back to live up here. I mean I assume he's hunky if he's related to Tom. Genetics, and all that.'

Harry shifted uncomfortably, stepping back and thrusting a hand in his back pocket, trying to look nonchalant. 'That sounds like a good idea. Poll is lovely.'

'She is,' Gavin agreed, 'But she's been single forever. Let's face it, Applemore isn't exactly thronging with eligible men.'

'I have to admit that's not really my department.'

Gavin grinned and raised an eyebrow.

'This cousin of Tom's,' Harry blurted out, surprising himself. 'He is decent, isn't he?' Something made him uncomfortable about the thought of Polly going off on a hot date with some random bloke.

'Course he is. I mean I haven't met him, but Tom says he's sound. He's hardly about to set her up with a serial killer now, is he?'

'Fair enough.' Harry made an open handed gesture, trying to let go of the uneasy feeling. 'I had no idea men were in such short supply.'

'Well, every time a single bloke appears in the village one of the Frasers snaps them up. I mean look at Beth's Jack – he's a bit of alright, isn't he? And now Charlotte and Rob are an item. The other women in the village don't get a look in.' Gavin chuckled at his own joke.

A Land Rover drove past at that moment, giving a beep of the horn in greeting. Harry and Gavin both raised a hand as Charlotte Fraser drove past.

'Probably off to see how work is doing on Midsummer House,' said Gavin.

'I hope she's remembered Kenny is mine for the next

month,' said Harry, watching as the Land Rover stopped at the junction at the end of the street before indicating right and heading out of the village. 'You know what Charlotte's like when she gets the bit between her teeth. I suppose it might be different now she's got Rob, mind you.'

Gavin looked at him with a dubious expression. 'You're expecting the most focused workaholic we know to be tempered by a multi-millionaire businessman?'

'Aye,' Harry rubbed his chin thoughtfully. 'You've got a point there.'

'I'm sure she's remembered. Anyway, Rob can always afford to get some big shot builder in from Inverness if he wants to keep things going.'

'True.' Harry pushed a hand through his hair, which was damp with sea mist. Down the road, he could see a worker from the Highland Council parking up alongside one of the streetlights that had been out of action for ages. Not before time, he thought.

Before long, the street would be lit up with the glow of strings of Christmas lights, as everyone decorated the shops and house windows to make the place look festive. Already Christmas trees were appearing in windows, and at night the village had taken on an expectant air. There were signs on the village noticeboard about school carol concerts and tree lighting ceremonies, and a special minibus was being organised to take the villagers on a Christmas shopping trip to Inverness. Thank goodness he didn't have to think about any of that. He knew he was doing a very good impression of the Grinch, but it was a relief to opt out of all things Christmas for once.

Harry had already decided he'd duck out of getting a tree, have a chilled out day at home, and maybe take his mountain bike out. This was one year he could pretend the festive season wasn't happening. He'd been invited to spend the day with his friend Lachlan and the rest of the Fraser clan up at Applemore House, but he'd resolved to try and put a bit of space between himself and Polly. Hopefully that way he might manage to get a handle on things. They'd spent an increasing amount of time together over the last few months, but something Lachlan had said a while back had given him the distinct impression he would have strong opinions about him making a move. That was even if Polly saw him as anything other than a good friend, which he was pretty sure she didn't.

'I better get off,' Gavin's voice broke into his thoughts.

Harry shook himself back to earth.

'Alright mate –' he tried to keep his tone light. 'If you're heading back to the shop, say hi to Poll for me. I haven't seen her for ages.'

Gavin gave him a fleeting glance, and Harry, feeling he was being observed, bent to pick up a stray piece of paper that was being buffeted in the wind.

'I'll tell her you were asking after her. Don't be a stranger, now.'

And with that, Gavin pulled up the hood of his hideous yellow mac and headed off down the street.

Harry stood for a moment watching him, a splash of colour in an otherwise grey day. He glanced down, seeing a flash of ginger fur. It was Pickle, the wildly anti-social half-feral cat who lived in an outbuilding beside the hotel, deigning to be fed once a day but refusing any other form of human contact. If I'm not careful, that's what's going to happen to me, thought Harry, turning to head back inside.

'You alright? You look like the end of the world is nigh.' Phoebe – who was an angel, and liked keeping busy – had taken down all the bottles from the mirrored shelf behind the bar and was wiping them all clean. 'Thought I'd do this so when we put them away before Kenny builds the new bar they won't get all sticky. This sloe gin stuff is like superglue.'

'It's all the sugar,' said Harry, absently. 'And yeah, I'm fine. Just got a lot on my mind.'

Phoebe's happy chatter distracted him as they worked together to clear up. Now and then they stopped to serve the occasional customer, catching up on locals and the odd tourist who appeared – damp and glad of the warmth of the fire – to have a drink and one of the bar snacks that were knocked up by the chef, Conor. He was experimenting with new dishes while they were quiet, and delicious scents were emanating from behind the swinging metal door.

'I'm ravenous,' said Phoebe, as they put the last bottles back up on the shelf. Conor, who'd popped out from the kitchen to grab a Coke from behind the bar, raised a finger.

'Wait two secs.'

A moment later he returned with a platter of miniature burgers in soft brioche rolls. Melted cheese oozed down the side of the patties, making Harry's stomach growl.

'I didn't think I was hungry. Now I am.'

'Tuck in,' said Conor, leaning a hip against the bar and crossing his legs. 'I want you to tell me which combo you like best.'

'They're not the same?'

'Course not.' Conor pointed to one. 'This is a chuck and brisket slider with double cheese, maple bacon, beef dripping red onions, homemade pickles and a steamed and buttered bun.' And – as if it was self-explanatory – he then pointed to the other, which looked remarkably similar. 'And *this* one is topped with American cheese, smoked streaky bacon, cherry rubbed pulled pork smoked with cherry wood, pickled red cabbage and a cherry cola barbecue sauce on a toasted mini brioche.'

'I'll have the cherry one,' said Phoebe, cheerfully. 'You can have the... whatever the other stuff was.'

Conor shook his head sorrowfully, passing one of the plates towards Harry, who bit into the burger. Conor stared at them both intently.

'My god, this is amazing,' said Harry, through a mouthful of food.

'Mmm,' nodded Phoebe. She wiped her chin.

'Excellent news,' said Conor, looking pleased with himself. 'I was thinking we might do some sort of street food menu in the summer. What d'you reckon?'

Harry wiped his mouth with the back of his hand. 'Yeah. Absolutely. Whatever.' The combination of tastes were astonishing. 'You know I'll go with whatever you want.'

'Within reason, I'm guessing,' said Conor, with a grin. 'No Wagyu steak burgers?'

'I'm not sure we're Wagyu steak level yet.' Harry took another miniature burger.

'Give it a couple of years,' said Conor, 'And we'll be getting prizes all over the shop.'

Harry frowned. He knew how ambitious Conor was, and how much of a difference he'd made to the hotel. Trying to keep hold of a chef who had the raw talent that Conor had was going to be hard. If the hotel was a success, hopefully they'd be able to make enough money to give him a decent pay rise and make staying worth his while. In the meantime, Harry had worked out that giving Conor his head and allowing him to have free rein in the kitchen – Wagyu steaks excluded – was the secret to keeping him on board. If they could get some decent publicity for the place when it re-opened, that would make all the difference. He needed some sort of miracle for that to happen. His new friend and investor Rob, meanwhile, was confident that they'd sort it out – but Rob had the innate confidence of a man who'd grown up with money, and who had the sort of wealth that Harry could only dream of. Harry, who'd grown up watching his parents struggle to keep the business afloat, understood the Highland economy was precarious, and they were reliant on people being willing to make the trek across the country from Inverness – a good hour and a half away by car – to visit.

'I reckon we'll have people queuing down the street for these,' he said, a moment later.

'That's the plan,' said Conor, looking gratified. He headed back to the kitchen, wiping his hands on his apron. Harry and Phoebe ate the rest of the burgers in a blissful silence. Conor really was good.

'If you're alright, Harry, can I nip off a bit early? I've got a date later.' Phoebe said, after her last mouthful of burger. She'd been seeing Danny, who was second in command at the outdoor adventure centre outside the village, for some time now. Harry noticed that whenever she spoke about him, her little heart-shaped face lit up.

'Things are getting a bit serious between you two, aren't they?'

Phoebe ducked her head, looking slightly pink-cheeked. 'A bit.'

'It'll be wedding bells next.'

'Shut up, you,' said Phoebe, with a giggle. 'Right, if it's okay I'll get going. Let me take these through to the kitchen.'

Harry watched as she skipped off to the kitchen, full of the joys of young love. Something inside him felt off, as if he wasn't quite right. Maybe it was the burger, he thought, as he settled himself behind the bar for the evening. Or maybe – he grimaced at his reflection in the mirror behind the bottles of gin – it was the prospect of Polly heading off on a date with some random bloke. At this rate, everyone in the village was going to be coupled up and he'd be left on his own. Somehow though, the thought of that didn't bother him as much as Polly ending up with someone else.

'Hello Murdo,' he said, as one of the village regulars appeared in through the door.

'I thought I'd better take advantage before you close down and I have to spend every evening with my wife,' said the old man, with a grim smile. 'You should think yourself lucky you've dodged a bullet on the marriage front, lad.'

Harry busied himself with pouring a drink for Murdo. He heard Lachlan's words echoing in his head – one of those seemingly innocuous conversations which held more weight than appearances suggested.

'You're not the settling down type,' Lachlan had said, laughing. Harry, who'd been holding Lachlan's baby girl at the time, had looked down at her and wondered how he'd somehow got stuck with that mantle, because he'd travelled the world and never found someone he wanted to be with long term.

'I might be.' He'd raised an eyebrow, jiggling baby Kitty and making her gurgle with laughter. 'You never know. Look at you and Rilla – you're all loved-up and settled.'

Lachlan had lifted a shoulder in a shrug. 'Yeah, but you're a free spirit. Girl in every port, and all that. I can't see you settling down to domesticity.'

Harry had glanced across the pub to the table where Polly had been sitting chatting to her sister, Charlotte. Lachlan's gaze followed, and there had been a fleeting

22

moment when they'd exchanged a look which Harry had interpreted clearly as *don't even think about it.*

He'd spent his whole life playing the field, and he'd had more than one opportunity to settle down. Until now, he'd always shied away from it. God knows why he was feeling so unsettled suddenly. He shook his head, handing over Murdo a pint of his regular. Maybe it was all the change in the air.

CHAPTER THREE

'THERE'S one of those Kardashians on the beach.'

Polly looked askance at Dolina, the village gossip, who was standing with her arms folded across her capacious bosom and the self-satisfied expression worn by someone who had a brand new piece of information to impart in a village where nothing happened.

'A Kardashian?'

Polly frowned, shifting the flat-packed cardboard boxes she was holding precariously under one arm, and leaned against the white-painted wall of the Applemore Hotel. The sun was trying to break through the clouds, and the wind had dropped. It had howled all night, blowing the branches of the trees outside her little cottage so hard that they crashed against her window, and whipping away the last remaining leaves. Dolina pulled the zip on her green anorak so it fastened tightly underneath her chin, her weather-beaten face with its rosy, weather-beaten cheeks looking for all the world like a Russian doll. All she needed was a headscarf, thought Polly, and suppressed a giggle.

'Aye. I saw her with my own eyes. She was standing on

a rock, all big lips and –' Dolina made an in and out motion with her hands, as if to indicate the swell of big boobs and an even bigger bottom, her pale eyes saucer-shaped with indignation.

'Are you sure it wasn't a mermaid?' There was actually more chance of that happening than a worldwide super-star turning up in the North West Highlands.

'As sure as can be,' said Dolina, with a decisive nod.

Polly felt her eyebrows raising involuntarily. This, after all, was the same Dolina who'd pronounced that Jack, her sister Beth's partner, had been a danger to the village when he'd arrived to set up the now hugely successful outdoor adventure centre. The story of his mysterious past had been blown up out of all proportions by the village rumour mill – started by Dolina, of course – and even after it'd been well and truly quashed, she'd said with narrowed eyes that there was no smoke without fire. Dolina had then had a field day in the summer when Rob turned up to do repairs on his aunt Frances' house outside the village, telling everyone that he was a billionaire who was planning to buy all the houses in the village and take it over. Rob – who had walked into the village hall meeting unheard – had pointed out with a wry grin that he was hundreds of millions short, and that he would be quite happy living in a tent as long as he had Charlotte for company. So it was with several sacks – not one grain – of salt that Polly took this latest newsflash.

'What's all this then?'

Polly turned, hearing the familiar voice. Tall and broad shouldered, tanned after a summer working front of house at the hotel, his sandy-red hair untidy as always, Harry pushed open the door of the hotel. He gave her a half-wink of greeting.

'Hello, stranger. I heard Dolina's voice,' he said, giving

Dolina a cheeky grin, 'and I thought I'd better check she wasn't making mischief.'

Dolina ducked her head and gave a little skittish giggle. She had a soft spot for Harry that she'd never managed to hide very well.

'Och, away with you, Harry Robertson. I was walking down the street to get my messages and I heard something going on down on the beach so I went to have a wee look. I was just telling Polly, but she thinks I'm seeing things. There's one of those Kardashians here in Applemore. Imagine. I tell you what, that's what happens when you start making all these changes.'

'All which changes?' Harry shot Polly a look of confusion. 'You've been reading too many of those gossip magazines. They're coming to life, aren't they?'

Polly giggled. 'Nothing to do with me.'

'You know fine and well what changes I'm talking about,' said Dolina, 'Opening shops, redecorating the hotel, that sort of thing. This village has been perfectly fine for long enough, and now we've got all sorts appearing out of the woodwork.'

Polly pressed her lips together, realising that if she wasn't careful she was going to start laughing and if she did, Harry – who couldn't help himself – would join in. Harry, noticing, arranged his face into an expression of polite concern.

'You don't want the village falling to rack and ruin, now, do you?'

Dolina gave a mutter of acquiescence.

'And you've got the mini-market now, so there's a shop for everyone who can't make it out to my place,' said Polly, reasonably. She'd opened the farm shop when the little shop in the village had closed down, and it was not without an pang of regret that she'd watched as one of the big supermarket chains had applied for planning consent to turn the little store into a mini-mart. Her takings had gone down, but she knew that it was practical for the older villagers who couldn't make their way out to the shop very easily, and after announcing that she'd boycott the place out of principle, she'd grudgingly conceded that it was handy to be able to get a bottle of sauvignon after a long day at work without having to drive the eight miles to the next town.

'So this Kardashian,' Harry said, carefully, 'Was it… alone? Travelling as part of a pack?'

Polly suppressed a snort of amusement. She watched as Harry, loose-limbed and rangy, settled in for the duration. He was leaning against the wall with one casual arm over his head, the other thrust into the pocket of his jeans. Beneath the black fabric of his Applemore Hotel branded polo shirt she could see the lines of his torso and felt a pang of longing. She shook herself, allowing her hair to fall over one eye, hoping neither he nor Dolina would notice the flush of pink she could feel rising on her cheeks. He was a friend, she reminded herself firmly, and nothing more.

'You make it sound like some sort of wild animal,' Harry continued.

'Are you making fun of me, Harry Robertson?' Dolina waggled a playful finger.

'Course not. I'm intrigued on so many levels. I had no idea you were au fait with the Kardashians and their oeuvre.'

Polly pushed her hair back behind her ear and caught his eye. He was sporting with Dolina now and his blue eyes danced with amusement, lines crinkling at their corners as the smile spread across his face.

'I don't live in a cultural vacuum, I'll have you know,'

said Dolina, crisply. 'Jenny and I love a bit of reality television, as it happens. Anyway, I was walking along minding my own business –'

First time for everything, thought Polly, trying desperately to keep a straight face. She bit the inside of her cheek and looked away from Harry, knowing if she caught his eye again she'd be doubled over with laughter at the madness of all of this.

' – and I looked across the beach and there they were, him taking photos and her standing on a rock posing away as if her life depended on it.'

Dolina arched her back and pouted to illustrate her point. Harry gave a snort of laughter which he tried to turn into a cough.

'Well,' said Polly, composing herself as best she could, 'I guess it takes all sorts. Harry, I was just coming to drop off these boxes. Gavin said yesterday that you needed as many as you could get your hands on for packing stuff up before you get going on the renovations.'

She braced for more remonstrations from Dolina about the renovations and all the changes that Applemore was being subjected to as the younger generation tried to drag the village into the present day.

'You,' said Harry, taking the boxes out of her arms, 'are an angel.'

His hand brushed hers and she felt the hairs on her arms stand on end, never more thankful that she was wearing a jumper as she was right then. Honestly, this was ridiculous. Focus, Fraser, she reminded herself. You've got a date coming up with someone else, and Harry Robertson is a friend, nothing more.

'So where are these mystery visitors now?' He cocked an eyebrow at Dolina. A light breeze ruffled the hood of her anorak, which lifted to halo her steely grey hair.

'I should imagine they're still down there on the rocks. I didn't like to interfere.'

Polly felt her eyes widening involuntarily at the prospect of Dolina choosing not to interfere, when it was her reason for living.

'So I just gave them a wee wave and headed up here to go to the shop. I must get on,' she continued. She gave them both a brief nod and bustled up the main street of Applemore, heading for the little mini-supermarket. It would be busy and full of customers nipping in before the school run, all of whom had no idea of the ground-breaking news broadcast waiting for them.

Polly stood by Harry, and together they watched as Dolina made her way into the shop.

'That's going to be round the village in about three seconds flat,' Harry said immediately and they both gave a burst of laughter. Polly watched as a huge smile spread across his face and he raised both hands in a gesture of confusion.

'I tell you what, every time I think this village can't get any weirder, Dolina manages to top it.'

Polly shook her head in bemusement. 'What d'you think she saw?'

'I have literally no idea, but I can categorically state that there's no way it was a Kardashian. Can you think of any reason why a multi-millionaire, or whatever they are, would be doing freezing their ass off doing a photoshoot on the beach?'

Polly stood on tip-toe, as if somehow that would give her the added height needed to see beyond the sea wall and down onto the rocky outcrops on the far side of Applemore beach, but all she could see was the steely blue-grey of the sea, and the white froth of little waves breaking far beyond the shore. Whoever Dolina had seen, they weren't visible from the Applemore Hotel, and much as she'd like to investigate, she'd promised her big sister Beth she'd collect the twins from school at three on the dot, and there was no way she could let them down.

'I need to go and get Edward and Lucy. Promise me solemnly that if anything happens, you'll call me with all the gossip?'

Harry chuckled. 'I'll have you on speed dial, don't worry. I'll see you later, Poll.'

Polly ducked her head, feeling suddenly and inexplicably shy. It was the strangest thing – when Harry had returned from a few years working in Australia, they'd fallen almost instantly into an easy-going friendship which seemed completely natural. Back then, Lachlan still lived and worked in Edinburgh running the brewery, eventually selling his part to secure the money for investment in the future of Applemore House. Not only for himself, but for the whole family and their descendants. Her middle sister Beth had been wrapped up in baby twins and a marriage which was hitting the rocks, and Charlotte, the eldest sister, had been so busy with work that somehow Harry seemed to find his way into her life just when she needed it.

With one last look in the direction of the beach, Polly hurried up the little lane that led to the Applemore Primary School. Whatever had happened of late, things had changed between herself and Harry. It was as if he'd sensed that her feelings for him were stronger and he was pulling back to let her down gently. Anyway, whatever it was she needed to pull herself together and stop hankering after something that was never going to happen. She paused to let a harried girl with red hair chasing after a tall grey and white Husky dog rush past, then pushed open the wrought iron gates of the primary school. Standing with the other parents and guardians, she wrapped her arms around herself as if to ward off the chill in the air. The grey sweater she was wearing was more pretty than practical, and a sudden wind whipped up the lane and swirled a discarded piece of paper around the playground, making her shiver with cold and look longingly at the glowing lights of the classrooms, warm butter-yellow squares decorated with artwork, which shone out from the cool stone walls. The night was growing dark and there was a frost already nipping in the air.

She'd waved a greeting to Miss Harris, the teacher, and was just hurrying them out of the playground, hand in hand with both twins, when she overheard a snippet of conversation.

'Aye, apparently they're shooting some film up here or something. That's what I heard in the shop a wee moment ago.'

Shaking her head in amusement, Polly led the twins back down the lane to the car.

'Why were you smiling at George's mummy, Aunty Polly?' Edward, who was rifling in his bag for a plastic toy dinosaur, looked up a moment later.

The twins didn't miss a trick. No wonder Beth and her partner Jack spent half the time spelling out words and talking in code.

'Oh, just something funny one of the other grown-ups said,' she said, turning the key in the ignition.

'Grown-ups are funny,' Lucy said, a frown on her little face. 'They laugh at things that aren't jokes.'

'I know a joke,' said Edward, looking pleased with himself. 'Why did the giraffe cross the road?'

'I don't know,' said Polly, looking at him in the rear view mirror, with a strong suspicion that she knew what was coming next.

'Because he's a poo?' Lucy gave a shriek of laughter.

'Yes!'

'You two,' said Polly as they laughed uncontrollably. 'One day one of your jokes won't end with poo, won't it?'

'Poo!' said Lucy, and Edward joined in with the chorus, repeating the word over and over. It was going to be a long afternoon. Polly turned down onto the main street, just in time to see a swish of expensively-highlighted hair and a denim clad (and very definitely curvaceous) bottom which sat atop long, slender legs and a pair of very high and completely impractical brown suede boots disappearing through the swinging door that led into the Applemore Hotel. She shook herself. There must be something in the water. First Dolina, now her. Whoever it was, it was guaranteed that there was more chance of one of Edward's dinosaurs coming to life than there was a Kardashian turning up in the tiny Highland village of Applemore.

CHAPTER FOUR

'THAT BOOKING HAS TURNED UP,' called Phoebe up the stairs of the hotel. 'They're in the bar.'

Harry, who was surveying a pile of ancient lever-arch files that his parents hadn't touched in about three decades, straightened up and dusted off his jeans.

'Can you deal with it Phoebe?' He was covered in dust and cobwebs, out of sorts because he was rattled by how he felt after seeing Polly, and absolutely not in the mood to be dealing with last minute guests who'd booked in just at the point when he was looking forward to getting the place sorted. He shook his head, annoyed that he hadn't updated the booking site online. If he'd remembered to do that, they wouldn't be in this situation. But –

'He says he wants to speak to the owner.'

Harry muttered something unrepeatable under his breath and pushed a hand through his hair, hoping he'd dislodged the cobwebs stuck there in the process.

'Give me a minute, I'll be there once I've washed up.'

He soaped his hands with warm water, looking at his reflection in the mirror of the little cloakroom that was set off the office. He looked a bit knackered and in need of a couple of weeks lying on a beach somewhere. Lucky he had six weeks of intensive renovations and no respite in sight, he thought, with a wry smile at his reflection. He puffed out a breath. No point in prevaricating any longer – he might as well bite the bullet and get these last guests out of the way.

Phoebe had switched the music when he wasn't looking and he could hear Mariah Carey crooning about what she wanted for Christmas. It didn't improve his mood.

Downstairs, standing at the bar, was a slim man tapping something into his phone. He was in his mid-twenties with jet black hair slicked back from his face with shiny product and a beard which had been carefully sculpted to enhance high, slanted cheekbones. He wore a black shirt with a white collar, which didn't have a single crease out of place, and he looked up at Harry after a moment with an apologetic smile.

'Sorry mate,' He said, with an East London accent. 'I had to upload something. You know what it's like.'

Harry, who made a mental note once again to take the bookings offline, nodded. 'I do, yes. How can I help? Phoebe said you wanted a word?'

'Ah right,' the man said. 'I wanted to have a quick chat with you before Ivy came back from the bathroom –'

'Baby, it's so sweet,' came a voice a split second later. 'They've even got tartan carpets. It's adorable.'

'Just as well you came this week,' said Harry, as the voice was followed into the room by –

'I'll talk to you later,' said the bloke, giving him a quick look which Harry interpreted as a signal not to say any more. But Harry was distracted by the arrival in the shabby, comfortable, laid-back lounge bar of the Applemore Hotel – which did indeed have tartan carpets, to go along with slightly battered teak tables that had come full circle and were, according to Phoebe, 1970s fashionable again – of a real live Kardashian.

Or near enough, anyway. The urge to grab his phone and call Polly to come and bear witness was almost overwhelming, but he squared his shoulders and slipped into front-of-house mode as if nothing could phase him.

'We made a booking online? For two rooms?' The man had that strange habit he'd grown used to when he lived in Sydney of ending each sentence as if it was a question.

'Two rooms?' Harry looked at the young woman who had sashayed across the room in a pair of impossibly high black suede boots and was now standing, her arm wrapped tightly around her partner's waist, and a huge, extremely toothy and very white smile.

'One for us, one for Felicity,' she said, cheerfully, patting at the side of her thigh. Hearing her owner's summons, a moment later what looked like a pom-pom on very short legs scampered across the floor, pausing only for a moment to sniff at a table leg.

'No you don't,' said the girl, scooping up the tiny dog and kissing it on the nose. It was wearing some sort of red and white snowflake-patterned woollen jumper. Harry dragged his eyes away, trying not to stare in frank disbelief. It wasn't the sort of dog that you saw in Applemore, which was all Labrador retrievers and mud-covered spaniels.

'Mummy has told you before about doing pee-pee on the carpet, hasn't she?'

Harry felt his eyes widening, but said nothing.

'She's used to her own little room,' the man explained. 'If you've got adjoining rooms that would be even better, because that way she can come into bed with us in the morning, but as long as she's next door, that'll be fine.'

'Two rooms,' said Harry, faintly. 'We do have adjoining rooms, yes, but they're – '

He was about to say that Phoebe had probably allocated two of the rooms at the back of the hotel which were still clean and ready to go, and not the front ones where he'd been slowly beginning the process of dismantling furniture and things getting ready for the big revamp project. Somehow, though, he found himself organising Phoebe – who was an angel – to sort out the rooms while he sent the couple to sit by the fire on the other side of the bar.

Once he'd poured them a drink he took a second to grab his phone and message Polly, wondering as he did so if he could manage to take a surreptitious photograph in order to illustrate his point, but decided that it would be pushing it.

Kardashian located, he typed, grinning to himself as a split second later before he'd even finished writing the second part of his message Polly had shot back a reply.

WHATTTT? I need info!

Harry looked across the bar at the unlikely sight. Applemore saw its fair share of tourists and visitors in the summer season, but they were all much of a muchness – hard core walkers dressed in practical weatherproof gear, families holidaying in the Highlands with their children, and since Jack had opened the outdoor adventure centre occasional groups of business people who came on corporate team-building weeks where they sat looking slightly out of place with brand new activity wear. But never in the whole time he'd been running the place – since he came back from laid back Sydney, where everyone was blond and bronzed and surf-chic – had he seen anything like these two. Ivy was petite, with a golden leonine mane of expensively curled hair – more hair than he'd ever seen on one person – and an outfit which would have been more suited to a night on the tiles than an afternoon on the beach of Applemore. As he watched, she took out her phone and passed it to Ben, leaning back with a practised pose and draping one arm across the back of the chair, turning her head to one side to look at the camera through lowered lashes, her extremely shiny lips puckered in a pout. Ben angled the phone and took several snaps of her holding the glass of wine which Harry had delivered a few moments ago.

His phone buzzed again. Harry looked away from the scene, once again dragging his eyes away, and saw Polly's message.

Come on, don't keep me in suspense, I need to know what's going on. What do you mean 'Kardashian located'???

Harry chuckled at the thought of Polly, knowing her fondness for those ridiculous gossip magazines she loved to read, and Dolina, who right now would be imparting her latest morsel of village gossip on the Applemore community Facebook group, which was more often than not filled with nothing more exotic than requests for people to leave their bins out on the right day.

I think, he typed quickly, half an eye on his new guests, *that Dolina sees a Kardashian as more of a concept than an actual person. A species, if you will.*

Sometimes you are really weird, Polly replied.

Okay - to spell it out, I think in Dolina's world anyone who looks like that probably means she's a Kardashian. I think she's one of those online influencers, by the looks of it. Posh hair, designer boyfriend, the lot. What the hell they're doing here is anyone's guess.

Ivy looked across at him and he put his phone down for a second, as if she could tell what he was writing. Where the hell had Phoebe gone? She said she'd only nip upstairs for a moment.

Oh my god, this is killing me. Of all the days… I can't come and look because I've got the twins. Wait – I could bring the twins?

Harry's phone buzzed again and as he read Polly's message, he grinned at the thought of her randomly turning up with Edward and Lucy, Beth's sweet but feisty little bundles of joy, on some spurious errand. Knowing them they'd make short work of the fluffy dog, smear ice-cream or something worse all over Ivy's posh suede boots, and spill Ben's beer.

'Right,' Phoebe said a moment later, 'You owe me one, Robertson, because I'm a miracle worker.'

'You've sorted the rooms?'

Phoebe nodded, her pink and blue hair swishing in its ponytail. 'To be fair they didn't need much, just a quick run over with the hoover and a bit of a dust. The beds were made up and I've moved the cardboard boxes into room 10. We're not expecting any more random social media stars for the weekend, are we?'

She peeked out from behind the pillar that stood at the edge of the bar, then ducked back again, hand over her mouth, eyes saucer shaped. 'I can't believe she's here.'

'Who?'

'Oh my god, Harry, I know you're old but you're not *that* old, surely?'

Harry gestured in confusion. 'Clearly, yes, I am that old. A dinosaur, basically.'

'It's Ivy Winter. She's got a YouTube channel all about make up and she's got like – hang on, let me check – ' Phoebe pulled her phone out of her back pocked and opened up the Instagram app, 'Over half a million followers on Instagram. Oh my days,' she said sliding the phone over to Harry, putting both hands to her cheeks. She looked like a brightly coloured version of Edvard Munch's Scream painting, he thought with amusement as he picked up the phone. On the screen was a photo of Ivy taken earlier – presumably when Dolina had spotted her – squatting on a rock in a pose that looked more than a little at odds with the rugged natural backdrop of Applemore Bay.

'She's actually here,' said Phoebe, picking up the phone reverentially and looking at the screen.

'Well, obviously,' said Harry, tipping his head in the direction of the fireplace on the other side of the room where the couple sat fussing over the little dog, completely oblivious now to Phoebe's fangirling.

'No I know she's *here*,' said Phoebe, as if talking to someone who was very simple and incapable of understanding basic English, 'I mean she's *actually here*.'

And she waggled the phone, with the photograph on the screen, as if somehow being on there made their presence more corporeal than actually sitting in the same room, breathing the same air.

'Sometimes I think you might be completely and utterly barking mad,' said Harry, with a shake of his head.

If you don't tell me more, Robertson, I'm going to spontaneously combust.

He looked down at his own phone, and the message which had just appeared from Polly. He wasn't completely sure what was going on, but it felt very much like the entire village was going completely mad, and he was the only one left with his feet on terra firma.

CHAPTER FIVE

POLLY WAS ABSOLUTELY DYING to bundle the children back into her car and head back into the village, but the twins had very strong opinions about the way their afternoon with their aunt was going to go, and peering at social media stars was very definitely not on their list.

Edward stood on the doorstep of her little cottage, thumb in mouth (a habit that she knew Beth was trying to stop, but Polly thought he looked really cute, so she didn't mind) and looked up at her through his ridiculously long, dark lashes.

'Aunty Poll, can we go to the café and get a cake and some hot chocolate?'

Lucy, who'd already scampered inside, scampered straight back down the hallway as if she'd read her brother's mind. The red and white bobble hat she was wearing was balanced on top of her curls, and she was trailing a matching scarf behind her. Together they looked at Polly with beseeching eyes.

'Please?'

'Oh you two,' said Polly, melting. She'd deliberately left

Jenny in charge of the Farm Shop so she could spend some time with her niece and nephew, and she'd bought some sticker books and a whole heap of carrot sticks and hummus for a Beth-approved after school snack, but…

'Oh go on then, Eddie, leave your book bag there and we'll come and get your things when Mummy comes back from the dentist.'

'Yay!' they chorused, dancing around her as if it was the biggest treat they'd had in months. She held out her hands and together, swinging their arms, they marched around to the courtyard behind Polly's cottage where the Farm Shop and Café – and now gallery, and bakery – were situated. Polly let go of their hands and the children dashed off and clambered up on the old tractor which was parked by the side of the Farm Shop, playing farmers for a little while and burning off some energy. She paused for a moment before they went inside, taking in how pretty it all looked now in the twilight – the huge arched carriage door had been replaced with a full height window which was strung with sparkling lights which glowed in the winter evening. A hand-painted sign announced Matt's Bakery, and she could see Mel, one of the gallery artists, hanging up a new set of her tiny miniatures which were so popular with locals and visitors alike. As if sensing she was being watched, Mel looked up and waved through the window. It was amazing to think that only a few years ago the little cottage had stood cold and empty, and the farm buildings and old dairy had been falling into disrepair. Now the place was bustling and full of life, and she never wanted for something to do – which was a blessing and a curse, living as she did on the premises.

The cottage stood at the entrance to the Applemore Estate. Rilla, her brother's partner, had returned to sort out the cottage where her father had lived after his passing.

She'd intended it to be a brief winter visit before she returned to her travels, working her way around the world teaching English language classes – but when she and Lachlan had rekindled their teenage romance, she'd put those plans on hold. Now she lived up at the big house with him and their adorable baby daughter, Kitty, who was all dark curls and long lashes, just like her mother. Polly, who'd been at a loose end since returning to Applemore, had grabbed the chance to renovate the old buildings and start the Farm Shop, and living in the cottage – leaving her brother and Rilla to settle happily into their new life – had been the perfect solution. Now they were blissfully content, running a little artisan brewery and gin distillery, and her sister Beth was happy with Jack, who'd arrived to run the outdoor adventure centre which was situated in the woodland which had once belonged to the Applemore Estate before it was sold off by one of their ancestors to pay for inheritance tax. And of course Charlotte was totally loved-up with Rob, her millionaire partner who'd recently invested in the Applemore Hotel.

She looked at Edward, who was climbing down from the seat of the tractor and had somehow managed to cover himself in mud. He was pink cheeked from the cold.

'Can we get some cake now?'

'Of course we can, darling. Let's go, Lucy.' Polly scooped up her niece and spun her around before depositing her, giggling, onto the gravelled courtyard. It was an inescapable fact. Everyone was happy, and settled, and paired off... except her. And she knew what was coming when she saw Gavin and Tom, who had already messaged her, excited at the prospect of a spot of match-making. She puffed out a sigh of resignation.

She went inside, and after a few moments of unfastening tricky zips and hanging coats and hats on the back of the chairs, she left the twins sitting at a table with some of the colouring-in sheets and bright chunky crayons in a shiny aluminium tin which Gavin and Tom provided for children to play with while their parents enjoyed a well-earned coffee and piece of cake.

'I'll be two seconds,' she said, dropping a kiss on the top of Lucy's head. 'Stay there and be as good as gold and I'll be back with one of Gavin's teddy bear gingerbread biscuits.'

'And hot chocolate with sprinkles on top?' Lucy looked at Edward with wide eyes.

'And hot chocolate with sprinkles on top.'

A couple had arrived at the counter before she got there and so Polly stood patiently, watching as Gavin and Tom worked together – one serving, the other efficiently preparing two flat whites on the huge, gleaming red coffee maker that was their pride and joy. Tom patted Gavin on the bottom and he grinned and said 'watch it, cheeky,' in his soft Welsh accent. The couple they were serving laughed, paid their money and headed off to sit in the little corner where there was a cosy sofa for two and a window that looked out over the fields towards the woods and the distant sea.

'I hear we've got strangers in our midst.'

Tom folded his arms and leant back against the counter. Gavin picked up two plates and without being asked, selected two of the gingerbread cookies and put one on each, and then lifted two of the tiny espresso-size cups and raised his eyebrows in unspoken query. Polly nodded and he got to work, steaming some milk for tiny, five-year-old size portions of hot chocolate.

'Strangers?' She suppressed a smile, knowing exactly what he was going to say.

'Well I have to admit I was disappointed to discover

that the Kardashians weren't filming a Christmas special here in the Highlands,' said Tom with an arch tone, 'But if Dolina is to believed that's what's on the cards.'

'I cannot believe this place, sometimes.' Polly shook her head.

Tom passed Gavin a silver container and watched as he sprinkled a generous layer of chocolate pieces on top of the twins' drinks.

'Some YouTuber or something?' Gavin put the drinks to one side and busied himself making a coffee for Polly. 'You probably know who it is, you're the one always reading Heat magazine and all the rest of them.'

'I'm not always reading them,' protested Polly. 'Just when I'm bored and there's nothing going on at work. I bet I've never heard of whoever this is.'

'And in the bath, you said the other day,' pointed out Tom. 'You're single-handedly keeping the magazine industry going. Everyone else is reading stuff online and you're still buying the real thing. They ought to give you an award for your dedication.'

'Anyway,' said Polly, pointedly, 'Getting back to the subject and away from my failings as a human being, I think they've missed a trick. They should employ Dolina as their gossip columnist. She doesn't miss anything. I can't believe word has made its way all the way up here already.'

'Oh there's something about it on the village Facebook group. Whoever it is has apparently landed at the hotel –' Gavin began, pulling out his phone to show her.

So that *was* the couple she'd seen heading in there as she left after picking up the twins, Polly realised.

'-ooh look,' he continued. 'It's on the 'Gram already. Look.'

Polly and Tom both leaned in to peer at his phone screen. Sure enough, there was a link to Ivy Winter's account, the photograph showing a an artfully casual-not-casual Ivy draped over one of the chairs in the Applemore Hotel bar, perfectly painted pout not quite sipping at the glass of red she held in her manicured fingers. In the background the Christmas lights were artfully blurred, giving the photograph an arty effect which also had the added benefit of disguising the ancient wallpaper and tartan carpet.

'Oh wow, look, it's Ivy Winter!'

'I told you,' said Tom. 'Those influencer types all look the same to me. Who is she?'

'Oh she's famous for YouTube videos about make up and trips to fancy places, and she has literally hundreds of thousands of followers on Instagram. I —' Polly stopped mid-sentence, realising that both Tom and Gavin were looking at her with amusement.

'Thought you said you wouldn't have a clue who she was?'

'Oh she's one of those ones that everyone's heard of. She's always going to amazing places and she used to date a footballer from Liverpool FC.'

Gavin and Tom shook their heads in unison. 'Nope.'

'I can see why Dolina thought she was a Kardashian,' giggled Polly, scrolling through the photos on Ivy's Instagram and showing the boys. 'I mean that's definitely the look she's going for. She's basically got the perfect life.'

'Has she now,' said Gavin, drily. 'And now here she is in Applemore.'

'What on earth is she doing here?'

'I haven't a clue, lovey. Here's your coffee, and the kiddies' drinks should be cool enough now. You can have a mince pie on the house — don't say I'm not good to you. We'll leave you in charge of finding out all the hot gossip from Harry.'

Polly was already formulating her message to him in her head. 'Don't worry, I will.'

She doled out cookies and hot chocolate to the twins, shifting Edward over gently to make space for her cup of coffee, and sat down to type a quick message to Harry.

Ivy Winter????

That was pretty much all she needed to say. Not wanting to ignore the children, she put the phone down and spent the next fifteen minutes chatting to them, laughing as they told her the news from their day at school and wiping up the inevitable spillage – not to mention the tears – when Lucy scribbled too hard with her crayons and sent the remains of her drink flying across the café floor.

Your guess is as good as mine, Harry had replied while she was busy. *Reports to follow. Unless you have any inside info that might help?*

Not a clue. She nibbled on her mince pie. Anna had been at work again, and it was utterly delicious, the pastry buttery and melting in her mouth.

Well, she's definitely not the last guest of the season I was expecting, Harry had replied.

Is that a good thing?

Harry didn't reply. She sighed. Not only was she trying to get her head round the idea that Harry saw her as nothing more than her brother's kid sister and a mate to have a laugh with, now he was going to be catering to the every whim of the most ridiculously uber-glam person in existence. She looked like a very dull and unexciting country bumpkin in comparison. She'd been so wrapped up in her little life here in Applemore for so long that the idea of someone as glamourous and interesting as Ivy Winter choosing to come here to visit seemed completely incomprehensible. Together with the stab of a reminder earlier that everyone was completely happy and paired off,

Polly was feeling distinctly flat by the time that her sister Beth turned up.

'Sorry, they did a filling and it took longer than I expected.' Beth, her long blonde hair tied in a plait beneath a grey hat and her collar turned up against the chill of the evening, stood in the kitchen of Polly's little cottage. 'Come on you two, Mummy's got a numb face so I want to get home and get into the warm.'

'What's a numb face?' Edward asked, as Polly helped him into his coat.

'It's what happens when the dentist puts special stuff in your mouth so she can make it better,' explained Beth, who had infinite patience when it came to the children. She gave Polly a fleeting sideways look. 'You okay?'

Polly nodded. 'Why do you ask?'

'I'm your big sister. It's my job to notice if you're not.'

'I'm fine,' said Polly, shooing them out of the door. Growing up without a mother, and with a loving but vague father who tried his best to juggle the four of them and the running of the dilapidated old house had meant that the siblings were close, and well attuned to how each other was feeling. It also meant, thought Polly, closing the curtains and turning on the television before sinking into the cushions of the sofa, that you had to be really good at your poker face or you had literally no privacy. And sometimes what she really wanted was to live her life as something other than the baby sister.

Her message to Harry had remained un-answered, a reminder that he was probably busy standing behind the bar ogling the tiny, petite, super-gorgeous Ivy Winter and definitely not thinking about her. She really needed to get a grip. And maybe make a bit more of an effort than she had been of late – she'd been so caught up with work that it had been forever since she'd sorted her eyebrows or painted her nails. Maybe it was time to start making some changes.

She went into the little bathroom with its white-painted wooden panelling and seaside decoration, turning on the bath taps and tipping in two big handfuls of the expensive bath salts she'd been given as a birthday present from Charlotte – who only ever used the best – and then tied her hair up in a loose knot, piling it on top of her head and wiping the steam from the mirror to look at herself with a critical eye. Now she was almost thirty there were some tiny lines sneaking in at the edges of her eyes that she hadn't noticed before, and – she peered more closely – was that a grey hair in amongst the blonde? She pulled it out and scrutinised it – no, it was just paler blonde. That was something, at least. But she needed to start some sort of regime besides her habitual get up, grab a shower, shove on some moisturiser. She looked in the cabinet and found a packet with a face mask inside, unwrapping it and smoothing it on so she looked back at herself like some sort of strange ghoul left over from Hallowe'en. Okay, Polly Fraser, she told herself, it's time to make some changes.

She waited until the bath was full up to the top and then climbed into the scented water, sitting back for ten minutes with her eyes closed, thinking.

After that she peeled off the mask, wiped her hands on the towel which hung beside the bath, and messaged Tom.

Okay, I'm in. You can tell the mysterious cousin that I'll go on a date.

His reply was instant.

Excellent. I'll give him your number.

Polly reared up out of the bath, almost dropping the phone in horror. She grabbed the towel again and tapped out a reply.

Not now! Tomorrow.

Bloody hell, woman, I wasn't about to send him round to yours for a nightcap

That's alright then, wrote Polly, who was already feeling like it was a very bad idea indeed. *I need some time to get my head round the idea*

Cool, sleep on it and we'll sort it in the morning.

Polly, who thought that she'd probably need about a hundred years to sleep on the idea, put the phone down on the bathroom windowsill and brushed her teeth. She had a feeling that this wasn't one of her better ideas, but she'd committed to it now.

CHAPTER SIX

LACHLAN FRASER – tall, bearded, with a blue cycling helmet atop his head – pushed open the side door of the Applemore Bar with a questioning expression on his face.

'You okay? Thought you said meet at the bottom of the hill. Jack's waiting, and you know what he's like for punctuality. I said I'd come and chase you up.'

After the morning he'd had Harry was quite impressed that he'd managed to locate his biking gear. He glanced up at the clock on the wall of the bar.

'Sorry mate, didn't notice the time.'

Lachlan, easy-going by nature, gave a vague shrug and held the door open, waiting for Harry as he screwed the lid on his water bottle and threw a couple of packs of salted peanuts from the shelf behind the bar into his bag.

'You all set?'

Harry grabbed his backpack and swung it over his shoulder. 'Yep, sorry, had a bit of a nightmare. I'm organising a staff rota.'

'There can't be that much to organise, surely? Thought you were on the wind down?' Lachlan said.

He moved out of the way as Harry lifted his bike off the rack at the back of the hotel where it hung, covered with a waterproof tarpaulin. He cast a quick eye over the tyres and squeezed the brakes experimentally. He hadn't even hosed off the mud after their last trip out, which was a cardinal sin in mountain biking world. No doubt Jack, who was a stickler for such things, would have words if he knew that he hadn't given the bike a quick maintenance check before they headed off on their bike ride, but after the night he'd had it had been the last thing on his mind.

He followed Lachlan, who was now wheeling down the street.

'Thought you'd forgotten we were going out.' Jack was leaning against the little picnic table which stood on a patch of grass overlooking the rocks that led down to a tiny secret beach. As they readied themselves to set off on their bike ride, they heard whoops of laughter from the little beach below. It was accessible only by scrambling carefully down and therefore hidden to most tourists. Lachlan shot him a grin of complicity, waggling his eyebrows in shared memory.

'Am I missing something?' Jack looked from Harry to Lachlan, amusement in his deep Glaswegian voice. 'Do you two want to share with the class?'

'I bet whoever is down there is up to no good.'

Lachlan chuckled. 'Maybe teenagers these days are better behaved than we were.'

'I doubt it somehow.' Jack, who had a daughter of his own who was in her late teens, and who'd caused him a headache or two in the past, shook his head. 'Don't you remember what a nightmare I had when I first moved up here?'

'I don't want to think about it.' Lachlan, thinking of his

baby daughter, groaned. 'Let's say I'm not looking forward to the teenage years.'

'You've got the terrible twos and the tricky threes to go,' said Jack, taking off his helmet and adjusting the strap before putting it back on his head.

'Cheers for that,' said Lachlan, drily.

'I speak from painful experience. The twins are pushing the boundaries at the moment. We're both knackered because they're not sleeping, and just as I'm winding down for winter Beth's got loads on with these workshops she's running at the gallery. I tell you what, I can't wait until Joan gets back from her holidays so she can give us a break.'

'You two aren't exactly selling the whole two point four kids thing,' Harry said, swinging his leg over his bike and getting ready to set off.

'Yeah, well, you're better off staying child-free, mate. Honestly, treasure those Sunday mornings in bed. You've no idea how good they feel until they're in the past.' Lachlan grinned.

'I'll tell Rilla you said that.' Harry tugged at the strap of his bike helmet, tightening it slightly.

'Oh believe me, she misses sleep as much as I do. Thank god we don't have to think about anything for the rest of the morning apart from staying upright.' Lachlan said, with feeling.

Together the three of them started the steady pedal uphill that took them out of Applemore village and towards the hilly wooded trail they'd earmarked for their fortnightly trip. It had started as a bit of a joke challenge – the super fit Jack, who spent all his working time doing outdoor activities and his spare time running and cycling had pointed out that both Lachlan and Harry were in danger of getting soft, working as they did behind a bar and in a tiny brewery respectively. They'd all enjoyed the challenge of getting out on their much-neglected mountain bikes and so it had become a regular date in their schedules. Today, though, Harry – who'd managed about four hours of sleep – could have happily stayed home and slept, given the choice.

The road opened out and he looked out over the faded green of the prickly gorse bushes which lined the roadside, the rock-strewn landscape clad in its winter garb of grey-green and brown. In the distance was the pine wood they were heading for today, where the trails cut through the trees by the forestry commission led to some steep and challenging paths which would take all their focus.

Right now though, his mind slipped back as they puffed up the hill to last night's disaster.

He'd finished pouring a second beer for Murdo who was sitting on one of the high stools by the bar as usual, flicking through the local newspaper and drinking his first pint in a leisurely manner. His wife Greta, who'd arrived to chair a meeting to organise the Christmas carol service, was re-organising some of the bar tables in the little side room in a slightly optimistic manner. Harry had privately suspected that turnout was going to be low, given it was a chilly, grey Thursday night and there was a brand new series of *Line of Duty* on television. He'd made a joke to that effect but Greta had brushed him off with a cheerful wave.

'I think everyone's looking forward to the Christmas carol service, and I'm certain that everyone will be flocking to do what they can to get a bit of community spirit going.'

Murdo had caught Harry's eye from over her shoulder and made a dubious face, which had made him laugh. Another fairly standard evening in Applemore, in other words, the only difference being that the restaurant was busier than expected because word had already got around that there was a media star in their midst. Ivy Winter and her boyfriend Ben were oblivious to the wide-eyed stares of the people at the tables around them. It was clear that the jungle drums had worked quickly. The clientele was younger and – Harry had noted with amusement as one table after another filled up with twenty-somethings he recognised from the village, none of whom were normally spotted eating in the restaurant apart from on family occasions. The place was rather more brightly coloured than normal, and the rainbow-haired Phoebe – who'd clearly summoned her people – was in her element. She was dashing from one table to the next, chatting happily and taking orders. They'd had to ring Jamie and Claire to come in and help with the tables, and Harry was standing with his arms folded surveying the scene when he heard a crash.

The noise from the kitchen was so loud that everyone looked up from their meals, all eyes landing on Harry.

'Don't worry,' he said, with a jokey tone to his voice, 'I'll go and sort out the mess.'

He strode across the little restaurant and headed in through the double doors and into the kitchen.

'Don't worry,' echoed Conor, his voice emanating from the passageway where the fridges and storage cupboards were located.

'Conor?'

'Down here,' said Kian, who worked alongside the chef. He was on his hands and knees, and had put a folded dishcloth underneath a prone Conor's head.

'What's happened?'

'Think I stood up too fast or something. Knelt down to get some pâté out of the fridge, everything went black when I stood up, and the next thing I knew – bang – I'm on the floor.'

'Sounds like low blood pressure or something like that.' Harry knelt and made to pick up Conor's wrist to check his pulse.

'Ahhhh!' Conor yelped.

Harry let go as if he'd been scalded. 'Sorry mate, what's wrong?'

'That's the problem,' Kian said, looking across at the stove where something was starting to boil over. He looked as if he was torn between tending to the chef and making sure the food didn't spoil.

'I'll sort Conor, you sort that.' Harry indicated the stove with a nod of his head and Kian shot off, rescuing the saucepan just in time.

Fortunately at that moment Phoebe had returned, and between them and the extra staff they'd managed to organise the rest of service, juggle the kitchen, and produce the – thankfully reduced - menu to a standard which just about passed Conor's exacting gaze as he sat on a hastily rescued office chair, an ice pack on his wrist.

Now, Harry followed the other two men as they turned off the road and bumped onto a rocky path which led down between two ploughed fields and on towards the forest. It had been the worst possible evening for something like that to go wrong. Phoebe had gleefully pointed out that the Applemore Hotel social media accounts already had several hundred new followers in the short space of time since Ivy had posted her location. If they'd screwed up dinner, a dodgy review would be all it took to undo all the hard work they'd been doing to try and make a difference to the place before he and Rob got to work on their partnership with the goal of bringing the hotel into this century.

Weirdly though, Ivy and Ben hadn't seemed to notice. They'd been wrapped up in each other all evening, happily accepting the free cocktails which Phoebe had brought them as an apology for their second course being more than a little late in emerging from the kitchen.

As they made their way into the forest Harry didn't have time to think about what had happened last night. The effort of scrambling through slippery mud and the layers of pine-needles which hid gnarly tree roots and bumps which sent the mountain bike ricocheting up and down took all his concentration. He skidded, mud flying up in an arc as he dropped a gear and then started climbing up through the narrow path between huge, stately pines. The sunlight filtered between them, lighting the way as they climbed up towards the brow of the hill and into the clearing.

'I think I might be on the verge of death,' said Lachlan, his bike landing in a heap as he jumped off to one side and doubled over, trying to catch his breath.

Jack gave a shout of laughter.

'I – can't – breathe,' groaned Harry, flopping forward over the handlebars.

'Bet you didn't think about work or stress though, right?' Jack looked pleased with himself. But even he was puffing. Together the three of them caught their breath and stood for a long moment looking down the hill that rolled away from them and down to the cliff edge far beyond, where the waves crashed white against the rocks.

'If this is work, though,' Lachlan said, looking at Jack, 'What do you do when you want to switch off?'

Jack shrugged. 'I don't.'

'What, you never want to switch off from work?' Harry said.

'Alright, I love this bit – the physical side of it. But the paperwork and all the admin, I could happily leave that behind. I've shunted as much off as I can, because I'd

56

rather be doing what I love. Taking people out, showing them this part of the world, letting them try new stuff … that's the amazing bit about this job.'

'Yeah, I'm the same, to be fair. Rilla and I split the admin stuff between us because neither of us like it. The only bit of work I'd happily never do ever again is cleaning out the compost loos on the wild camping site.' Lachlan made a face.

'That sounds revolting.' Jack grimaced. 'Never thought about that when you started the wild camping site.'

'You should see the toilets of the Applemore Bar after the annual Halloween party,' Harry said with feeling. 'Believe me, that's not a job for the faint hearted. But anyway, can we change the subject to something less gruesome? I haven't eaten and my stomach's churning now.'

'How can you run a hotel and not have time to eat?' Jack shook his head, laughing.

'Long story.' Harry took off his bike helmet and ran a hand through his damp hair, leaving it standing in spikes.

'Too busy catering to the every whim of our superstar visitor?' Lachlan grinned. 'You can always send her our way. We could do with the publicity.'

'Don't you start,' Harry laughed. 'As soon as Rob heard, he was on the phone pushing for me to get her to do some sort of promo. He's a hard taskmaster, that man.'

'I bet Polly will be utterly star struck as well. You know what she's like, reading all those magazines full of gossip and photos.' Lachlan rolled his eyes. 'She's such an airhead, sometimes.'

'Hardly,' said Harry sharply. 'She works her fingers to the bone running that place. I think you lot don't realise how much she does. She's a brilliant businesswoman.'

He noticed a brief look pass between Jack and Lachlan and turned away, fiddling with the gears on his bike. It annoyed him sometimes how dismissive they could be of Polly, teasing her and not realising what she put in to make the farm shop a success.

'I bet Rob will be all over it,' said Lachlan, a moment later. 'He and Charlotte are a force to be reckoned with.' He shrugged the backpack off his shoulders and rifled inside for a cereal bar.

'Oh yeah, I know that.' Harry had calmed down. 'But we were all set to wind down, and the next thing I know she turns up and somehow I've reorganised bedrooms for her to stay in, not to mention one for her blooming dog, and then the restaurant's fully booked…'

'My heart bleeds,' said Jack, grinning. 'Isn't that what you're aiming for?'

'Not when it ends with my chef flat out on the tiles with a suspected sprained wrist.'

Jack and Lachlan looked at him with curious expressions.

'It's a long story.'

He told them the whole saga, explaining that once he'd somehow managed to blag his way through the rest of the evening and deal with the Christmas carol service meeting – which had as he predicted had a minuscule turn out – and then clear up the kitchen without the help of Conor it was so late and he was so wound up that he'd ended up lying wide awake staring at the ceiling for hours, unable to sleep.

After they'd had a drink and a breather, they started the second half of the route back to the village, lungs full of fresh air and bodies pumping with endorphins. Harry mused as they coasted down the road. He caught a glimpse across the fields of the white-painted buildings at the entrance to the Applemore Estate which made up the Farm Shop, gallery and bakery, not to mention the little cottage with its blue windows and a curl of smoke twisting into the air. He realised he hadn't mentioned to Jack or Lachlan that part of the reason he'd been lying awake most of the night was because he couldn't get Polly Fraser out of his mind, no matter how hard he tried.

CHAPTER SEVEN

POLLY WAS HAVING one of those mornings. She'd woken after a broken night of weird dreams to the sound of her alarm, which almost never happened – she was usually up and out of the cottage like a lark, and it was unusual for her to be bleary-eyed and chugging back coffee to try and jump start her brain. Jenny had called to say she was running late because of a doctor's appointment, there was a delivery of meat due from Gregor the butcher, and the freezer which should have been full of the delicious home-baked ready meals had broken down overnight, meaning she was down hundreds of pounds worth of stock *and* had a new freezer to sort.

'And you know as well as I do that nothing happens at speed round here,' she said, nodding in response to Tom's finger pointing at the coffee machine. She was still finishing one flat white as he was preparing another.

'Anything we can do to help?' Tom reached over, taking a cup from the shelf.

'Find me a new freezer?' She was joking, but it was the last thing she needed. Insurance would cover it, but the faff of sorting it out, not to mention the excess and all the rest of it meant that she'd end up barely breaking even, if she was lucky.

'Leave it with me,' said Tom with a wink. 'I bet I can sort something. Meanwhile, you get this coffee down you and get back to work.'

She decided that the only thing for it was to try and Christmas herself into a better mood. Selecting some cheerful Christmas pop songs, she switched on the speaker and glanced at herself in the mirror in the little shop office. God, she looked tired. A swipe of lipstick and some mascara helped a bit, and she brushed her hair and tied it back in a ponytail, adding a colourful sprig of red tinsel. Fake it 'til you make it, she told herself firmly.

The morning whizzed by. Jenny had rallied, returning with the news that there had been a drama last night at the Applemore Bar.

'Apparently Conor passed out,' she said, as Gregor the butcher pulled up in the yard outside. They headed outside into the cold to help him with the boxes of meat, carrying them into the shop and putting them down by the fridge where they'd be displayed beside the local produce which brought customers in from all around the area. Jenny chatted away the whole time. 'So there I was at the Christmas carol service meeting – thought you might have been there, Greta sends her love and Joan was asking after you – and the whole place was buzzing because there was this big calamity going on but Harry and Kian managed to keep the kitchen going like troupers. And meanwhile the place was heaving because of that Ivy Winter and she's put something else on her Instagram page about the dinner and –'

But Polly had paused, hearing her phone buzz, and looked down at the message on the screen.

'Sorry,' she said a second later. 'I just …'

Jenny, who had impeccable gossip radar, stopped dead and looked at Polly with an inquisitive expression. 'What's up?'

Polly shook her head. 'Oh nothing,' she said, casually, pocketing her phone and turning to smile at Gregor.

'That's your lot,' he said, taking out his iPad and offering it to her to sign. She typed in her details on the delivery screen and he headed back out into the frosty morning with a cheerful wave of his hand. 'Don't forget to let me know how many turkey orders you're wanting for Christmas.'

'I'll email you later. We've got the list somewhere behind the till,' Polly called, and with a tinkle of the bells on the door, he was gone.

'I'll get these sorted, you go and email those turkey numbers before they slip your mind,' said Jenny, rolling up the sleeves of her red and blue checked shirt.

'If you're sure?' Polly, who was reeling slightly, stepped back.

'Course I am. You getting enough sleep? You look worn out.'

The lipstick and mascara clearly weren't having much effect, thought Polly as she sat down on the tall wooden stool behind the cash register. She took out her phone and looked down at the screen.

Hi, this is Giles. Tom gave me your number. Wondered if you'd like to have dinner tonight at the Applemore Hotel?

Brilliant, that was exactly what she needed. A date, on a night when she looked like death warmed up, in the restaurant of the hotel owned by the person she was trying very hard to pretend she wasn't in love with. Perfect.

Woman up, Polly Fraser, she told herself. She typed a

reply and hit send before she had a chance to have second thoughts.

That sounds lovely. 8pm?

Perfect. I'll book a table. See you there.

She put the phone back in her pocket and closed her eyes. Well, that was that done.

The day sped by with a constant stream of customers bustling around, filling their baskets with the usual food and drink and loading up with gorgeous hand-made decorations and Christmas gifts. With not long to go until the day itself, it felt like Applemore had moved up a gear and the shop was full of chat about needing to get organised and making plans for all the traditional events that dotted the village calendar. Polly closed the door on the last customer with a sigh of relief and a warm glow – maybe small village life wasn't so bad after all.

'I hear you're off out on the town,' called Tom, who was sweeping up the café. Polly put a finger to her lips with her eyes wide open.

'Shh,' she said, jerking her head in the direction of Jenny who was cashing up behind the till. For once, though, Jenny's gossip radar appeared to be on the blink because she carried on singing along to Elton John and doing a little dance, completely oblivious. If her mother, Dolina, got wind of the news, it would be round the village like wildfire.

Tom beetled across the room, leaving the broom balanced against one of the tables.

'Got to give my cousin Giles his due, he didn't hang about.' He gave a nod of approval. 'I think you'll like him.'

'I'm sure I will,' said Polly, who had to admit that she hadn't even given the date a moment's thought since. She wasn't sure if that was a good sign or not.

'Nervous?' Tom eyed her carefully.

Polly shook her head. 'Should I be?'

'I'm sure you'll have a fab time. I haven't seen him in years but he's lovely. When my mum said he was coming back to Applemore after his divorce I thought straight away *who can I pair him off with* and you were the first person that came to mind, given you're perma-single.' Tom beamed.

Polly scanned him for any indication that he was joking, or perhaps that he realised he was putting his foot in it. Nothing.

'Perma-single?' Polly said with a slight edge to her voice.

Tom chuckled. 'Well, let's just say every other member of your family has paired up since we've been living back here and you're still flying solo.'

'I'm picky, not desperate.' Polly released her hair from the ponytail and flipped it over her shoulder.

'Well, tonight might be your lucky night, duckie.'

Polly glared at his retreating back as he made his way back over to the broom, singing along to the music which Jenny had turned up now the customers were gone.

Feeling distinctly unimpressed with pretty much every-one, Polly headed home. She needed to get herself into date mode, but it had been so long (she grudgingly admitted to herself) since she'd been on one that she'd forgotten how.

She was standing in the kitchen in her dressing gown when she heard a bang at the door. Rubbing her wet hair with a towel, she walked into the hall to a familiar call.

'Hellooo? Polly, you in?'

Rilla's dark curls were unruly as ever as she popped her head around the door.

'Ooh sorry, didn't mean to bother you. Just wanted to let you know that Lachlan and I are getting the frozen stuff out and taking it up to the house. Well, Lachlan is. I'm here, avoiding the hard work.' Rilla laughed.

She'd completely forgotten in the business of the day that she'd rung Lachlan and asked if she could stick all the frozen meals up there. As soon as the freezer had gone off, health and safety rules meant that the food couldn't be sold, but most of it had been salvageable.

'You are an angel.' Polly smiled at Rilla, whose pretty freckled face was drawn. She looked even more tired than Polly was. 'You okay?'

'Just a bit worn out,' said Rilla, drawing her hand across her face with a groan. 'Kitty isn't sleeping. I have no idea how Beth did this with twins. I must admit I can't wait for Joan to get back from her trip and give us a break.'

'I'll come and take over baby duty for the night soon and you two can get away. Why don't you go over to Inverness or even down to Edinburgh? You could see Gus.'

She knew that Lachlan still missed hanging out regularly with his old uni friend and business partner, and Rilla looked as if she could really do with a break.

'That would be amazing.' Rilla flopped against the wall, looking as if she was ready for a chat. Polly glanced up unthinkingly at the clock above the archway that led into the little sitting room.

'Oh god, am I keeping you?' Rilla said, putting a hand to her mouth.

'Not really,' said Polly, politely. 'It's fine. I'm going out in a bit, but I need to get dressed.'

'Ooh, anything exciting?' Rilla lifted an eyebrow in query. 'I don't know why I'm asking you that. I assume it's nothing exciting.'

Polly shook her head. 'Nothing exciting,' she agreed. Rilla blew a kiss goodbye and Polly headed back towards the bathroom. Wiping steam from the mirror above the sink, she looked into her own eyes and gave herself a stern talking-to.

'Right, Polly Fraser,' she said aloud, 'you need to pull out all the stops. Even your family doesn't expect you to be doing anything exciting.'

She took longer than her usual five minutes putting on her make-up, applying a soft grey kohl liner and layers of silvery eyeshadow, finishing off with two coats of black mascara which emphasised her blue-grey eyes. It was more of an effort than she'd made in – well, in forever. Back when she'd lived down south and hung out with her university friends she'd followed this getting-ready ritual every night before they went out clubbing and partying, but since her dad died and she'd returned to Applemore she'd become more and more understated until a slick of lip gloss and some mascara had felt like enough of an effort for a night out. When you were only going to see the same people you hung out with in the village all week, it hardly seemed worthwhile getting glammed up to have fish and chips and a glass of wine at the Applemore Hotel quiz night.

Carrying on this theme, instead of the pale blue top and dark jeans she was planning to wear, she pulled out a grey dress of the softest cashmere with a scooped neck and three-quarter length sleeves which was nipped in at the waist and flared out, ending above the knee. She'd bought it ages ago and it had been hanging in the wardrobe, but she'd never found the right occasion to wear it. Pulling on some black tights and a pair of chunky biker boots, she gave herself a twirl in the long mirror in the hall and laughed at herself. Not bad, she acknowledged. She would do. Now all she had to do was get there.

It was only when she'd set off and was driving in the darkness towards the softly glowing lights of Applemore, nestling in the little harbour and embraced by the hills that it suddenly struck her – how on earth was she going to know what Giles looked like?

She pulled up on the road outside the little white cottages where old Mrs Mackay, who'd taught her at primary school, still lived. She hadn't drawn her curtains – lots of the villagers didn't – and Polly could see her sitting inside watching television in the glow of a fire, her feet up on a padded stool, a ginger and white cat sitting on a tartan blanket which was spread over her knees. Applemore looked gorgeous in the pale light of summer, when it never quite got dark and the sky glowed pink and lilac, but Polly had always loved it best in winter, when the windows of the houses shone out with their warm yellow light, and especially in the festive season, when lights were strung from the lamp-posts which lit up the lanes between the cottages and shops, and the place sparkled with the promise of Christmas magic. Soon the village tree would be lit, and the carol service would take place, and there was a funfair and fete on the horizon as well. She gave a little happy shiver with the cold and the excitement of it all, her breath clouding in the air as she made her way towards the hotel.

It was only as she put a hand to the door of the bar that she felt a sudden bolt of nerves and her stomach lurched. Gritting her teeth and squaring her shoulders, she pushed open the door.

CHAPTER EIGHT

WITH CONOR OUT OF ACTION, Harry had found himself wearing far too many hats. So much for winding down to a few weeks of quiet when they renovated the place ... he was currently overseeing the kitchen, keeping an eye on the running of the whole place, dealing with enquiries from Kenny the builder who was raring to get going and who'd been delivering all the materials to the back of the hotel all day long, creating a noise which had not gone un-noticed by one or two of the more *particular* guests. Talk of the devil, he thought, as he straightened up having been digging about in the back of the filing cabinet for an order form that he was pretty sure had been missed when he'd sent stuff off to the accountant the day before. His head was banging and he needed about three weeks on a desert island. Instead though he was not exactly delighted to discover that Ben, Ivy Winter's boyfriend, was standing at the reception desk with what they all referred to a *could you just* expression on his face. There were some guests who you could tell from the minute they arrived that they were going to need just one more of whatever you offered them.

So far they'd had to provide extra blankets ("Ivy feels the cold"), a porcelain dog bowl ("she doesn't like to drink from metal") and two hot water bottles ("she likes to have warm toes"). Not to mention ordering off-menu for breakfast ("I wonder if we could ask a *tiny* favour?") and this afternoon's request for an eye mask, which had made Nina at reception roll her eyes so hard that she'd almost sprained them as she pointed out with the faintest hint of ice behind her best customer service voice that they were quite some distance from the nearest beauty supplies shop, but that they'd do their best. Thankfully Phoebe, still utterly star struck, was more than happy to attend to Ivy Winter's every need. She'd rushed home and retrieved one from her own bathroom, dashing up the stairs to deliver it to a grateful Ben. Ivy, apparently, was having an afternoon bath. Phoebe had taken out her phone to illustrate this point, scrolling through social media until she found an arty snap of the silver-polished taps of the old fashioned bath in the en-suite bathroom.

'Look! You can't pay for this sort of promo,' squeaked Phoebe, delighted.

'Glad we did a good clean before she took the room,' Harry had remarked. He had to admit that Ivy's social media presence had made a marked difference in the short time she'd been staying in Applemore, but despite Jack's exhortations that they should be making the most of it he was so focused on getting on with the refurb that he was mainly fantasising about a few days hence when he could close the door on all the guests, take off his game face, and breathe a sigh of relief.

But meanwhile, Phoebe had gone off duty for the evening, and so Harry was stuck with being a concierge.

'I wonder if you could give us some pointers,' said Ivy Winter's boyfriend, Ben. He was standing by the little reception desk with a pair of completely superfluous sunglasses perched on his glossy black hair. Harry clocked them with a fleeting look. It had been cloudy all day, and now it was pitch dark outside. Presumably they were part of the whole look.

'What kind of pointers?' Harry straightened one of the little piles of business cards which covered the desk, advertising local wares to guests.

'Well, we've got another couple of days. I thought it might be nice if we did some activities in the area, maybe – I don't know if you've seen,' said Ben, looking slightly bashful, 'But we – well, Ivy – has a bit of a profile on social media.'

Harry warmed to him slightly. The bloke, despite his slicked-back hair and rather wide boy appearance, was clearly more humble than he looked.

'I had clocked that, yes,' Harry felt the corners of his mouth twitch. 'We doubled our Instagram following overnight, and I've had enquiries about bookings already.'

'Cool,' Ben gave a nod. 'We're hoping to maybe try something a bit different –' his eyes landed on the colourful postcard which advertised Jack's outdoor adventure centre. Images of white water rafting, mountain biking, kayaking were displayed on one side, and he flipped it over to read the contact details on the other.

'Not sure that's quite the sort of thing you've got in mind,' said Harry, mindful of Ivy's immaculate hair and manicured nails. They wouldn't last ten minutes if Jack got hold of them.

'I'd love it.' Ben pocketed the card.

'There's a wreath-making workshop up at the gallery,' said Harry, thinking that it would probably be more Ivy's sort of thing.

'Wreaths? What, like funeral wreaths?' Ben recoiled. 'That's a bit niche, innit?'

Harry laughed. 'No, Christmas wreaths. For the door, that sort of thing.'

'Oh, right.' Ben looked embarrassed. 'I forgot about Christmas wreaths.'

'Wish I could,' said Harry, watching as Kian walked past with a box of decorations. There had been a rush of last minute bookings for the restaurant, and the was pub busier than expected because word had got round that Ivy Winter was staying and people wanted to have a look for themselves. Kian and Phoebe had pointed out that his winding-down plans were all well and good but the rest of the village was getting into the Christmas spirit and the place was looking weird with no decorations up.

'But we're closing on Saturday,' he'd protested.

'Which means we have four days to make the place look festive,' Phoebe had said firmly. 'I'm getting the stuff out of the storage cupboard and we're decorating whether you like it or not.'

Harry had growled assent. 'Fine, but I'm having nothing to do with it. I told you all I was having a year off Christmas.'

'Anyway,' he said, pulling himself back to the present. 'Sorry. Where was I – oh yes. Wreaths. My friend Beth is running the workshop, she's great. Hang on – ' he rifled through the cards on the table until he found one in understated brown card, with a pretty line drawing of a flower on the front.

'The Flower Farm,' Ben read. 'That sounds right up Ivy's street.'

'It is pretty cool,' Harry agreed. 'You should see it in summer when everything is in bloom.'

'These are a good start. I'll take them up to Ivy now,

and we'll have a think. I really appreciate you sorting room service for tonight. We're both absolutely worn out.'

Harry did a double take, which he somehow managed to turn into a nod of acknowledgement. 'Room service,' he said faintly, 'Yep. Right. Absolutely. No problem.'

'Cool,' said Ben, again. 'Just give us a knock and leave it outside the door.'

Harry was left standing with his mouth hanging open. It was only after he heard Ben's retreating footsteps on the stairs that he glanced behind him and realised he'd completely forgotten to mention Polly's Winter Market which was taking place on the weekend. That would have been right up Ivy Whatsit's street, he suspected. Making a mental note to remind them the next day, he headed towards the kitchen, still muttering to himself about Phoebe and her terrible habit of bending over backwards to make sure they were catering to Ivy Winter's every whim.

'Room service?' said Harry, a moment later, hooking a chef's apron around his waist.

'Oh yeah, Phoebs said before she left,' Kian looked up from the stainless steel counter where he was assembling little bowls of side salad, ready to be garnished as needed. 'For Ivy and Ben.'

'We don't do room service,' said Harry, through gritted teeth.

'We do now, apparently.' Kian wiped the surface and with a flourish of the cloth turned his back, striding down towards the grill. 'We've got a full house tonight, by the way. Apparently the last table was booked earlier in the afternoon. Oh and Charlotte and Rob are in.'

Harry, his head full of everything he had to do, nodded without really listening. He'd had to call in favours to get extra staff on board when he'd already wound down, and it had been ages since he'd done a night in the kitchen. It didn't help that his backer Rob and his partner Charlotte had booked a table. Charlotte was a lifelong friend, but Rob was, well, he still had a feeling of complicated pride about taking the financial backing from Rob, and while they got on well, Harry was determined to prove that he was worth the investment.

'Right, let's get this show on the road.' He looked up at the clock. There was no time for navel gazing when there was a restaurant to run.

CHAPTER NINE

THE WARM AND familiar scent of delicious food and the burning logs on the fire welcomed Polly as she made her way into the Applemore Hotel. Normally she'd stop at the bar, hitch herself up onto one of the stools and sit chatting to Harry or Phoebe or whoever was working, catching up on village gossip and comfortable in her familiar environment. The bar was busier than usual for a midwinter evening, and she noticed Greta and Murdo sitting by the fire, him reading his newspaper while his wife chatted away, a pile of crochet squares sitting on the table beside her. The boardgame club was parked in their usual corner, a motley gathering of men who met once a fortnight to drink craft beer and spend hours on a complicated strategy game that made no sense to outsiders. She gave a brief wave to a couple of her regular customers who smiled hello and returned to their drinks. Phoebe was sitting – off duty for once – with her boyfriend Danny, who worked alongside Jack at the outdoor centre. She looked as if she was on high alert, presumably keeping her eyes peeled for Ivy Winter who was still floating around the village if her

Instagram account was anything to go by. The pub really was the hub for the whole community, and she realised with a pang how much everyone would miss the place when it was closed for refurbishment.

But today wasn't about hanging out with the locals. She gave a brief wave to Phoebe who spotted her and gave a motion to indicate that she liked her dress. Then, taking a deep breath, Polly strode towards the little archway that led through to the tiny restaurant, butterflies dancing a jig in her stomach.

'I'm meeting someone – ' she began to say as an unfamiliar young girl of about eighteen appeared, her long hair tied up in a bun, wearing the familiar Applemore Hotel logoed polo shirt and a black knee-length skirt.

'Oh yes,' said the girl, smiling and stepping forward, beckoning Polly towards the little dark alcove table which sat slightly apart from the rest of the room, 'You'll be having dinner with Mr Donaldson?'

Polly scanned the room fleetingly. Almost all the tables were already full, but as she approached the alcove table a man with short cropped brown hair stood up, putting out a hand in welcome.

'Polly?'

'You must be Giles.' She went to shake his hand as he moved in to kiss her on the cheek, meaning that he landed a kiss somewhere in the region of her ear. That's a good start, she thought, sitting down as the waitress hovered to one side of the table.

'Can I get you a drink?'

'We'll have a bottle of the house white,' said Giles, decisively, passing the wine menu back to the young girl.

Polly opened her mouth to say that she was driving, and that she'd prefer her one drink to be a glass of red, but then closed it again. She thought for a moment, realising that she wasn't a meek little creature living in 1950 and then opened it again.

'Actually, I'd prefer red,' she said, lifting her chin slightly.

Giles waggled his eyebrows. 'A woman who knows her own mind, I like it.'

Polly suppressed a grimace. Don't judge on first appearances, she told herself, firmly.

'So, I gather you've got a little business,' he said, leaning back as the waitress returned with two bottles of wine. 'Tom says you've made quite a success of it.'

Polly felt her nostrils flaring and wondered if it was alright to judge on second appearances.

'Well yes,' she said, lifting the glass to her lips almost as soon as the wine had been poured, 'You could call it that. So what do you do, Giles?'

'Oh, I'm a writer,' he said.

There, Polly said to herself. That was better. Interesting.

'Oh, what do you write?' She was going to ask if he'd have written anything she'd have heard of, but bit her tongue remembering an article she'd read where an author had said it was the question they all dreaded most.

'Well, I'm working on a novel at the moment. I've recently come back to Applemore to – well, I would say to find myself, but that sounds a little bit fanciful, doesn't it?' He gave a laugh which was more of a giggle, slightly higher pitched than she'd expect. Polly had a sudden flash-back to her sister Charlotte describing in painful detail the moment when she realised that the man she was dating – a perfectly inoffensive farmer – had made her blood go cold with horror. At least Charlotte had managed more than five minutes into a date. For goodness' sake, Fraser, she reprimanded herself, you haven't even placed an order yet.

'What's the novel about? Which genre?'

'I don't like to define it by anything as pedestrian as a genre – it's more conceptual. I'd like to think that it's going to find a place all of its own.'

'Oh, right.' Polly, who liked reading romance novels in the bath in which nice people met, fell in love, and lived happily ever after, suspected that it might not be her sort of thing. 'And what did you do before that?'

'Well my ex-wife ... ' Giles' face dropped 'We had a business together, which I left with her when we split, but I'm still very involved in the behind the scenes, although I'm sure she'd rather I wasn't ...' he gave a slight chuckle. 'Long story. One for another day.'

Polly picked up the menu, lifting it up so her face was hidden, aware that her terrible poker face was probably going to give her away. She was going to *murder* Tom when she saw him at the café.

'I don't fancy a starter, do you?' She crossed her fingers under the table, hoping.

'Oh I was thinking we could have the sharing platter.' Giles ran a finger down the menu. He had long fingers tipped with slightly too-long nails. Yuck, thought Polly.

'It's huge,' she said, trying to put him off. 'I promise, you won't have room for a main course if we have that.'

'I'm so sorry,' said the waitress, a moment later, 'I completely forgot – we're a bit busy, as you can see – that we're running a slightly reduced menu tonight.'

'Of course,' said Polly, looking up at her. 'How is Conor?'

The girl blushed slightly, and looked uncomfortable, as if she wasn't quite sure she was supposed to give away trade secrets.

'It's fine,' said Polly, confidingly. 'I'm friends with Harry.'

'Oh,' she said in her soft Highland accent, looking relieved, 'He's fine, just a sprained wrist, but he can't cook and Harry's going bonkers in the kitchen trying to keep everything going. You know what he's like.'

Polly grinned at a vision of Harry – frazzled, still managing to make a joke out of the situation, his dry sense of humour keeping everyone's spirits up. 'I do. Very well.' She looked across at Giles, who looked slightly put out not to be involved in the conversation. 'Sorry, I should perhaps explain that it's a friend of mine who owns this place.'

'I see,' said Giles, shaking out the menu and squaring his shoulders as if to reassert his authority. 'If I'd known they weren't operating on full power I'd have suggested we meet elsewhere.'

'Oh no, the food here is amazing.' Polly felt defensive. 'I'll have the steak and ale pie with mustard mash, please.'

'I'd like the fish and chips – can you tell me if the batter is gluten free?'

'I don't think so,' said the girl, twisting her mouth in an expression of concern. 'I can ask?'

'If you wouldn't mind,' said Giles. 'I don't agree with gluten,' he added to Polly as the waitress headed off to the kitchen.

'Can you get gluten free batter?' Polly frowned. 'Isn't it made from flour?'

'Well yes of course,' he said, and launched into a detailed lecture about the benefits of a gluten free lifestyle. Polly, who had a friend who was coeliac and had to avoid gluten or else risk serious illness, listened with a polite expression on her face.

'So besides avoiding gluten and writing books, what else do you do?'

'I'm a real ale buff,' he said, not noticing the expression on Polly's face.

Of course you are, thought Polly, and said, knowing as she did that she was deliberately winding him up 'Isn't there gluten in beer?'

'Well yes,' said Giles, but as he opened his mouth to continue his explanation the waitress returned with a cheerful smile and said that yes, they could do a gluten free batter, and was there anything else he might like to know about their specialist menu?

A moment later Polly felt eyes boring into the back of her head, and a sibling sixth sense made her turn, only to discover her sister Charlotte was sitting at a table behind with her boyfriend Rob, who also turned to give her a wide-eyed look of surprise. Charlotte raised her glass slightly in a toast of greeting. Polly made a face which said *shut up*. Charlotte made a zipping motion across her mouth.

As dates went, this one was up there in the top ten of disasters. Giles prattled on about the plot of his genre-less novel, and complained about his ex-wife. He was living, it transpired, with his mother. Better and better, thought Polly, who excused herself to go to the bathroom.

'Hello stranger,' said a deep voice as she scuttled along the narrow passageway that led to the loos. Polly crashed straight into the broad chest of Harry, who took her by the arms and looked down at her with a crooked grin on his lovely, handsome face. Oh god, thought Polly, this is the last thing I needed right now. She glanced over her shoulder, feeling horrified at the prospect of him meeting the unutterably awful Giles.

'Hi,' she squeaked. 'How's it going?'

'Oh fabulous,' said Harry, drily. 'I've got no chef, a prima donna upstairs demanding peeled grapes on tap, and now someone's requested gluten free fish and chips so I'm trying desperately to discover what Conor did with the gluten free flour and how to make up the batter mix. Knowing my luck it's probably a restaurant critic in disguise.'

Polly grimaced. 'It's definitely not a restaurant critic.' She glanced sideways and caught sight of Giles who was poking something out of his teeth with his finger.

'Have you developed psychic powers?' His eyes twinkled in amusement.

'Something like that.' Polly rubbed her nose, then remembered that was a tell for lying and stopped suddenly, twitching her mouth instead.

'You okay? You look like you're having some sort of allergic reaction. You're not developing a gluten sensitivity as well by any chance?'

'Definitely not.' More like an allergy to bad dates.

'Right,' said Harry, 'I better get back to work. See you after service?'

Polly thought for a moment that he looked slightly reluctant, then decided she was imagining it.

'Um,' she began, not quite sure how to fudge the fact that no, she wouldn't be hanging around at the end of the bar chatting to the usual suspects and waiting for Harry and the rest of the kitchen staff to finish before they all chucked their aprons in a heap, grabbed a plate of leftovers and relaxed after a busy evening. 'Maybe, yeah,' she said, lamely.

'Cool.' Harry let go of her arms, which she hadn't quite realised he was still grasping. The sensation of his big hands left a feeling of warmth and... something else she shook her head to dismiss.

'Catch you later,' he said, disappearing down the passage.

The gluten free fish and chips were pronounced a triumph by Giles, which delighted Polly.

'I'll have to tell Harry,' she started to say, then closed her mouth rapidly. That probably wasn't what Giles wanted to hear, although she wasn't completely sure that Giles wanted to hear anything apart from the sound of his own voice. Worried they were going to run out of things to say at the start of the date, she'd worked out pretty quickly that all she had to do was ask a vague question and he'd go off like clockwork for about fifteen minutes on pretty much any topic, and then he'd go off on a tangent and spout forth on something else. He had very strong views on Scottish Independence, Religion, the Royal Family, politics in general and the government in particular, and was getting started on the damage caused to the Highlands by the reckless drivers who were tearing up and down the North Coast 500 route when the waitress returned to ask if they'd like to see the dessert menu.

'I'm fine, thank you, no,' said Polly, as Giles said, 'Definitely, yes,' taking it from her hand before she had the chance to put it down on the table.

'I'll have the Highland toffee pudding with lavender cream,' he said.

Please, muttered Polly under her breath.

'Nothing for me, thank you,' said Polly, looking up at the waitress with an expression which she hoped said, 'Please save me from this, the very worst date in the history of bad dates,' but clearly said nothing of the sort. The waitress gave a shy smile and ducked her head slightly before disappearing off towards the kitchen. At least let the pudding come quickly, prayed Polly, fiddling with the edge of her napkin.

'As I was saying, I think the North Coast 500 is causing no end of damage to the environment and it's giving nothing back,' Giles continued, as he poured himself another glass of wine. He waved the bottle vaguely in her direction as an afterthought.

'No thanks, I'm driving,' Polly repeated, putting her hand over the almost empty glass which held the dregs of the red wine she'd eked out, alternating with sips of water from the table. If she'd had a good night and decided to have another glass or even share a bottle she knew perfectly well that Charlotte or Rob would have given her a lift home, or she could have spent the night – as she'd done countless times before – tucked up under a duvet on Harry's sofa in the little flat above the hotel kitchen. Funnily enough, though, she had felt absolutely no desire to do so.

He was still ranting on about wishing tourists would leave their part of the Highlands alone. Polly felt faintly queasy at the lascivious expression on Giles' face as he licked his lips as the pudding arrived.

'I have to disagree,' said Polly, managing to get a word in edgeways as he lifted a loaded spoon to his mouth. 'First of all, tourists bring a huge amount of money to our economy which is much needed. I wouldn't have a business without them, nor would anyone in my family. Or –' she was about to continue, but she realised that Giles was distracted and patting at his head and then looking at his hand. 'Are you alright?'

'I think I felt a spot of water. There – another one.'

Polly looked up at the ceiling. Directly above his head was a distinctly damp circle of grey on the otherwise white plaster. Another drip hung waiting, gathering mass.

Polly pushed back her chair at warp speed. This was the escape she'd been hoping for.

'Oh my goodness, I must go and tell someone there's a leak,' she said, tossing her napkin down on the table and leaving a frantically mouthing Giles looking from the remains of his dessert to the ceiling.

Polly had dashed into the kitchen and grabbed Harry.

'Something's leaking upstairs.'

'What? Where?'

'I don't know. Over the alcove table if that makes sense?'

Harry groaned, putting a palm to his forehead. 'The shower in room nine. I knew it was going to blooming go. Why does everything happen when we're short staffed?'

'Can I do anything?' Polly said, spying a chance to cut the worst date ever short.

'Count these – ' he shoved a pile of papers which held the orders from each table for the night. 'If you don't mind? You are an angel.' He dropped a kiss on the top of her head and strode out of the kitchen, the doors swinging violently in his wake.

Polly stood exactly where she was, holding the stack of papers in one hand, while the other reached up to gently touch the place where he'd kissed her.

CHAPTER TEN

CHARLOTTE AND ROB were standing by the bar, both doubled over with laughter.

'So what happened then? I saw you shoot off at ninety miles an hour, then the next thing you reappeared and gave your hot date the Spanish Archer.' Rob straightened up, still chuckling.

Charlotte looked at her partner with a puzzled expression. 'The what?'

'El Bow,' said Rob. 'As in giving him the push. Can't believe you've never heard that expression. Anyway what's the deal, Polly?'

Harry, who had appeared behind the bar, leaned his chin in his hand and gazed at Polly, both brows raised quizzically. 'Yeah, what's the deal? And how come I'm the last to know about you having a date in the first place?'

'It's not that big a deal,' said Polly, who – having been offered a space on Harry's sofa – was now having a very large and much-needed gin and tonic. She caught them up on the horrors of the evening, making everyone groan and then laugh in recognition.

'We've all been there,' said Charlotte, with feeling. 'Until I met Rob I seriously thought that was it and I was going to spend the rest of my life with Nero.

'Some people would say a Golden Retriever was a perfectly nice life companion,' said Phoebe, who'd perched on one of the bar stools with her boyfriend Danny, enjoying the chance to relax and be off duty for once. Rob gave her a jokey shove.

'Watch it, you.'

'I'd take it if I were you, mate,' said Danny, who'd arrived a couple of years before with Jack to run the activity centre. 'Once they start taking the mickey out of you it's a sign you've been assimilated.'

Rob glanced at Charlotte, who flipped her long blonde hair over her shoulder as she gave a smile and a nod of agreement. She laced her fingers through his. 'He's right, you know.'

'Do you mean about Nero being a good life companion, or about being accepted as part of the village?' Rob raised his eyebrows.

'Bit of column a, and a bit of column b,' said Harry. Everyone roared with laughter.

Harry was putting glasses into the washer and wiping up the back of the bar while they chatted, and Polly slid off her stool and without being asked wandered around the tables, picking up leftover glasses and bringing them back over for him to wash, then gathering up soggy cardboard beer mats and shoving them into the bin. They worked well together, having spent many late evenings long after official closing hours chatting and laughing with the usual local suspects until they were shooed off home in the darkness of the small hours.

As she pottered about, she wondered how on earth she was going to break it to Tom that his *really great* cousin had been anything but. It had first appeared that Giles had been on a completely different date, because when Polly had returned from the kitchen to explain that she was needed to help out and thanks for a nice evening he'd wiped a dribble of caramel sauce from his mouth and stood up, asking when she was free next and whether she wanted to come fishing with him on the weekend. Polly had recoiled, taking an actual step backward, and then tried to arrange her face into a polite expression as she let him down gently and said that no, she didn't think that would be a good idea and that actually, although it had been very nice to have dinner that would be that. Giles had bristled slightly and waved the waitress over with an imperious arm.

'Can we have the bill, please?'

'Of course.' The waitress, glancing at the still-dripping ceiling with alarm, rushed off and returned moments later. She looked from Giles to Polly momentarily. Giles took the bill, muttered a calculation under his breath and then passed her his credit card.

'I think it's only fair we split the bill, don't you?' Polly said.

The waitress cast her a fleeting glance of surprise as Giles stalked out of the restaurant while she was still fishing in her bag to find her wallet.

Handing her card over, Polly giggled. 'I wouldn't mind but he drank all the wine *and* had pudding. Still, it's worth it for a lucky escape.'

The waitress, who'd clearly seen and heard enough of Giles to work out that he wasn't exactly the catch of the century, had joined in with Polly's laughter.

'Right you lot,' said Harry, half an hour later, 'I'm knackered. Sod off to your own beds.'

Polly glanced up at him for a moment. 'You sure you

don't mind me staying over? I can always ask Charlotte for a lift home or stay at her place.'

Harry tipped his head in the direction of Rob and Charlotte, who were standing by the door, heads close together, chatting. Rob lifted a long strand of Charlotte's hair and tucked it behind her ear, leaning in to kiss her on the cheek. Charlotte blushed and ducked her head. It was lovely to see her workaholic big sister so happy and madly in love with someone after so many years on her own.

'I think you might be a little bit surplus to requirements, don't you?' Harry lifted an eyebrow.

'I think you might be right.' Polly hitched herself back onto the bar stool. 'Looks like you're stuck with me for the night.'

'I'm not complaining,' said Harry, softly, and Polly felt her stomach flip with something she wanted very much to tell herself wasn't desire. She looked down into the bottom of her empty glass, spinning it on its edge carefully.

'I'll even fill that up for you. Come on, we'll turf this lot out and head upstairs with a pint of ice-cream and watch something terrible on Netflix. I think there's a new thriller that looks so bad it's got to be good.'

Harry's flat above the hotel had been his family home, and there were still remnants of his parents to be found all over the place. Old school photographs showing a gap-toothed six year old Harry still lined the stairs which led up to the flat. Polly paused for a moment, laughing at the terrible haircut he was sporting in one of them.

'That is such a good look,' she teased. He turned, one arm on the wall above her head, towering above her with a look of amusement on his face.

'I begged mum to take me into Ullapool for those blond highlights for ages, I'll have you know.'

'You look like a reject from the 1980s.'

'That was what I was aiming for. It was cool at the time.'

'At least you were cool once,' teased Polly, as they continued climbing the stairs.

'Watch it, you. There's still time for me to drive you back to Applemore. I haven't had anything to drink.'

Polly, who'd had two large gin and tonics in quick succession, hiccupped.

'And by the sounds of it I better catch you up.' He opened the door to the sitting room which was cluttered with boxes and had a stack of paintings balanced against one wall. 'Sorry this place looks even more like a bomb site than usual. These are the new pictures I've got for the bar when it's done.'

He left Polly looking through them as he went over to the kitchen which was through an archway. The pictures were colourful abstracts, painted by Nick, who worked from the gallery. She recognised his work immediately.

'Here you are.' Harry had poured her another drink and got himself a tumbler with two fingers of his favourite malt whisky.

'Have you bought these?'

'Some of them, yes. The others we're planning to have up for sale.'

'Oi, you're going to be nicking the gallery's business.' Polly took a sip of her drink, the bubbles bursting on her tongue.

Harry shook his head. 'Quite the opposite. Nick is hoping that it'll work as a bit of cross promotion. People will see what we're selling, and head up to the gallery to find out more.'

'That's a really good idea.'

'I'm full of them.' He headed towards the big L-shaped

sofa, collapsing on the cushions and tossing her a fluffy blanket. 'Here, you get under that, I'll find the remote.'

'Is it missing?'

'Everything is upside down here at the moment. I haven't a clue where it is. Saw it on Monday, but since then I've been stuck watching the BBC News Channel.'

Polly shook her head, laughing. Harry lifted the back cushion of the sofa, peering down the back of it with a hopeful expression.

'No sign?'

'Nope.'

She lifted a pile of newspapers. 'These are from the Sunday before last?'

'Yeah, I was going to have a relaxing evening with my feet up reading the papers.' Harry gave a slight chuckle. 'It didn't happen, you'll be surprised to hear.'

'On a plus note,' said Polly, brandishing the remote, 'We're not stuck watching BBC News for the rest of the evening.'

'Well, there's a silver lining to every cloud. I'll find the terrible film I was talking about. The ice cream's in the freezer, bring two spoons.'

As usual they talked all the way over the top of the film, which was as terrible as Harry had predicted.

'So how are the plans for the winter market going?' Harry shifted over so he could pass Polly the ice cream.

'You've eaten all the cookie dough,' protested Polly. She shoved him with her shoulder, feeling the sturdy bulk of his body and the warmth of his skin radiating through the wool of her dress.

'I'm saving you from yourself.' Harry tapped on her knee with his spoon. 'Nobody likes cookie dough, really. It's a myth.'

'It's my favourite thing,' said Polly, digging into the tub. 'Ah look, you haven't nicked it all. There's loads in here.'

'Of course I wouldn't steal all your cookie dough,' said Harry, squinting at the screen as he spoke. 'Is he –'

They both paused for a second in horror and watched as Ryan Reynolds was eaten alive by some sort of alien space creature.

'That's enough to put anyone off their ice cream.' Harry made a face.

'Not me.' She looked thoughtfully at the melting spoonful for a second then devoured it. 'I love ice cream too much to be put off by a minor little detail like a flesh eating space octopus.'

'…is a sentence I never thought I'd hear you say.'

Harry hadn't moved, so she was hyper-aware of his closeness. Polly's heart was thumping so loudly that she was certain that he must be able to feel it. This was ridiculous. She'd known him all her life, and he saw her as nothing more than a mate – his best friend's little sister, who'd come back to Applemore at the same time as he'd returned from his travels. She needed to shake herself out of this ridiculous fantasy that he might feel something else for her, just because she did.

'So,' he began, his expression solemn, 'Are you going to be seeing Giles again?'

Polly turned to look at him and realised he was teasing her. 'No I am not. In fact I've resolved to stay single for the rest of my life, if that's the alternative.'

CHAPTER ELEVEN

THERE WAS A LONG SILENCE. Harry looked at the screen as if the film had suddenly become the most fascinating thing ever. He was painfully aware of Polly's physical proximity, and of the floral scent of her hair which brushed past his face as she leant over to put the ice cream tub on the table. She looked bewitching tonight, dressed up far more than normal, in a silver-grey dress which seemed to cling to all her curves and show off her figure. She'd pushed up the sleeves as usual, and for a moment he imagined how it would feel to take her hand, turn it to expose the pale skin of her wrist and drop a kiss there, surprising her.

He shook himself and cleared his throat. 'So you're going to become an old maid like Frances from Midsummer House?'

'I don't think she's done too badly. She's travelling the world and having the time of her life by all accounts,' said Polly, picking the ice cream up again. 'Maybe I'll have one more spoonful.'

'I would.' He drained the last of his whisky.

'I don't think the world is going to end if I'm off the

dating scene,' said Polly, offering him the almost-empty tub. He shook his head.

'I'm alright. Whisky and ice cream is a pretty weird mix.'

'Gin and ice cream is too.'

'D'you want another?' He clambered out of the deep cushions of the sofa, looking down at Polly, who was curled up like a cat, her long legs tucked underneath her, the dark eye make up slightly smudged now. She scrunched up her nose.

'I probably shouldn't. I've got tons to do for the winter market. But – oh, go on. One for the road.' She patted the cushions beside her. 'Or the sofa, even.'

He mixed her a drink, long on tonic and short on gin, mindful that she had to be up and out in the morning, and that he'd have to drive her home.

'So what's the plan then?' Polly looked at him expectantly.

'With?'

'The hotel. I mean once you get rid of all the guests.'

'It's pretty straightforward really. We're doing two phases – the last thing we want is to be out of commission for too long, because the natives will get restless. You know what Applemore's like when people start making changes. So, the first stage is redecorating the bar, replacing the soft furnishings, that sort of thing. We'll have that done in a couple of weeks, all going to plan.'

'Is that the delivery that I saw arriving the other day?'

Harry nodded. 'Yeah, it's all being stored up in the old barn at Jimmy's farm. Once we've got the bar done and the decor, we're going to open – but leave the restaurant closed for January while we get the rest of it done.'

'I thought you were going for a grand re-opening for

Hogmanay?' Polly swirled her drink so the ice cubes clinked gently against the edge of the glass.

'That was the plan. But Rob and I had a talk with Kenny yesterday. We were rushing to get it done when really it's the quietest time of the year – bar New Year's Eve, of course but we'll take the hit on that – and it made more sense to wait and make some bigger changes.'

'What about planning permission and all that stuff?'

He shook his head. 'We're not doing anything structural. Decided that we'll stick with the place the way it is, because we've got our eye on something else. Lochinver House is on the market, and Rob reckons we could set it up as a destination restaurant.'

'Competition for Lochbay?' Polly's eyebrows lifted. 'That'll put the cat amongst the pigeons.'

'It will. But it'll also mean we've got somewhere for Conor to grow into. And of course we're still planning the seafood shack for next spring.'

'That wouldn't go down well with my date this evening.'

He shook his head, still marvelling that someone as unremarkable as Giles had managed to snare an evening with Polly. 'Not a fan of seafood?'

'I suspect he's probably got strong opinions on seafood, to go with his strong opinions on everything else. He disapproves of tourism in the Highlands.'

'Ah,' Harry nodded. 'So he wants to come up here and enjoy it but not actually do anything to keep the economy going?'

'Pretty much.'

'I can see why you gave him the nod,' he said, giving Polly a sideways look. She giggled.

'Yeah, not my best move. As I said, I'm going to stay single forever. It seems like the best option.'

'I'll drink to that.' He tipped his glass towards hers, and for a moment her blue eyes met his and something in her expression made him wonder if —

'Right,' said Polly, jumping up from the sofa with an unexpected burst of energy. 'I'd better get some sleep or I'm going to be like the living dead in the morning. Have you got a t-shirt or something I can sleep in?'

'Don't I always?' Get a grip, man, he told himself, pulling himself together and heading for his bedroom. He found a grey marl t-shirt with Sydney Sailing Club printed on the front and brought it through, along with one of the little hotel packs they kept behind reception for forgetful guests, which contained a toothbrush and toothpaste, a little pot of moisturiser cream, and a crisp white flannel cloth. 'Let me grab you a towel. Two secs.'

'Okay, I'll just get organised.'

The advantage of living in a hotel was that there was a permanent supply of freshly laundered white towels folded in his bathroom closet. He pulled out a big bath sheet and a smaller hand towel and went back to the sitting room, pushing open the door without thinking.

'Oh – sorry.' He stepped back again, pulling the door to quickly, feeling the blood rushing in his ears. Polly was pulling on the t-shirt, her back to him as he walked in, and he'd caught a glimpse of long pale legs and a flash of black lace. He puffed out a breath and shook his head as if to erase the picture.

'Sorry,' echoed Polly, calling to him through the door. 'I was getting changed. I'm decent now, don't worry.'

He walked in to find her sitting hugging her knees with the fluffy blanket covering them, looking perfectly modest and innocent.

'Two towels,' he said, abruptly. 'I'll wake you at seven, okay?'

Polly gave him a quizzical look. 'Yes, that's perfect.'

Harry jumped in the shower, turning the dial up so the water ran like hot needles against his skin, eyes closed in the hope that he could wash away the image he'd seen, but to no avail. He lay in bed for a long while trying to sleep, hyper-aware that Polly was lying in the room just next door. What the hell was wrong with him? She'd slept over on the sofa countless times over the last few years since he'd taken over the hotel and she'd returned to Applemore after her father's death. He needed to get focused on something other than what he couldn't have, or he was going to end up screwing up a friendship that meant everything to him.

It took a long time to fall asleep.

'Morning,' came a cheerful voice what seemed to be ten minutes later. He opened one eye, then another. It was still pitch dark outside.

'I woke up at half six for some weird reason,' said Polly cheerfully, flicking on the bedroom light, 'so I jumped in the shower and thought I'd make us a coffee.'

Harry pulled the duvet close and shifted up the bed, pulling himself upright and awake at the same time. 'You're an angel.'

'I am,' agreed Polly, happily. 'I even figured out your weird super snazzy new coffee maker. I assume these are some of Tom and Gavin's magic coffee beans?'

Harry reached out, taking the mug from her and sipping gratefully. 'Nicaraguan special roast, yeah. I didn't know you'd become a coffee afficionado.'

She shook her head, long hair – which was tied back in a pony tail high on her head – swishing back and forth for emphasis. 'I haven't a clue about it. They keep making me try all these amazing new beans they've imported and I honestly can't tell one cup from the next.

I only make the right noises because I know it makes them happy.'

'Like me when Beth turns up with different flowers for the hotel. She's always on about the new cultivar she's grown and pointing out the difference.'

Polly laughed at that. 'Yeah, I'm the same with the flowers, too. Basically my approach is along the lines of *do they look nice?* Or *does this coffee stop me falling asleep in the middle of the day?*'

'It can be our secret,' he said, watching as she wandered over to the window and looked outside into the darkness of the morning. He'd slept – as was his habit – with the curtains open, and the sky was dark but streaked with vivid pink streaks of light as the sunrise lit up the distant hills.

'This view is really pretty, isn't it?' Polly turned, perching her bottom on the edge of the window ledge. 'We're lucky to live here.'

'We are,' he agreed. 'Guests always want the sea view, but I think the back view over the hills is far more interesting. Especially in the morning when the sun is rising over them like that.'

'I think so too. It's why I love the cottage, even if it does mean living on top of the shop.'

'We're in the same boat.' He glanced at his phone, checking the time. As he picked it up, the alarm sounded. 'Seven o'clock. I better get a move on. The lads are doing breakfast but I've got a beer delivery coming and I think we're first on his list because he's heading from the brewery down this way before he heads to Inverness.'

Polly picked up her mug. 'I'll go and tidy up the sitting room while you get ready. Have you seen my car keys?'

Fifteen minutes later, having pulled up all the sofa cushions and searched behind the bar, they were none the wiser.

'Do you want me to give you a lift back?' Harry stood up, having checked under the last of the bar stools. 'I bet someone's picked them up by mistake.'

'If you don't mind. I've got spares somewhere. I'll catch a lift back into the village with someone later and pick the car up then.'

They were both surprised when they headed out to his car to bump into a woman in a woollen hat and a thick padded coat, the only other person up and about at that time of the morning. She was bent over, stroking the normally feisty and half-feral Pickle, who suddenly reverted to type and shot off hissing, tail like a bottle-brush.

'Hello,' said Polly, hovering for a second, a concerned expression on her face. 'Are you okay?'

The girl nodded, and he realised that there were tears – reflected in the glowing amber light of the street light – shining on her cheeks. 'I'm fine, yes, thank you.'

Only on hearing her Manchester accent did he clock that it was Ivy Winter, who looked completely different in outdoor gear.

'What's going on there?' He started the engine and looked across at Polly as she fastened her seat belt.

Polly shrugged. 'Dunno. Maybe they've had a fight?'

'Trouble in paradise.' He rubbed his chin thoughtfully. 'I guess I'll find out when I get back.'

'She looked really sad. Let me know what happens?'

'I'm sure it's just a quarrel.' Harry changed gear as they pulled out of the village and up towards the farm shop. 'But yeah, I'll keep you posted. Hopefully she won't decide that it's the curse of Applemore and write a bad review on her Instagram page saying she's had a terrible time.'

'By all accounts that's not likely. You couldn't pay for the sort of promo you're getting from all her stories and posts about what a fab time she's having. She's making Applemore look amazing.'

'It *is* amazing,' he protested with a chuckle.

'Oh, I know that,' said Polly, shoving her phone in her bag and straightening the hem of her dress. She'd changed, which was a pity in Harry's eyes, because her blue eyes and sleep-tousled mermaid hair were the perfect foil for the simple grey t-shirt.

The security light flashed on as they pulled into the courtyard outside the cottage.

'Right, no rest for the wicked, unfortunately.' Polly leaned across, planting a kiss on his cheek. He felt the soft brush of her lips against his day-after stubble and her hair brushed against him again as she pulled away.

'Lucky I've got a house key under the mat. Thanks for a lovely evening. It made up for the date from hell.'

'Any time.' He leaned across and opened the door for her. 'See you soon.'

'Come up and see the winter market tomorrow?'

'I'll try.'

Polly slid out of the passenger seat and stood for a second looking in at him. 'That would be lovely. Right, I'd better get to work.'

She blew him a kiss and headed towards the cottage. Harry watched her go, realising he'd miss her, then pushed that thought away as he started the drive back to the hotel. He wondered what sort of drama was waiting for him, and whether he'd find that his social media superstar guest had made an unexpected early departure.

CHAPTER TWELVE

'I GATHER that Ivy what's-her-name is away off on a nature trek with your Beth's Jack,' said Dolina McCloud, folding her arms over her capacious bosom, as was her wont, and leaning back against the counter of the farm shop.

Polly looked up from the counter where she was wrapping a box of hand poured candles in brown paper. 'She is?'

Dolina pounced. There was nothing she liked more than to be first with news of any sort, and especially when it came to the Fraser family. Even though it had been many years since the Frasers had owned much of the village and the farms and land surrounding it, she still seemed to hold on to a strangely feudal attitude which Polly found slightly disconcerting.

'She is indeed.' Dolina settled in, shifting herself slightly so she was leaning comfortably against the counter, mouth pursed, nodding slightly like a magpie, her bright eyes still taking everything around her in as she spoke. 'I was outside the hotel first thing when she and her fancy man came out all dressed up to the nines in brand new gear, all spotless and expensive-looking, and your Beth's Jack came along in his big pick up truck and took them up to the adventure centre. It's closed, you know, so he's doing them a favour.'

Polly, who was aware that Jack had wound down the centre for the winter months, nodded politely as she tore off a piece of Sellotape with her teeth, sticking it down carefully on the package and turning it over to smooth the paper down. 'That's nice,' she said, absently.

'Not sure what kind of nature she thinks they're going to see in the middle of winter,' continued Dolina, who was on a roll. 'Everything's dead.'

'That's not strictly true,' said Polly, who having grown up spending all her time outside, was very aware how much there was to see all year round. 'He'll probably take them down to Scrabie Bay to see the seals, and there are the eagles up on the moor, and –'

'Och yes,' said Dolina, 'Sure enough, I forgot the seals. I was thinking of flowers and that sort of thing.'

'Beth would tell you there's plenty out there as well. She's gathered loads for her wreath workshop,' said Polly, steering the conversation round to something productive. 'In fact I think there are a few spaces left on it, if you fancy spreading the word around?'

'Who me?' Dolina brushed away some imaginary crumbs from the front of her grey waterproof coat. 'And who am I going to spread the word to?' She chuckled to herself as if the idea was completely preposterous.

Polly shook her head faintly, and put the brown-paper-wrapped parcel into one of the bags with Applemore Farm Shop stamped on the side in black ink. She made a mental note that she needed to check they had enough for the market. There was so much to do – and Lachlan still hadn't brought the blooming Christmas tree.

'Will we be seeing you tomorrow for the market?'

Dolina nodded. 'I hear there's going to be mulled wine and Gregor the butcher doing a stall selling hot pork rolls.'

'That's right,' said Polly, handing over the bag. 'And loads more. We've got lots of the local makers coming together to sell stuff for Christmas, and there's a band playing, and toffee apples, and – well, you need to come and see for yourself. I'm hoping it'll be a success. It's a bit of a risk trying something new,' she said, almost more to herself than to Dolina.

Dolina put out a reassuring hand and squeezed her on the arm. 'Don't you worry, I'm sure you'll do a grand job. I'll see you tomorrow.'

Polly watched as the older woman made her way across the shop towards the exit, veering right at the last minute when she spotted someone she knew through the archway into the café.

'You'll never guess what I've just seen,' Polly heard her say as she disappeared out of view.

Outside in the courtyard, the wooden stalls were being assembled by Matt from the bakery along with Anna, who baked the delicious chocolate brownies that sold like hot cakes (Polly always giggled to herself at that) from the shop every day. She'd privately suspected that the flirtation between Matt and Anna must be on the verge of tipping over into something more, if it hadn't already. Anna had insisted when they'd been chatting the other week that nothing had happened, but the swoony expression on her face suggested that she was hoping it was only a matter of time. Sure enough, when Polly walked towards them she sensed that there was an atmosphere which was charged with something other than the excitement of Christmas.

'How's it going?' She looked at Anna and raised one eyebrow, her face hidden from Matt by the long curtain of her blonde hair. Anna widened her eyes almost imperceptibly for a second in an unspoken acknowledgment of the situation.

'Well, once *someone* acknowledged that it would be easier to assemble these stalls if we actually followed the instructions,' said Anna, pink cheeked and laughing, 'It's started going a lot better.'

'Shush, you,' said Matt, giving her a playful shove. Despite the cold he was in a t-shirt and a red checked flannel shirt, the sleeves of which were rolled up to reveal the strong arms of a baker who spent every day kneading dough the old-fashioned way.

'Well I'm glad I've left it in your capable hands,' said Polly, drily. 'No sign of my brother with this extra tree he promised?'

'Rilla stopped by on her way into town half an hour ago when you were serving someone. She said she couldn't stop, but that Lachlan was out with a chainsaw as we speak and would be dropping it off shortly. I said – ' Anna gave Matt a shy glance from under her cloud of wavy dark hair 'That we'd decorate it, if you give me the lights and stuff?'

'That would be absolutely amazing.' Polly, who was trying to coordinate everything and feeling slightly last-minute-ish, gave a sigh of relief.

The shop was busy right up until closing time, with lots of locals popping in for their usual supplies. Polly noticed that everyone seemed to find a reason to pause outside, taking in the industrious scene of Matt and Anna working together to decorate the tree, their breath rising in the cold air and the tiny pin-prick dots of golden light sparkling through the branches of the huge pine that Lachlan had cut from the wood. By the end of the day the courtyard was ringed with the canopied wooden stalls, each hung with strings of glowing fairy lights. The tree sparkled in one corner, and even the tired old tractor which had been parked in the yard for as long as Polly could remember had recently been given a coat of red paint and someone had tied tinsel around the steering wheel. She hovered for a while after everyone had left, taking it all in. She was normally so busy that she didn't have a moment to stop and think about everything that she'd done, but tonight she paused, looking at the white-painted buildings glowing under the lights, and through the huge arched window into the shop and café. Her dad would have been impressed with everything they'd done to drag Applemore out of the dire financial straits it'd been in when he'd died. She glanced up at the sky, where the crescent moon peeped out from behind a cloud and the stars shone brightly, and gave a little nod. If he was out there, somewhere, she hoped he was looking down and smiling.

The sound of a car pulling up woke her before the alarm had a chance to go off. Fifteen minutes later, showered and yawning, she headed out, feeling butterflies of excitement in her stomach. They'd never tried anything like this before – was it going to be a success, or would she end up being the laughing stock of the village for having ideas above her station?

The lights were on in Matt's Bakery – he gave a wave through the window, where she could see him directing Euan, his young seventeen year old apprentice, to put a huge metal shelf on the cooling rack. The window was slightly open despite the icy chill of the still-dark morning and the smell of freshly baked sourdough bread was mouth-watering. She knew that he would've been up since the small hours, determined to get everything just right for today – he was a perfectionist when it came to his baking, and even more so when there was a chance that maybe Ivy Winter might turn up with her camera ready to take some arty shots and promote his work on her ultra-popular Instagram page. Polly, who was still wondering why she'd been in tears the day before, crossed her fingers and hoped that whatever the drama was, the nature trip with Jack had been enough to cheer her up. She felt slightly guilty that she was mainly hoping she was going to turn up at the market and do a bit of free promo, but there was a decent sized portion of her heart which felt sympathetic. Even people with seemingly perfect lives must have their fair share of heartache.

She headed into the shop and flicked on the lights, still thinking about Ivy Winter. She was making judgements based on appearance, like people who didn't know her assuming that she'd grown up with vast riches because of the size of Applemore House. It was easy to look at the outside and make assumptions, but the reality was that she'd grown up with her single parent dad trying desperately to make ends meet in a crumbling, freezing cold castle they couldn't afford to sell, and no money for anything exciting like holidays abroad or nice clothes. She'd been dressed in hand-me-downs from her sisters, which had been patched together by Joan, the housekeeper who'd held the family together after their mother had left when Polly herself was tiny. She smiled to herself remembering that Joan – who divided her time between Applemore and Aberdeen, having found love with George, a retired teacher – was on her way home today. Hopefully she'd be back in time to pop up and see the market for herself. Polly automatically straightened up the glass jars on one of the shelves. Joan was a stickler for neatness, and she wanted the place to look as good as it could, so she'd be proud of her. She was the closest they had to a parent now, and Polly adored her.

'This is obscenely early,' said Rilla, breaking her

reverie. Polly spun around to see Rilla, her hair tied off her face with a pretty red and white gingham scarf, standing in the doorway. She was wearing a thick woolly Christmas jumper and dark blue jeans, and put down a box on the counter with a clatter of glass bottles.

'I didn't want to start unpacking them until I knew for certain which stall was ours. Lachlan's up at the house with Kitty – would you believe she actually slept though the night? I feel like I've had about three weeks at a health spa.' A huge smile spread across Rilla's freckled face. 'And we've got Gillian from the nursery coming to look after her for the day so we can focus on selling all this –' she pointed to the box 'and Lachlan's bringing down a load of beer in the Land Rover when she gets there. I said I'd come down and get organised, by which I meant sneak off and have a coffee and one of Matt's pain au chocolat uninterrupted.'

'That sounds like the best idea ever. Tom and Gavin aren't here yet, though, so it'll have to be instant coffee.' Polly headed for the little office at the back of the shop. 'I'll put the kettle on, you go and see if you can wheedle a couple of pastries out of Matt. Ask them if they want a coffee, too.'

Coffee was a nice idea in theory, Polly thought two hours later, when she dashed into the office to find a roll of tape to stick up the fairy lights which were refusing to stay put on the edge of the wooden stalls. She looked down at the mug she'd made which was still sitting, half-drunk and looking distinctly unappetising, alongside the half-eaten pain au chocolat which she'd abandoned when Gregor the butcher's pick up and trailer had started reversing into place down the side of the shop. He'd arrived at the crack of dawn to get ahead with the hog roast, and no sooner had she got him organised, Ben, the woodcarver who exhibited at the gallery, had turned up asking for something. Now outside was a hive of activity – it was almost nine and the stalls were nearly finished, each stacked with locally made products, looking enticing. It had been cold so she'd put on fingerless gloves to keep herself warm, but as she worked she'd cast off layers and was now just in a shirt, despite the temperature being almost freezing and the sky having a faintly purple tinge which hinted that they might be in for snow later. She paused on the threshold of the shop, looking out at the market, which was thrumming with a sense of anticipation. Everything was ready to go. All they needed now were some visitors. She turned around, hearing footsteps behind her. Gavin dropped an arm around her shoulders and gave her a squeeze, his eyes kind.

'What's the matter with you, cariad?'

She smiled at the Welsh endearment. He had such a way of making everything feel okay.

'What if nobody turns up?' Polly bit her lip. 'And we've got all these people here and it's a complete disaster?'

'And the likelihood of that happening is…?' Gavin cocked his head gently.

'Fifty fifty?'

'For a smart girl, you can be pretty blooming stupid sometimes. There's nothing else to do in Applemore, it's a gorgeous winter day, and everyone's got their Christmas shopping to do. I promise you, you'd be fighting them off with a stick before you know it.'

Polly stomach fluttered with nerves. 'I hope you're right.'

'Trust me, my love. I am.'

He gave her shoulder a little squeeze and headed out across the courtyard and into the bakery, returning a few moments later with a tray of freshly baked pastries which filled the air as he passed with a scent of cinnamon and sweet vanilla.

'Have one last wander round and take it all in,' he warned, 'Because I will lay money on you being so busy in about half an hour that the next time you draw breath it'll be the end of the day and the place will look like a plague of locusts has been through it.'

Polly – still unconvinced – decided to take him at his word. She picked up her phone and started snapping some pictures for their social media accounts. First there was sisters Susie and Jo, who made the hand-poured candles scented with essential oils which she sold in the Farm Shop. Their stall smelled delicious, a mixture of wintergreen and eucalyptus mingling to create a Christmassy scent which was irresistible. There were glass bottles of bath oils with sprigs of rosemary suspended inside, and little jars of hand creams and skin salves, all made in a converted barn in their old family farmhouse.

Rilla and Lachlan were chatting and laughing with Beth, her sister, who was carrying armfuls of greenery which she was taking into the workshop alongside the gallery. She was planning a display of her wreath-making class, as well as selling pretty little wicker baskets planted with hyacinths which were almost ready to bloom in time for Christmas. Her flower farm business had started off as a summer-only affair, but over the last few years – and with Jack as moral support, cheering her on in a way she hadn't had when unhappily married to her ex – she'd branched out until there was something going on all year round.

Rilla was straightening out little hand-written cards which she had placed beneath sample bottles of the gin that they distilled here at Applemore, using an old copper still that had been – not altogether legally - used in the old days by an ancestor.

'Made with herbs and botanicals grown here on the Applemore Estate,' read Polly, aloud. She looked at the other side of the table where serried rows of the craft beer which Lachlan had recently started brewing again stood neatly, their labels printed with a simple, understated font. 'I hope this lot isn't going to explode like the first batch.'

'You and me both,' said her brother, grimacing.

'Is that a possibility? Should we be warning Susie and Jo they might be assailed by flying beer bottle lids?'

Lachlan rubbed his bristly chin. 'Nope, you're good. This batch is a success. Can't believe you're doubting my brewing ability.'

'Can't believe you're taking me seriously.' Polly grinned. 'You're good enough that your first brewery was sold off and made you a fortune.'

'Oh, you are such a smart arse,' said Lachlan, shaking his head.

Polly giggled, and stepped back to take another photograph. When she turned to get a photo of Matt's bakery stall, she heard the first crunch of tyres on gravel and felt a shiver of excitement.

'We're on,' said Rilla, brushing down her Christmas jumper and straightening the little cards once again.

'I think they're probably as straight as you're going to get them,' said Lachlan, laughing. He closed a hand over hers and squeezed gently and Rilla looked up at him.

Polly turned away, feeling surplus to requirements once again, and felt herself wishing that Harry was here to see how the market was looking. But he'd be hard at work, on the last hotel day of the season, probably watching the clock and looking forward to tomorrow when he could check out the very last guests and close the doors and get on with the renovations. She was certain that the last thing he was thinking about was her little Christmas market.

CHAPTER THIRTEEN

HARRY WATCHED out of the bar window as one of the village fishing boats headed out of the bay. The sea was like glass. The sky was the strange lilac blue that it turned when there was a chance of snow, and there wasn't a cloud to be seen. It was the perfect day for Polly's Christmas market. He crossed his fingers unthinkingly, turning to look down the road which led out of the village and on towards Applemore and the farm shop where he knew she'd have been working hard for hours. Behind him he could hear Katie and Phoebe chatting away as they tidied the glasses underneath the bar, counting and making note as they did a stock take in preparation for the renovations. There were only three guests now - Ivy Winter and Ben, and a quiet elderly man who'd disappeared after breakfast with a pair of binoculars around his neck, explaining that he was heading off to the moor in the hope of spotting some rare birds. This time tomorrow he'd have the place to himself, although it would be anything but quiet. He hoped it would be full of the sounds of industry as Kenny and his gang got to work.

Bring on Radio Scotland and football chat blaring out and the sounds of hammering and sawing. He wasn't looking for peace and quiet – he wanted to get on with making changes without any guests to consider. It was funny that having grown up in the hotel, he'd become accustomed to always putting the needs of the guests before himself. This was the first time in as long as he could remember that the Applemore Hotel would be closed. He gave a happy sigh. Not having to deal with the myriad requests of visitors was going to be a blessed relief.

'If we're going to be opening up for people to collect drinks at night, do we need to keep any glasses out?' Phoebe called, and he turned back to attend to her.

'Box up all of them bar about twenty or so. I've said we'll do beer boxes, but I can't see anyone coming along and having a drink in the freezing cold outside, can you?'

Katie and Phoebe exchanged glances. 'I think if you give Murdo and Jock the chance to escape their wives for half an hour they'll be installed on the picnic table across the road setting up an unofficial pub before you know it.'

Harry shook his head. 'That's not the deal and they know it. I'm only offering this as a service because they're all so stuck in their ways. They can take their beer home and watch it in front of Coronation Street or Eastenders or whatever they like. For once, I'm not going to be responsible for keeping them off the streets.'

'Fair enough,' said Phoebe, with a shrug. They were so delighted to have the run up to Christmas off on full pay that Harry suspected he could have said anything and they'd have agreed quite happily. He and Rob had talked it through, and both agreed that taking the hotel and pub out of commission at this time of year wasn't the choice of the staff, and so it had been agreed that not only would they be paid as if they were working, but they'd be given a

Christmas bonus as well, in lieu of all the tips they'd normally receive working in the restaurant and bar, which were usually divided between all the staff.

The door opened and all three of them looked up.

'How's the injured soldier?' Katie said, as Conor walked into the room, his arm in a sling.

'Getting there,' said Conor, wiggling the fingers which peeked out of the end of his bandage. 'I'll be fine by Christmas.'

'You've got until the end of January before the restaurant is open again,' Harry reminded him, firmly, 'And I don't want you injuring yourself meanwhile.'

'No white water rafting in the holidays then?' Conor gave a cheeky grin, his eyebrows steepling.

'Not if you want to wow everyone when we re-open. At this rate with all the new social media followers we've got thanks to Miss Winter we're going to be booked up well in advance.' Harry had to admit that she had an amazing effect – every time she posted a picture online the hotel gained a flurry of new followers, and the booking enquiries were coming in surprisingly fast. Given everything, he'd grudgingly acknowledged that Phoebe's desire to bend over backwards for her social media idol seemed to have worked wonders. He wondered how the no-nonsense Jack, with his gruff Glasgow sense of humour and practical attitude had got on with their nature walk yesterday. He wasn't the sort to have any time for someone like Ivy.

'Talking of which,' Conor said, adjusting his arm in the sling, 'Has she checked out or is she still here? I saw her Instagram photos of the seals. You've got to admit she's pretty good at getting decent pictures.'

Harry gave a brief nod of acknowledgment.

'Yeah, she and Ben are heading up to the market at Polly's shop, apparently. Hopefully she'll work her wonder and get a load of new eyes on the stallholders' businesses, too.'

'Cool.' Conor gave a nod. 'I'm going to head up in a bit too, if I can catch a lift. Can't drive one-handed. I mean I could, but…'

Harry raised a hand to stop him. 'Don't even think about it. I'll give you a lift. I was looking for an excuse to go and check it out anyway.'

'Brilliant.' Conor beamed. 'Gimme a shout when you're ready. I'll supervise Phoebe and Katie sorting this place out meanwhile.'

Ten minutes later they set off out of the village, Conor shuffling awkwardly into the passenger seat with a brief growl of discomfort as he managed to whack his wrist on the doorframe.

'You sure that's definitely only a sprain?' Harry shot him a look.

'Yep, had it x-rayed at the clinic. The doc started making noises about why I'd blacked out but I pointed out that a day with no food and four hours sleep will do that to a person.'

'No more burning the candle at both ends,' warned Harry. 'I've got plans for you. When we get the renovations done at the end of January I want to do a big opening, get some press up – maybe I'll even invite Miss Winter to come back again.'

'Sounds like a plan. Then you can get her back when we get the Airstream caravan sorted and the seafood shack is up and running for the summer season.' Conor sounded excited at the thought.

'Yeah, and if our other plans come off… we can –' Harry stopped mid-sentence. He hadn't told Conor about Rob's plans to buy the Lochinver estate and turn the house into a luxury restaurant with rooms.

'Can what? What plans?' Conor shifted his body, still guarding his arm and looked at Harry as he turned off the road and onto the single track driveway that led up towards the farm shop.

Harry contemplated how much to give away, not wanting to get Conor's hopes up when everything was still up in the air. He glanced up at the big wooden sign which announced APPLEMORE WILD CAMPING AND FARM SHOP was hung with starry silver decorations and tiny glowing fairy lights which swayed gently in the breeze.

'Watch this space,' Harry said, finally. 'Let's say if this comes off, you'll not be bored.'

Conor raised both eyebrows and gave a nod. 'Mum's the word.'

'Yeah, don't say anything.'

'I can't say anything about nothing,' Conor laughed briefly. 'I mean you haven't given me much to go on.'

'You know what the jungle drums are like round here. It's not you I'm worried about, it's people like Dolina. If she gets wind that we're making plans she'll be spreading rumours like wildfire.'

'Loose lips sink ships and all that jazz.' Conor put the index finger of his good hand to his mouth and made a zipping motion. 'I won't say a word.'

Harry flashed him a grin. 'That's the spirit.'

They swung round a tight bend on the road and Harry slowed the car with an exclamation of surprise.

'Look at that!'

'Aye and Polly was worried it wouldn't be a success?' Conor gave a low whistle.

Cars were parked all along the grass verge on the lead up to the farm shop, lining the road on both sides. Harry reversed back, parking his at an angle behind a familiar pick-up truck with the logo of Jack's outdoor adventure centre painted on the sides. On the back seats were the twins' car seats, the windows smudged with tiny sticky finger prints. Harry pointed them out to Conor.

'Looks like Jack's on stepdad duty. I think Beth's doing some sort of floristry demo.'

They both caught a waft of roast pork which was floating on the breeze as they strolled up the road towards the shop, moving out of the way as another familiar vehicle went past, sounding its horn in greeting. An arm extended from the open window and gave a wave as Lachlan's Land Rover sped off past the entrance to the shops and headed up towards Applemore House itself.

'You've got to give it to Poll, she's done a bloody good job of all this.' Conor thrust his hand in his jeans pocket as they paused at the entrance to the courtyard, taking in the throng of visitors who were milling about, soaking up the festive atmosphere.

Harry's heart squeezed as he caught a glimpse of Polly, long blonde hair tied up in a ponytail and a pair of brightly coloured bauble earrings swinging against her neck. She was dressed in a garish Christmas sweater, her long legs encased in jeans. He watched her as she bent to chat to one of Jack and Beth's twins, a huge smile on her face, completely focused on what they were saying. Harry dragged his gaze away, realizing Conor was looking at him sideways with a knowing expression.

'Right then,' said Harry quickly. 'I don't know about you but I could do with one of Gregor's hot roast pork rolls with apple sauce.'

'That sounds like a plan.' Conor fell into step beside him.

There was a long queue, which snaked around the side of the farm shop and café, falling into line behind couples and families who were patiently waiting. Gregor's hog roasts were famous in Applemore, and nobody minded waiting when they know how crisp the crackling would be, or how deliciously succulent the meat, which was so tender that you could cut it with a fork. His stomach growled as he stood waiting beside Conor, who was scrolling on his phone and typing a series of messages. He hoped that he wasn't furiously texting his girlfriend with news that Harry and Rob had secret plans for expanding the business, but dismissed the thought with a shake of his head. No, Conor was as reliable as they came, and that was one of the reasons that they saw him as cornerstone in their plans. Rob was drawing up the financial details and working with an estate agent friend from back in Edinburgh to put together an offer for the Lochinver estate. It was mad to think how much money he had, considering how easy-going and laid-back he was. He was the perfect match for Charlotte, Polly's eldest sister. He'd thought how happy they'd looked the other night when they came in for dinner, totally wrapped up in each other, finishing each other's sentences and sloping off into the night leaving him to spend the last hours of the evening with Polly after her date from hell. He grimaced, thinking about how it had made him feel to think of her dating someone else. Maybe he needed to bite the bullet and tell her how he felt – and in doing so, risk their friendship. And Lachlan's. The line moved forward a few paces as a family who had just been served wandered off, carrying their hot pork rolls, laughing and chatting happily. Polly was so sweet with her niece and nephew – she'd make an amazing mum. The thought of that left him with a painful stab of realisation that if he didn't do something before too long, it would be too late and she'd have found someone else. The prospect of having to watch her spend the rest of her life with another man was... he glanced down, realising he'd balled his hands into fists. Sort it out, Robertson, he thought to himself, you're setting yourself up for a fist fight with a non-existent sparring partner. You need to get a grip, and fast.

'Alright, stranger?'

A familiar deep Glaswegian voice broke through his thoughts and he turned, pleased to have the distraction. Jack stood, a huge giant with close-cropped dark hair, clad in his habitual outfit of practical Scandinavian-style outdoor gear and enormous hiking boots. Flanking him on each side, one hand holding onto Jack and the other clutching a toffee apple, were Beth's son and daughter.

'Guess what, Harry,' said Edward, grinning up at him with a gap-toothed smile, 'Look what happened to me last night.'

'It's not fair,' said Lucy, stamping a furious little foot. 'My tooths aren't even a tiny little bit wobbly and now Edward had the tooth fairy come and visit and I didn't even get to see her because I was asleep.'

'Is that so?' Harry laughed.

'I think she might come back again tonight,' said Lucy.

Edward widened his eyes at the thought. 'She might. Maybe I could leave her a note and tell her I'm trying to make my other tooth fall out.'

'*She* might be a *he*, for all you know,' said Jack, meeting Harry's amused gaze. 'It's been a long morning,' he added as an aside.

'Beth busy with flower stuff?' Harry peered across the courtyard in the general direction of the converted farm building which now held the gallery and art studio where she offered her courses.

'Oh yes,' said Jack, with meaning, keeping his voice low so the twins couldn't hear. 'We got up when she did at half five this morning – thank goodness the tooth fairy had already been for his or her visit. Then we did breakfast, dropped Beth up at the farm to get organised, headed home, watched approximately fifty four hours of children's tv, painted thank you cards for the mysterious tooth fairy, made chocolate and banana pancakes for breakfast, and somehow got up here for eleven. I feel like I've been awake for five days on the trot and it's not even lunchtime. Speaking as a survival expert, it's easier spending a night bivouacking and drinking rainwater than doing this as a job. Whatever they pay teachers, it's nowhere near enough.'

Harry and Conor both snorted with laughter.

'I hear you've been in the wars,' said Jack, turning to Conor. 'Been drinking on the job?'

'Something like that.'

The queue moved forward again. Harry gave a sideways nod, indicating the wooden picnic tables over by the edge of the field. One had become free as a family of four finished eating and headed off towards their car, their arms full of bags from a morning's shopping at the market stalls. He'd noticed Conor rubbing his shoulder, which was clearly aching despite his protestations that it was nothing.

'You go and grab a seat, I'll get us something to eat.'

Conor headed over, followed by the twins who scrambled up onto the benches and sat chattering beside him, faces increasingly sticky from the toffee apples.

'So how'd it go yesterday?'

Jack put his hands in the back pockets of his trousers, arching his back to stretch it out. 'Good, yeah, surprisingly so. From what Beth had said I was expecting to have to cater to some super-glam princess type, but Ivy and Ben were a good laugh.'

'Really?' Harry felt his eyebrows shooting upwards in surprise.

Jack nodded. 'Yeah. She got covered in mud when we went over the moor to see if we could spot the deer, and it turns out she knew quite a bit about our wildlife. Got some really good photos, too.'

'I guess appearances can be deceptive.'

'Yeah, well, we all know Applemore can be a bit quick to judge people,' said Jack, with meaning.

'Mmm.' Harry had witnessed first-hand the judgements people had made when Jack had arrived in the village to set up the outdoor centre.

'Anyway she's put a link to the centre on her social media and I've had loads of enquiries already, so I'm definitely in her corner. She really knows her stuff when it comes to all that stuff.'

'Sounds like Ivy Winter's got a brand new fan club member.' Harry grinned.

'Don't knock it, mate,' said Jack, as they finally moved forward to give their orders to Gregor at the front of the line. 'I tell you that lassie has her head well screwed on.'

CHAPTER FOURTEEN

'I NEVER THOUGHT I'd be saying this but we're running low on stock,' said Rilla as Polly approached her stall. Rilla's dark hair had come loose from the band she'd tied it back with and dark curls were hanging in untidy tendrils around her face. Lachlan was underneath the table of the stall removing the last bottles of Applemore Gin from the wooden crates they'd brought earlier that morning.

'Do you want me to nip up to the house and get some more?' Polly glanced around. The courtyard was packed with shoppers, and over on the wooden picnic tables groups of people were sitting having Gregor's pork rolls and drinking steaming hot cups of hot apple cider and mulled wine. The air was full of delicious smells and the sounds of happy chat. For a second she allowed herself to give a tiny sigh of relief that it looked like she'd actually pulled this thing off and the Christmas market was a success.

'Or man the stall and I can nip up?' Lachlan straightened up and pushed his scruff of hair back from his face.

A second later a tall grey haired man with an untidy

beard materialised at Polly's side and started quizzing Lachlan in a thin, nasal Edinburgh accent. He lifted one of the bottles and examined the label, turning it around before putting it down on the table a moment later.

'What was the original gravity post mash?'

Polly looked at Rilla, who gave a shrug which indicated that she didn't have a clue what he was on about either. Given the choice between dealing with real ale geeks and leaving the market to its own devices for ten minutes, she knew which option she preferred.

'If anyone needs me, tell them to call me,' said Polly to Rilla, after taking instructions on what was needed and where it was.

She was turning the key in the ignition of Lachlan's Land Rover when she looked up to see Harry standing there, one hand on the roof, the corners of his eyes crinkling in amused welcome.

'Hello, stranger. Are you making a fast getaway?'

'Lachlan needs more beer – can you believe they've sold it all already?'

'Are you suggesting your brother's beer is terrible, or marvelling that your Christmas Market is a success?'

'The latter.' Polly shook her head, laughing. 'Shouldn't you be working? Haven't you got a hotel to renovate?'

'I've left Phoebs and Katie sorting out the bar, but we're on the wind down. Your social media superstar is heading this way, apparently.'

Polly gulped. 'Seriously?' Somehow, besides bumping into a tearful Ivy Winter, she'd managed to miss spotting her at all on her visit to Applemore, and with her heading back to Manchester tomorrow it was now or never. 'Hopefully she'll come and work her magic up here as well. We could do with a bit of free promo.'

'Better come and give you a hand with this beer then,

hadn't I? Otherwise you'll take twice as long loading it into the Land Rover and by the time you get back she'll have been and gone.'

'Hardly,' Polly protested, then closed her mouth as Harry headed round and climbed into the passenger seat beside her, slamming the door shut and looking at her expectantly.

'Come on then, wagons roll.' Harry grinned. 'Let's get this show on the road, as your old dad used to say.'

They had to pause halfway up the drive towards Applemore House to allow a little group of sheep to trot across their path, heading in towards the shelter of the wood.

'Are they supposed to be there?' Harry watched as they scampered off.

Polly nodded. 'Lachlan and Rilla got Jimmy to drop them off a couple of weeks ago, they can't get out because of the cattle grid and they've fenced off the woodland.'

'Cheaper than a lawnmower?'

'Something like that.' They turned the corner and Applemore House rose up from behind the trees, the tall turrets pale against the lilac sky. She parked by the back door, reversing the Land Rover up to the long stone steps to make it easier to load up with the heavy boxes of beer.

'Amazing the difference those two have made to the place, isn't it?' Harry stood for a moment looking upwards. She followed his gaze.

'It looks a lot better, doesn't it?'

'Makes me think about how different the hotel will be once we've finished. It's got good bones, but the whole place is tired.'

'I know how it feels.' Polly yawned. 'But I need a bit more than a coat of paint and some damp-proofing. A couple of weeks in the Maldives would do it.'

'You need to change career then, and start doing what Ivy Winter does. I had a look at her Instagram account and she's been on about seven holidays this year.' Harry stepped back as she pushed open the door. Conscious of the narrowness of the dark passageway, she pressed herself against the wall as she slid into the house, but even so she could feel the closeness of his body and sense the heat which emanated from him in contrast to the winter cold in the air.

'Rilla said it's in the old cold store.' His footsteps on the flagstone floor echoed behind her as they traipsed down the passage until she opened a big wooden door, pushing it as it creaked in its frame. Once upon a time in her grandparents' day this had been the old larder where the cook would have stored all the meat and dairy products for the family but now it was filled with a jumble of old wooden pallets and wooden crates stacked with Lachlan's craft beers and the artisan gin that he and Rilla created together as one of their many money-making ventures.

Harry sized up the room, having a look inside one of the boxes.

'Right, that's gin. If you take that –' he lifted it up, passing it to her, 'I'll grab one of these crates of beer.'

The bottles clanked gently as they carried them back along the passageway. Polly slid the box into the back of the Land Rover, shoving a couple of dog leads and some old walking boots out of the way.

Together they worked quickly, loading the back of the Land Rover.

'Think that's enough?'

'Probably more than,' she said, looking at the carefully stacked boxes. 'But we've got all afternoon to go yet.'

'You've done well,' said Harry, looking down at her

thoughtfully. 'All that stressing about it being a washout – I knew you'd make a success of it.'

Polly felt her cheeks getting warm as she flushed with embarrassed pleasure. 'Thanks.'

'I mean it,' said Harry, as they climbed back into the car. 'You're amazing. You've done all this by yourself.'

They pulled up outside the farm shop, and Rilla – who'd had the presence of mind to block off a parking spot with a couple of old crates – moved them back out of the way and stood with her hands on her hips looking at them as Polly and Harry climbed back out of the car.

'Saved by the bell,' she said, pretending to mop her brow. 'That bloke Lachlan was talking to ended up clearing us out of beer.'

'Polly,' called her sister Beth from across the courtyard, 'Can you give me a hand with this stuff?'

'What it is to be in demand,' joked Harry. 'I'll give Rilla a hand with this stuff. See you in a sec.'

Polly headed over to see what Beth was wanting, feeling reluctant to have to leave Harry's company. She turned to see him talking to a small blonde-haired woman with a thick Icelandic sweater on and felt a pang of envy. Sometimes it felt like she'd done the most amazing job of making a success of everything in her life apart from the stuff that mattered.

'Sorry,' said Beth, brushing down the grey apron she was wearing and then hooking her pale blonde hair behind her ears. 'Can you grab this? I would have asked Jack but he's taken the twins back to the house – they were having world war three over tooth-gate.'

Beth pointed to a pile of jute sacks. 'Jack dumped this here but it all kicked off with the twins before I got a chance to put it in the studio.'

They lifted them into their arms and ducked behind

the market stall where Anna was re-organising her wicker baskets of cakes and chocolate brownies. Someone had changed the music and now Michael Bublé was warbling away through the speakers. 'Ow!' Polly yelped as a holly leaf poked through the sacking and jabbed her finger. 'Tooth-gate?'

'Lucy's green with envy because the tooth fairy didn't come and visit her.'

'Oh poor Luce.'

'Don't you start. I'm always trying to make things realistic with those two and show them that sometimes one will get something and the other won't and it'll even out.'

That was her practical sister all over. She'd always been determined that Edward and Lucy would be seen as people as their own right, although she'd long since given up on her resolution never to refer to them as "the twins" which all the Fraser siblings still teased her about.

'Thanks for that,' said Beth a moment later as they tipped the contents of the sacks out onto a huge wooden trestle table. She moved quickly, setting out individual floristry scissors and secateurs at intervals along the table. 'I've got a special guest joining in - fingers crossed it'll go okay. I'm feeling the pressure this afternoon.'

Polly gave her a curious look. 'Why this afternoon?'

A moment later there was a hesitant knock at the door to the studio and a hesitant voice said, 'Am I early?'

'No,' said Beth, cutting a few extra lengths of floristry wire, 'Come in, you're fine.'

She looked up and caught Polly's eye for a fleeting moment, lifting her brows in an almost imperceptible movement which Polly clocked immediately. She turned, and gave an audible gasp of surprise.

'Hello,' said Ivy Winter, smiling back at her.

'Um, hi.' Polly glanced back at Beth. This must be the

extra person she was talking about. She was surprised to notice that Ivy was wearing hardly any make up, her long blonde hair tied back from her face. She looked younger and far less intimidating than she did on her ultra-posed Instagram photographs.

'Is it okay if I take some videos? I thought it might be nice to put them up on my stories.'

'Oh yeah, wow, yes that would be amazing.' Beth beamed, 'Just tell me if you want me to do anything.'

Polly did a double take at her practical, no-nonsense sister sounding star-struck and tongue tied and shook her head with a grin. 'I better get on, we've got the band starting in a moment and I said I'd announce them in the hope people will sign them up for parties. Good luck with the wreath-making, I'll come and have a look at how you're doing later.'

Beth gave her a beady look and a wave. Ivy, who was moving the items on the table in front of her to make them look good for a photo, didn't notice her leaving. It was odd to see her looking – well, normal, really. She looked like everyone else when she wasn't dressed up in all her posh gear and with her hair and make up immaculate.

Over by the old tractor, the band were tuning up their instruments on the makeshift stage that they'd rigged up with a stack of wooden pallets. They'd played a couple of sessions at Harry's bar on a Thursday night, and as she looked across the courtyard she could see Harry leaning back against the tractor, one long leg crossed over the other, hands thrust in his pockets. He looked up for a moment and spotted her, a lazy smile spreading over his face. Polly felt her heart skip with longing then a second later it sank like a stone when she realised that there was someone heading in her general direction with a determined expression on his face. Oh god, where the hell had Giles sprung from? She'd hoped that after the date from hell she was never going to see him again.

She ducked behind Rilla and Lachlan's stall, making herself as small as possible as she sidled along the wall of the farm shop, then speeded across the open courtyard dodging between groups of shoppers as she made her way towards Harry, who greeted her with a slightly confused expression.

'I need to borrow you,' she hissed, grabbing his hand.

'Sorry lads,' said Harry, giving a fleeting wave of apology to Joe, the singer of the band, who was adjusting his guitar strap. 'Duty calls.'

Polly towed a nonplussed Harry towards the bakery, muttering that she needed him to look at something. She had her eyes on stalks, looking over her shoulder and peering around in case Giles had somehow noticed her.

'Okay, you're going to have to tell me what's going on,' said Harry when they stopped in the doorway of the bakery, which stood ajar. Matt had set up at one of the wooden stalls next to Anna and she could see the two of them laughing and chatting as a lull in the proceedings gave them a moment to talk.

'Over there.' Polly whispered, as if somehow Giles was going to hear over the sound of shoppers chatting and the crunch of footsteps on gravel and the band striking up with 'I'm Dreaming of a White Christmas'.

She watched as Harry scanned the market, trying to work out what the problem was.

'It's Giles. The date from hell.'

'What's he doing here?'

'Well that's the thing. He sent a text this morning saying he thought we'd got off on the wrong foot and maybe we could have another date.'

'I thought you said it was hideous?' Harry looked down at her, the corners of his mouth twitching with amusement.

'It was. Utterly.'

'So which part of no is he having trouble with?'

'All of it, apparently.' She pushed a hand through her hair, flicking it back from her face and then tying it back up in an untidy knot on top of her head.

'Sounds like a bit of a knob.' Harry spotted him and inclined his head to indicate to Polly where he was situated. 'We need to make sure he gets the message you're not interested.'

'Exactly. I mean you might argue that stating clearly that I wasn't interested was pretty much as direct as I could be, but…'

'Men are idiots,' said Harry.

'Present company excepted?' She laughed.

'Most of the time.' Harry's eyes narrowed in thought. 'Believe me, I've been a complete arse more times than I'd care to admit.'

'You're lovely,' protested Polly.

'Not always.'

Polly raised a finger to his lips. 'Shush. Anyway – oh god, he's coming this way. He's spotted me.'

Harry pulled her into the doorway of the bakery so they were out of sight from the market, invisible to everyone except for the rapidly-approaching Giles. He looked down at her, his eyes meeting hers in silent communication, and she gave an almost imperceptible nod.

'There you a-' began Giles.

But he stopped midway through his sentence, as he looked on at the sight of Polly wrapped in Harry's arms, his mouth coming down on hers.

'-Oh. Right. Well.'

Polly's heart was banging so hard against her rib cage

that she was certain that it was going to burst out and fly off around the room. Harry had dropped the gentlest of kisses to the side of her mouth, his stubble grazing her cheek, holding her close enough that it looked from Giles' angle as if they were caught in a passionate secret embrace. She felt his mouth curving into a smile against her skin as Giles stomped off, his footsteps disappearing down the path that led back to the car park.

'Well,' said Harry, pulling back and holding her at arm's length, a mischievous twinkle in his eye, 'that ought to do it. Sorry, it was the best I could do with a moment's notice.'

Polly shook her head, half laughing, half wanting nothing more than to pull his arms around her again and soak up every delicious sensation so she could replay it over and over again. 'I'm not complaining.'

Harry crooked an eyebrow at her. 'Really?'

She shook her head again, emphatic this time. 'I mean I'm glad we've put him off. Sorry for borrowing you to get him out of my hair.'

Harry gave a shrug. 'No probs. That's what friends are for, right?'

'Exactly.' Polly wriggled out of his grasp. 'Right, I better get on with running the show.'

'Cool.' Harry took a step back and thrust his hands back into his pockets. 'I'm going to go and make sure Conor isn't getting up to any mischief or breaking any more limbs. Catch you later?'

'Definitely.'

CHAPTER FIFTEEN

POLLY WATCHED as Harry strode over towards the band. The singer didn't break stride but somehow managed to give him a nod and a grin of acknowledgement as he burst into the chorus of "Wonderful Christmastime".

I am blooming well not, she thought, turning on her heel and heading back towards Beth's workshop with a horrible churning in her stomach. It was as if someone had offered her everything she wanted on a plate for a micro-second, just for long enough for her to realise that yes, that was it. And then whoosh, it was gone, and the moment was lost. She gave the longest sigh, and opened the studio door.

Inside, Beth was standing at the front of the room holding an armful of vibrant, trailing green ivy. She looked up and smiled a welcome.

'Perfect timing. My sister Polly can give us a hand. We're weaving the greenery onto the frames, and once we've got the base looking perfect we can start to make it pretty. Polly, can you give anyone who needs help a few pointers?'

Polly hovered for a second, wondering if she should be

doing something more useful outside. But the market seemed to be up and running, and everyone was quite happy. She wanted to hibernate somewhere where she wouldn't have to deal with looking at Harry or trying to avoid either the awful Giles (who she'd noticed was still floating around) or worse still Tom, who'd set her up with him in the first place and was no doubt going to have something to say about the whole situation. She'd managed to avoid the topic so far but she knew that Tom and Gavin, who loved nothing more than a bit of hot gossip, would be all over the news that she'd rejected his cousin, not to mention – she cringed inwardly – the fact that for all she knew he was off telling all and sundry she'd been caught in a secret clinch with Harry.

There was nothing more to it, she'd have to front it out and wait for it all to blow over. Hopefully there'd be something else for everyone to get their teeth into before long.

'I'm having trouble trying to get this laurel to stay in place,' said Ivy Winter in her soft Manchester accent. 'I knew I should have made Ben stay and give me a hand, he's way better at that sort of stuff than me.'

'Here,' said Polly, leaning over. 'You need to tuck it in like this,' she pushed the leaves underneath the metal and twisted the floristry wire with practised fingers.

'You make it look really easy,' said Ivy.

'I've done it loads before, that's all. If you asked me to do all the stuff you do, I'd be stumped.' Polly said it without thinking, then wondered if she was supposed to act as if she didn't know who she was talking to. 'So what sort of look are you going for with the wreath – traditional, or something more modern?'

'I want it to look really traditional. When I was growing up my Grandma always had one that she got from her friend Rita who had a florist's shop. This is the first

Christmas I've had without her.' Ivy's eyes shone brightly with tears which threatened to brim over and spill down her cheeks.

'Oh I'm sorry. I think the first Christmas is the hardest. Well, the first everything, really.'

'Exactly.' Ivy fiddled with a sprig of mistletoe and two of the berries fell off and rolled across the table. 'I'm sorry, I'm guessing you must've lost someone too if you know how it feels.'

'My dad died a few years ago. My mum too, but – well, that's a bit complicated. She left when I was little so I didn't know her. But Dad was harder. I still miss him a lot.'

'I bet you do. I never knew my parents,' confided Ivy, picking up a piece of scarlet ribbon and trimming the edges carefully with scissors. 'That's why losing my grandma was so hard. She was the only family I had and now it's me and Ben.'

Maybe that's why she'd been crying the other day when they'd left the hotel first thing in the morning. Grief had a funny way of sneaking up on you when you least expected it. Polly helped her wire some sprigs of holly, the berries jewel bright, and fastened them carefully into place.

'You're so lucky living here. It's so beautiful.'

'It is,' agreed Polly, automatically.

Ivy chattered on about how much she'd enjoyed their nature trip the day before with Jack, and how she loved the cuteness of the Applemore Hotel.

'We came up here to scatter Grandma's ashes, you see. She and Grandpa were married here years and years ago.'

Polly, by far the most romantic of the Fraser siblings, put a hand to her heart. 'Oh, that's so sweet.'

'Isn't it? We took them both up – Grandma kept his all those years so they could be scattered together, and we took them over to the beach and did it yesterday before we went off for the day with Jack. He's lovely, isn't he? He told me to come and do this with Beth, said I'd enjoy it.'

'Where's Ben today?'

Ivy giggled. 'Well, even I couldn't persuade him to do a Christmas wreath making workshop, although I know everyone thinks he does whatever I want. He's gone off on one of Jack's mountain bikes for a trip up to some woods. Phoebe's looking after Felicity at her house. Jack gave him a map and he's got lunch in his backpack. I hope he doesn't get lost.'

'I'm sure he won't.' Polly looked over at Beth who was busy demonstrating how to tie a decorative bow with a couple of older women she recognised from the next village. 'And yeah, I can't really see this being his cup of tea.'

'The funny thing is we've got on so well since we've been up here. I mean we do anyway, but it's like all the pressure's disappeared. That's why we decided that we want to get married here in Applemore, at the hotel.'

Polly had an instant vision of the village packed with all the starry people she'd spotted on Ivy's social media and had to suppress a gasp of excitement.

'Oh really?' She tried to sound casual.

Ivy paused for a moment, putting her chin on her hand and staring dreamily out of the window. 'Yeah, it's so gorgeous and romantic up here. And I feel really close to Grandma and Grandpa, too, so it feels right. And the nice thing about Scotland is you can get married anywhere, it doesn't have to be in a church or a register office.'

'That's true,' Polly nodded. 'Where are you thinking?' She had visions of them hiring one of the big country estates – one of their neighbours had recently started hiring hers out as a huge, scaled-up version of AirBnb. It wasn't Applemore, of course, but it was close enough. Or there was always the super-posh Lochbay restaurant with rooms, but it was tiny.

'Oh the Applemore Hotel, of course,' said Ivy, as if it was glaringly obvious.

'The Applemore?' Polly turned to look at her.

'It's where they spent their honeymoon. That's why we came up here.'

'Oh that's so romantic.' Polly sighed. Beth, who was holding up a finished wreath to demonstrate how to create a hanging loop, shot her a look and shook a finger to indicate *more wreath making, less chatting.* 'Oops, we're getting into trouble from my big sister for chatting when we should be onto the next stage. Here, let me tape up some of that eucalyptus.'

They renewed their efforts, working together in an amicable silence. By the time they'd finished, the moment of closeness had passed and Polly felt awkward bringing the subject up again. Ivy held her wreath up to show it to Beth.

'What d'you think?'

She'd woven through the tiniest fairy lights which were threaded on silver wire so the whole thing glowed prettily and Beth clapped her hands in delight.

'You're a natural,' Polly heard her sister saying as she left the studio, having been summoned by Gregor's helper who couldn't find the liners for the bin. Muttering to herself about returning to her unglamorous life, she headed off to give them a hand, leaving a shyly smiling Ivy taking photos of the finished wreath.

It was mid-afternoon and the initial rush was over. The stalls were looking depleted now, with the sellers reorganising their wares to try and make them look good for the slowing trickle of visitors who were still making their way from Applemore and the surrounding villages and towns.

Polly helped out, bringing the leftover greenery from Beth's workshop and arranging it on the wooden table-tops to fill in the gaps where earlier in the day there had been baskets filled with scented candles, Anna's delicious chocolate brownies, and Rilla and Lachlan's artisan gins.

'Well I have to give it to you,' said a familiar voice in a soft Highland accent 'When you put your mind to something you do a good job. Your dad would be amazed with what you've done to the place.'

'Joan!' Polly spun round, dropping a long strand of ivy to the ground as she was embraced in a huge hug by the closest thing to a mother she'd ever known. 'Where's George? How was the trip?'

'Och it was out of this world. He forgot his glasses, so he's gone back to the car park to pick them up. I swear that man would forget his head if it wasn't attached.'

Joan chuckled and pushed her own specs up her nose.

'I see you've got a new pair.'

'Aye,' Joan did a little jokey preening motion. 'Italian designer, no less. What do you think?'

'Gorgeous.' Polly's heart glowed with love as she reached out and gave Joan another tight squeeze before letting her go. 'Oh, I've missed you. How was Italy?'

'Amazing. All those handsome Italian men,' Joan chuckled, her eyes sparkling with amusement, 'But none of them a patch on my George, of course. Talk of the devil, here he is.'

Polly turned to see the tall, patrician George striding across the courtyard, wearing a tweed flat cap over his steel-grey hair. She'd put a bet on it that underneath his sensible waterproof coat he'd be wearing a shirt and tie beneath a Scottish Lambswool sweater, his habitual uniform, which he'd worn every day as a science teacher at a big school in

Aberdeen. Even now, years after retirement, he still had the ability to make Polly want to stand up a little bit straighter and check she'd handed in her homework on time. He was a man of few words with a dry sense of humour, but when he made a joke there was a warm twinkle in his eye and a twist to his mouth that made sure she knew he was only teasing her.

'Well, missy,' he said, as he approached, leaning across to give Polly a kiss on the cheek. 'Look at all this. When Joan said you were planning a Christmas market I was expecting a couple of stalls and a bit of tinsel, but this looks like a miniature version of the one we visited last year in Hamburg. Well done.'

Polly beamed. 'You should have seen it earlier before all the stuff was cleared out. It's looking a bit diminished now and lots of people have left.'

'Don't do yourself down,' said Jack, who'd returned with the twins, their faces no longer sticky with toffee apple and their bad tempers sorted. They squealed with joy on seeing George and towed him off by the hand to watch the band playing as, much to their delight, he pulled a lollipop out of his pocket for each of them.

'Nice to see you back,' he said, kissing Joan on the cheek. 'Although I'm not sure Beth will be so happy to discover George is plying them with sweets when I've just managed to get them off this morning's sugar high.'

Joan put a finger to her lips. 'What Beth doesn't know won't hurt her. Is she hard at work?'

'She's been doing a wreath workshop.' Jack said, proudly. 'Sold out. In fact she even had to squeeze in a couple of extras.'

'She did brilliantly,' added Polly.

'And Charlotte? Where's she?'

Polly frowned then. 'I don't know actually, I thought

she and Rob would have been here. Maybe they're over at Midsummer doing some work?'

'Talking of Midsummer House, we met up with Frances while we were in Tuscany. She's having a whale of a time over there, and still dining out on her matchmaking skills. She's telling anyone that'll listen how she got her nephew together with one of the Applemore Frasers and how they're turning her old place into a respite house.'

Jack grinned at Polly. 'That's sweet, isn't it?'

'Cute,' she agreed. 'Although, I suspect from what I heard from Charlotte one night when she'd had one too many gin and tonics, that she and Rob might have had history…' She put a hand to her mouth in horror. 'I didn't say that. Forget I said anything.'

Joan raised her eyebrows to the heavens. 'Well, that's put the cat among the pigeons. I'll have to hear more about that another day. I'd better go and say hello to Lachlan and Rilla over there. Where's my wee Kitty?'

'Back at Applemore with one of the girls from the nursery school. I get the feeling that the two of them are enjoying a bit of baby-free time.'

Joan rubbed her hands together and beamed. 'Well, Granny Joan is back now, so there will be plenty of baby-free time for them when I get my hands on that little angel. I've got a month's worth of baby cuddles to catch up on.'

Polly and Jack watched, both smiling fondly, as Joan beetled off across the courtyard towards Lachlan and Rilla, spreading her arms out wide in greeting and wrapping them in a huge three-person embrace which startled the bearded man who arrived at their stall the same time, narrowly missing being incorporated into the hug.

'Nothing like a quiet entrance,' said Jack, wryly. 'You'd be hard pushed to miss the fact that Joan's back in town.' He turned, elbowing Polly gently in the ribs to get her attention. 'It's just as well George is the strong silent type. I bet he never gets a word in edgeways.'

Polly giggled. George was now sitting on one of the wooden picnic benches, Lucy dancing at his feet and Edward leaning against him with his thumb in his mouth, legs swinging in time to the band, who played a jazzed-up version of We Three Kings. Jack dropped an arm around her shoulder and gave it a brotherly squeeze for a second.

'You've done good, our kid.' His tone was teasing but when she looked up at him he gave her the ghost of a wink and the expression on his face told her that he meant it. Tough Glaswegian Jack wasn't one for doling out praise unless it was due.

'Thanks,' said Polly, simply. For a moment, she paused and took it all in – it had been such a lot of work, but somehow they'd pulled together to make it come off. It was exactly why she loved living in Applemore, and as she stood watching the community gathering together to take part in what she knew right then was going to be a new tradition, she realised just why Ivy Winter – and her grandparents before her – had fallen for the place.

CHAPTER SIXTEEN

'HARRY MY MAN!'

Conor, taking advantage of the fact he wasn't driving, had availed himself of one too many of the spiced apple ciders and hot mulled wines on offer. He swayed slightly before toppling gently sideways to rest at an angle against the interior window of the café.

'I wondered where you'd got to,' said Conor, allowing Harry to adjust the sling which had somehow come loose and was hanging around his neck like a scarf. 'Thanks for that,' he added, thickly.

'No problem. I was just giving Matt a hand with the bakery shelves while I was here. He's sold out all the bread and they've been meaning to move some stuff around so I thought we might as well get it sorted while I've got a bit of free time.' He looked at his watch, pointedly. 'But we need to be getting back.'

'Thought you said that you were only doing dinner for the three guests tonight and the restaurant was closing?'

'It is,' said Harry, realising with dismay that Conor was angling to hold on to the bitter end, or the bottom of the mulled wine barrel – whichever came first. 'But I need to get back and let Phoebs and Katie off shift, and you look like you could do with putting your feet up in front of Sky Sports and chilling for a bit.'

'Who's putting up their feet?' Rob said, walking into the café with impeccable timing.

'This one,' said Harry, indicating Conor with a jerk of his thumb. 'Before he knocks back any more mulled wine and ends up breaking the other wrist and then we'll really be in trouble.'

'I'm not any trouble,' hiccupped Conor, sliding down the wall slightly.

'See what I mean,' said Harry, quietly. Rob grinned and gave a nod.

'I tell you what, why don't you get a lift back with me and Charlotte in half an hour if Harry needs to get off. Deal?'

Harry mock-glared at his new investor. 'If he ends up three sheets to the wind…'

Rob shook his head. 'I assure you, I have no more intention of sabotaging our prize chef than you do. But I think –' they paused for a moment as Conor hefted himself upright and swayed his way gently across the café floor towards Tom and Gavin, who were clearing up behind the counter. 'If we make him think it's his idea we might have more chance of getting him home in one piece. Plus he was telling me the other day he was dying for a ride in my new car.'

Rob, who had been teased incessantly for his spotless Range Rover when he'd first arrived in the village (which was now as mud-splattered and covered in dog hair as all the other Fraser family cars), had recently treated himself and Charlotte to an expensive four-seater convertible for their trips down to Edinburgh for meetings and the like.

'I wouldn't mind a drive in it either,' said Harry, laughing.

'We can deal with that once we get our errant chef back home in one piece.'

'Fair enough.'

'Where is Charlotte? Is she here?' Harry glanced over Rob's shoulder.

'Yeah, she's outside talking to Polly and what's her name, the glamour chick.'

'You mean Ivy Winter?'

'That's it. I keep forgetting her name. I swear she made it up.'

'Apparently not, Phoebe informed me.' Harry followed Rob out into the courtyard. Dusk was falling and the little market stalls looked beautiful in the light. Polly was standing over by Rilla and Lachlan's stall with Charlotte, chatting happily to Ivy, who had several bags by her feet and a huge evergreen wreath in her arms. He rubbed his hands together. 'It's her real name. If you want to know anything about her from her shoe size to her favourite meal you can ask Phoebe. I swear she could do a degree on the subject of social media stars.'

'The whole thing is beyond me. I can't imagine anything worse than having my whole life on display,' said Rob. 'Still, she's given the hotel a bit of a boost in off season. Let's hope all these social media followers get booking for the new year.'

'Wonder what he makes of it all?' Harry tipped a head to indicate Ben, who had just arrived and was kissing Ivy on the cheek, pulling her close with an arm around her waist. He reached over and shook Polly's hand, and Harry smiled to himself, watching as Polly tried to look nonchalant. Her game face was terrible. They stood chatting for a moment, everyone focusing intently on the couple, then there was a gasp of delight from Polly. Whatever they'd said to her had caused a stir - even the normally level-headed Charlotte looked quite giddy, clapping her hands to her cheeks, eyes bright with excitement.

Charlotte beckoned them over a second later, calling to them with a wave of her arm. 'Harry, Rob, guess what?'

Rob and Harry exchanged glances. 'If there's one thing I've worked out,' said Rob with a roll of his eyes, 'It's that Charlotte's "guess what" usually isn't quite as straight-forward as you'd hope.'

Harry, who'd known her all his life, gave him a fleeting nod. 'That's your beloved you're talking about.'

'Yes, I know,' grinned Rob, 'I'm the one who chose to spend the rest of my life with her. I also know that look on her face. I sense trouble...'

'Work, more like.' Harry chuckled, as they made their way over.

The couple were tiny in comparison to the tall, long-limbed Fraser siblings. As she emerged from behind the back of the market stall he realised that even Rilla towered over Ben. Polly caught his eye and waggled her eyebrows meaningfully.

'Rob, this is Ivy and Ben,' said Charlotte, who'd taken over the situation in the way that she always did. Harry glanced at Polly unthinkingly, checking on her. As the youngest in the family, he'd always felt that Polly had some-thing more to prove to actually be taken seriously, and much as he loved all the Frasers, he felt fiercely protective of her especially today, knowing how hard she'd worked to make the market come off.

'This is my partner Rob,' said Charlotte, moving out of the way as he shook hands with Ben and gave Ivy a brief nod of welcome.

'How many of you are there?' Ivy giggled. 'Everyone I meet seems to be connected to the Fraser family somehow.'

'Oh, they used to own everything round here,' Harry said, giving Polly a teasing wink. 'Until they ran out of money and had to sell it all off. Basically if you went back a hundred years we'd all be tugging our forelocks in greeting when we saw them.'

Ivy looked surprised, her eyebrows – which were thick and dark, like her unfeasibly thick eyelashes – raising skyward.

'He's joking,' explained Polly, shaking her head and giving him a warning look, eyes dancing. 'It's just his jokes aren't actually funny.'

'Harsh,' Harry said, laughing.

'Fair point though,' said Lachlan. 'Anyway, it's pretty simple – Charlotte runs the holiday cottages, Beth's in charge of the flower farm, Rilla and I are trying to make a go of the brewery –'

'And the wild camping and the gin,' Rilla added, her curls bobbing as she nodded in emphasis.

'And that, yeah. So we've kind of covered all bases. Except hotels. That's his job.' Lachlan pointed at Harry.

'Guilty as charged,' he said, thrusting his hands into his pockets. He was getting cold, and he really needed to get back. Nice as they were – and to be fair, they hadn't proved to be as prima-donna-ish as he'd expected – all he could think about was the glorious moment when he closed the doors on everyone and got to work on the renovations. There was a countdown clock in his head and the seconds seemed to be ticking by slower and slower as the day went on.

'You still here?'

Harry turned, hearing Jack's amused voice. 'It's like the Hotel California. You can never leave.'

'I'd make a run for it now if I were you. The terrible two are on their way over with Joan and George.' Jack yawned. 'I tell you what, I don't know how teachers do it. I'm knackered.' He turned to say hello to Ben. 'How was the bike trail?'

'Great, thanks. I suspect I'll feel it in my thighs tomorrow.' Ben bobbed up and down in a half-squat, as if testing his leg muscles.

There was a brief interlude while everyone had a chat about the route Ben had taken on his mountain biking adventure and how he'd found the difficult section on the north end of the course. Taking advantage, Harry shifted across in a casual movement, moving to Polly's side, bending slightly so his mouth was close to her ear. He could smell the faint floral perfume on her hair.

'You alright?' He kept his voice low, not wanting to be overheard.

Polly looked up at him, fiddling absentmindedly with the silver horseshoe pendant round her neck. 'Yeah, I'm fine. My feet are killing me though. I thought you were going home?'

He noticed that Charlotte had taken over the conversation again and was chatting animatedly to Ivy and Ben. Rob was standing with his hands deep into his back pockets, nodding intently.

'I was,' he started, wishing he could scoop her up and take her home. 'But we had to sort Conor. I'm on my way now, though.' Despite her insistence she was fine, he couldn't help noticing that she had shadows under her eyes. He could tell that she was flagging. It had been a long day for everyone, but there was no denying it had been a huge success.

'Aha,' her mouth curled into a conspiratorial smile. 'Don't go just yet.' She put a finger in the air and turned back to the group. Ivy and Ben had been given a cup of mulled wine each. He watched as Ivy looked at Polly for a moment with a questioning expression. Polly met it with the slightest nod, taking his arm and giving it a squeeze. 'We've got a little bit of news,' said Ivy, in her soft northern accent. Dimples appeared prettily in her cheeks as she turned to smile at Ben, swinging his hand in hers.

'You have?' Harry noticed that everyone else was looking at him, not them, for some reason.

Ben nodded. 'We came up here because it's a place that means a lot to Ivy, and we have a bit of a special request. I know you don't normally do it, but...'

There was a pause, where he got the distinct impression that everyone seemed to know what was coming, and Harry felt his heart sinking at the prospect of yet another *could you just* request from the couple. He had to admit that despite his pre-judgements, they hadn't been as awful as he'd expected – they were quite nice, actually - but he'd almost reached the end of his tether when it came to hand-baked dog biscuits and off-menu room service requirements.

'Go on,' he said, trying to look enthusiastic and hoping that he didn't look as knackered as he felt. This time tomorrow it'll all be over, he told himself, silently.

'The Applemore Hotel is where Ivy's grandparents spent their honeymoon. They're gone now, but she – we – we'd really love to remember them when it comes to our own wedding.' Ben looked at Ivy and laced his fingers through hers, and she looked up at Harry with shining eyes.

'We'd like to get married at the Applemore Hotel.'

Harry's shoulders dropped in relief.

'Is that all?'

Everyone seemed to let go of the breath they'd been

144

holding. The sense of delighted celebration in the air was palpable. Bloody hell, was he that much of an ogre? He must really need a holiday if everyone thought he was that cantankerous that he'd say no to a perfectly acceptable request. A wedding at the hotel would be a brilliant way to celebrate the re-opening.

'Funnily enough, we've been contemplating whether we should offer weddings,' he said, glancing over at Rob who had a slightly odd expression on his face. 'As you might know the good thing about Scotland is you can get married anywhere at all, as long as you can find a registrar willing to conduct the ceremony. Sounds like an excellent idea.' He raised both thumbs. 'Cool. I'm in.'

Then he glanced briefly at his watch again, aware that Phoebe and Katie needed to get off. Polly squeezed his arm and looked at him starry eyed. Who knew that agreeing to host the wedding of a couple of social media types was enough to make her this happy? Women could be very strange, sometimes. He cocked his head slightly in confusion, still looking at her. Polly beamed back.

'Oh my goodness,' said Ivy, putting her manicured fingers to her cheeks in surprised delight. 'I can't believe you said yes just like that.'

'Well that makes it nice and easy,' said Charlotte, brushing her hands together as if she'd just done a day's hard work. She turned to Rob and gave him a look which Harry recognised very clearly as her *told you so* expression.

'We're checking out at noon – that's right, isn't it?' Ivy looked at him for confirmation.

'Yes,' Harry suppressed the urge to fist pump the air at the prospect. 'We're closing down at noon tomorrow.'

'That's great,' said Ben, who'd taken out his phone and was tapping rapidly on the screen. He looked up. 'Would you rather we pick up the keys tomorrow?'

Charlotte shook her head. 'Oh, we have a little key safe outside. But don't worry, I'll be there and we can go through everything.'

'Keys?' Harry looked from one woman to the other, confused.

'For the cottage,' said Charlotte, as if talking to someone who was very stupid indeed.

'They can't very well stay at the hotel if it's being done up, can they?' Polly tugged at his arm, giving him the look you'd give someone who was very slow and not keeping up with the conversation at all.

'You alright, mate?' Jack grinned. 'You look like you're a bit dazed.'

Rob chuckled. Charlotte folded her arms and looked at him steadily. Lachlan raised his eyebrows briefly in a look which clearly stated none of this was his idea. Rilla had somehow slipped away and was busily tidying up her stall, quite definitely not catching his eye.

As he took in the scene, glancing from one member of the Fraser family to the other, the slow realisation that he'd been stitched up dawned on him.

'When you say a wedding...'

CHAPTER SEVENTEEN

'A CHRISTMAS WEDDING.' Ivy beamed.

Polly looked up at the sky, which had been threatening snow all day. Now, it was almost dark and she could swear she felt the tiny melting sensation of a first flake on her forehead. She let go of Harry's arm to brush it away. He rocked back on his heels, and she could tell he was trying to find the words. Maybe springing it on him hadn't been such a good idea. She looked at Ivy and Ben, who were still smiling, but slightly more hesitantly, as the news sunk in.

'Hang on,' he said, eventually.

Polly watched as Rob shot a fleeting look at Harry and raised one finger almost invisibly in the briefest of warnings. Harry saw it too, and cleared his throat.

'We can iron out the details later,' said Rob, smoothly, putting an arm around Harry's shoulder and steering him across the courtyard in the direction of his car. 'Meanwhile, congratulations, both.'

Ivy's smile dropped into a little pout of concern. 'Is he okay? He didn't look very excited at the idea.'

'Oh,' said Charlotte, airily, 'He's a Highlander, they

don't tend to show much emotion. I can guarantee that he's smiling on the inside.'

Ivy's face lifted again. 'Oh that's nice to hear,' she said, cheerfully, bending to pick up some of the bags of shopping. She handed them to Ben. 'Shall we get back? We need to make sure that Felicity is okay. We left her with a dog sitter,' she added.

Lachlan raised his eyebrows. She watched her brother suppressing a grin. 'Oh yes, we do that with ours all the time.'

Rilla thumped him on the arm a moment later when Ben and Ivy had headed back to their car. 'You are such a wind-up merchant. Dog sitter my backside. They're all fast asleep in front of the Aga.'

'That's what I meant,' said Polly's brother, grinning.

'I despair of him,' Rilla said, shaking her head.

'He's your responsibility now.' Polly played along with the joke, but her mind was elsewhere. She wanted to run after Harry, who looked shell-shocked. As soon as she'd got this market cleared up, she'd nip down to the hotel.

Despite Harry's hopes that the last night of the hotel being open would be a quiet, low-key affair the villagers of Applemore had decided to go out in style. Polly pushed open the door into a bar which was thronging with people and noise.

'Shut that door,' shouted Murdo, who was clearly quite merry and holding a frothing pint of beer. 'You'll be letting all the cold air in.'

'Is it still snowing?' Phoebe, who was standing behind the bar, called over to her. She'd dyed her hair again and it was now pale pink and green, knotted on either side of her head.

'No, it's stopped.' Polly squeezed past Old Jimmy, the farmer, who nodded a hello and shifted his bar stool slightly to let her past.

'Shame.' Phoebe looked at her questioningly. 'What can I get you tonight? You driving?'

Polly nodded. 'I didn't come for a drink, I wanted a quick word with Harry. Is he about?'

'Changing a barrel in the cellar and muttering about it. He's in a right old grump.' Phoebe tipped a couple of glasses into the sink then popped them in the glass washing machine, wiping the surface as she went. 'Go and find him, you might be able to cheer him up. If anyone can, it's you.'

Polly headed through the back and down the narrow dark staircase which led to the cellar. The hoppy beer smell hit her first, just before the cold did. Harry was leaning against the back wall, staring into space. She'd made it all the way down the stairs before he seemed to shake himself out of his reverie and realise she was there.

'Penny for your thoughts?' She stood on the bottom step, hovering.

Harry made a face and shrugged. 'Just wondering how I've been railroaded into a bloody Christmas wedding in a closed hotel.'

'You weren't railroaded,' she said, realising as she did that he was genuinely aggrieved. It was rare to see Harry looking anything other than his habitually cheerful self and, as she did, her heart melted. She crossed the floor to stand toe to toe with him, looking him directly in the eye. He lifted an eyebrow, and a the smallest smile tugged at one corner of his mouth.

'Oh for goodness' sake, I can't even be cross at you for a second,' he said shaking his head. He dropped her gaze, pushed his hair back from his face, then looked back at her, the lines at the corners of his eyes crinkling as he smiled – properly this time. 'I swear you could charm the birds off the trees, Polly Fraser.'

Despite the cold, she felt a warm glow inside as she looked at his face, the jaw etched with stubble, and his wide, generous mouth. Realising that the warm glow was shifting into a tug of longing she stepped back, flipping her hair over her face for a second then pushing it back in her habitual manner. 'I think that's unlikely,' she said, diffidently.

'Right, well,' he said, pushing himself away from the wall where he'd been leaning, 'much as I'd like to hang out here in the unheated cellar with you and avoid the frankly ridiculous crowds upstairs, I don't think I can. Shall we?'

He gave a wave of his arm, motioning for her to go first in a gentlemanly manner. Polly scuttled up the stairs, crashing into Conor, who was coming back from the loo, his shirt hanging loose over the arm which was in a sling.

'I thought I took you home?' Harry sounded disapproving.

Conor leaned against the wall, looking distinctly dishevelled. 'Wanted to check that you'd made a decent job of dinner.' He rubbed his nose with his free hand. ''Lo, Poll. How's it going?'

'Good thanks,' said Polly, glancing behind her to see a thunderous-faced Harry looking distinctly unimpressed.

'I was only catering for Ivy, Ben and Mr Jacobs, the birdwatcher,' said Harry, 'And I've cleaned up after myself, naturally,'

'Aye,' said Conor, 'You left the knife out on the draining board, though. Health and safety, and all that.'

Harry growled. 'Out,' he said, but he was laughing.

Conor bumbled off towards the middle of the bar, swallowed up by a crowd of locals he'd known for years.

'He's a control freak when it comes to that bloody kitchen,' said Harry, shaking his head.

'Takes one to know one,' said Polly, laughing. 'You're only in a strop because you wanted this place closed up quietly and instead everyone's decided to have a last hurrah.'

'You're not joking.'

She sat down at the side of the bar, chatting to him while he served beers and poured drinks, game face on and not a sign that he'd rather be doing something else. It was all part of being in a customer facing job – and she knew that he loved it, despite his grumbling tonight. So it shouldn't be that difficult to persuade him that he'd make a go of Ivy and Ben's Christmas wedding. In theory, anyway.

Harry came over, taking advantage of a lull in proceedings to help himself to a large glass of lemonade. He rarely drank alcohol when he was working behind the bar. Without asking, he poured her a glass and handed it over, his fingers brushing against hers as he did so. Polly cupped her fingers around the cold glass, trying to focus on that sensation and not the goosebumpy feeling she'd had when he touched her. This was ridiculous – he was an old friend, and nothing more. She squared her shoulders and looked at him.

'Right. I came here on a mission,' she said, taking in his expression of mild alarm.

'You have?'

'Yes. About this afternoon. I was talking to Charlotte and Rob after you headed home –'

'Rob.' Harry gave a slightly dismissive snort and shook his head. 'I dunno, I think I might have made a mistake there.'

Polly looked at him closely. He'd narrowed his eyes and was gazing across the bar to the table by the fire, where Rob and Charlotte were deep in conversation – laughing and chatting quite happily – with Ivy and Ben.

'What kind of mistake?'

'Agreeing to have him come in as an investor.' Harry's mouth twisted as he paused for a moment, choosing his words carefully. She knew he was thinking that as her sister's partner, Rob wasn't someone she'd want him to be insulting.

'Go on?'

'I grew up in this place – for better or worse. Spent all my teenage years working behind the scenes, went to uni, came home, had to deal with my parents doing things their way whilst knowing if I could get my hands on it I could make a difference. They were totally stuck in the past – not that I don't love them, but – ' he gestured to the bar, and the faded décor. 'You know what I mean.'

'Course I do.' Polly picked up a beer mat and flipped it over, trying to get it to balance against another one. 'And now you can do things your way.'

'Yeah, well, that was the plan. Except Rob's – I mean he's a great bloke and everything – but he's all guns blazing for this Christmas wedding idea and I think he's got no idea what's involved. He's all *you can't buy this sort of publicity.* All I can think is if we screw it up, it'll be all over social media and that's the last thing we need.'

Polly reached over, putting a hand on his arm without thinking. Then she realised what she'd done, squeezed gently and then pulled away, feeling suddenly self-conscious. This was ridiculous.

'Why on earth would you screw it up?'

'Just the minor matter of a bar that's about to be ripped apart, bedrooms that are going to be renovated, a restaurant that's out of order…' He shrugged, but he was half-smiling. 'I don't know what I'm stressing about. It all sounds perfectly feasible when you say it out loud, doesn't it?'

'It's not that difficult. All you need is one bedroom and the bar sorted, and you've got everything you need.'

'And the kitchen. They're going to want feeding, aren't they?' Harry said, as Phoebe threw him a drying cloth. He started polishing some of the glasses, absently.

'You're not doing anything to the kitchen.' Polly lifted a finger and started counting off items one by one. 'Beth can do the flowers, Anna can make a cake, Charlotte's provided her with the cottage –'

'Alright, you've got me there,' he admitted. 'I still don't get it.'

'Which bit?'

'It feels like this Ivy Winter turns up and snaps her fingers and you're all eating out of her hands. I don't get it.'

'What did Rob say?'

'He came in earlier and was full of it, telling me what a difference it could make, that it'd be a springboard for our other plans, blah blah blah. You're all bloody star-struck.'

'You don't think he's talking sense?'

'Oh, I think he's making perfect sense, that's half the bloody problem. It's just that we've got four weeks to turn this place around when we were supposed to be opening up at the end of January, and I know as well as you do that any kind of building work takes twice as long and costs twice as much as you think it's going to.'

Polly reached over and poked him squarely in the chest. 'You, Harry Robertson, are a grouch. A tired grouch. And you're not happy about having your plans changed at the last minute.'

He put his hands in the air. 'Guilty as charged.'

'Have you managed to persuade him that this is the most amazing opportunity we've had yet?'

Polly turned. Rob and Charlotte, hand in hand, were standing behind her, cheeks pink from the heat of the flames of the log fire.

'Persuade me?' Harry eyed her beadily. 'Are you on a secret mission?'

Polly shook her head. 'I'm not, but I happen to think they're right. As do you, grumpy face.'

Harry groaned. 'Alright, alright. I think you're all insane, and if it all goes pear-shaped, I'm going to take great pleasure in saying I told you so, but – well, fine. We'll make it work, somehow.'

Rob grinned. 'I told you,' he said to Charlotte, with a knowing look on his face. 'Leave it to Polly, I said, and she'll charm him into doing it.'

Polly felt her cheeks prickling as they turned as pink as if she too had been sitting by the fire for a couple of hours. She ducked her head. 'It wasn't charm,' she protested, 'Just common sense.'

Rob and Charlotte exchanged a glance. Harry shook his head, still laughing.

'Murdo, what can I get you? Another pint?'

'Aye, that would be grand. I need to stock up before you leave us in the lurch. Can't believe you're going to be closed until the end of January. What's a man to do without his pub to escape to?'

'Ah,' said Harry, talking to Murdo but looking at Polly directly, his eyes twinkling and an expression on his face that let her know he'd given in completely, 'About that...'

CHAPTER EIGHTEEN

'So that was it?' Rilla lifted baby Kitty out of her high chair and popped her down on the floor, where she started banging one of her toys with a wooden spoon, delighted at the noise she was making.

'Pretty much, yeah.' Polly shoved a handful of dog treats from the jar beside the Aga into her pocket. 'If you ask me, it was a bit of a territory thing. Harry and Rob are still learning to work together and the next thing he knows Rob's just gaily said yes to a Christmas wedding at the hotel when it's supposed to be shut for renovations.'

'Gently, darling.' Rilla replaced the wooden spoon with a pink and white striped teddy bear, which Kitty embraced happily. 'It's a lovely noise but not when Mummy's talking to Aunty Polly.' She lowered her voice. 'It's a terrible noise but never mind. Anyway, so it's all sorted?'

'Yep. Harry's put a rocket up Kenny, told him they need to get the bar sorted before anything else, and now he's all systems go on getting the place ready. I spoke to Beth about it earlier. She's full of ideas for Ivy's wedding bouquet.'

'Cute.' Rilla wiped the high chair down with a cloth and tossed it in the direction of the big Belfast sink. It missed and flopped onto the floor, where Hugh, her rescue spaniel, picked it up in his mouth and wandered off to lie down on the rug with a heavy sigh, placing it carefully between his paws and looking up at them with a resigned expression.

'You sure you don't mind taking this lot out?'

Polly shook her head. 'I could do with a decent walk. The trouble with running the shop is I never actually stop, and I never get the chance to blow the cobwebs away and have a bit of space. I probably need a big beach walk as much as the dogs do.'

Rilla reached down, rubbing each of the dogs on the head, eliciting a drum symphony of wagging tails beating against the floor.

'They'll love you forever. Me too. Taking this little one out when it's freezing cold takes so long, and then inevitably we get halfway through the woods and she needs a change and nobody wants to strip off when it's freezing cold outside, do they, Kitty?'

Kitty looked up at her mother with a wrinkle of her nose and a cheeky smile, and shook her head.

'Right, then, you three. Let's go exploring.'

Leaving the warm, homely atmosphere of the kitchen of Applemore House behind, Polly wrapped her red woollen scarf more tightly around her neck and pulled on her gloves, turning up the collar of her padded coat against the cold. It had been unusually chilly for the last week – normally Applemore missed the harsher weather, but there had been a succession of below-freezing nights and days which had left the trees in the woods rimmed with a hoar frost, leaving everything looking sparkling and breathtakingly pretty. She crunched down the path, heading towards the wooden stile where the dogs scampered ahead as she climbed over, holding on carefully. The sun was low and shone pale through a haze of thin cloud, and her breath clouded as she walked, reminding her of childhood days when she'd run along pretending to be a steam train as they played in the woods. It had been a wild sort of childhood where they'd been free to do what they pleased, messing about on the loch and playing on the beach in all weathers, with Joan tutting in gentle disapproval when they came home soaking wet and covered in mud no matter what the season. Her dad had been loving but absent-minded, and had always seemed rather befuddled by parenthood despite having four children. Harry's parents, in comparison, had been busy day in and day out running the pub, kindly but always slightly distracted in another way. They were happily retired now and living in a little bungalow in Auchterarder – 'just as well,' Harry had remarked, the other day 'or they'd be having kittens at the prospect of this wedding idea.'

At least he seemed to be on board with it now. She'd dropped in to see how the work was getting on when she was in the village the day before, opening the bar door to a cacophony of shouting, the whine of a mitre saw, and music blasting from Kenny the builder's little portable radio which travelled with him wherever he worked. Harry – covered in sawdust and with his hair sticking up on end, his face dusty and streaked with sweat despite the freezing cold weather outside – had beamed at her in greeting, and taken great delight in showing her how they'd already stripped off the dated wood panelling and filled a skip outside.

She marched on, passing the hedgerows hung with frozen spiders webs and still decorated with red berries and the last of the deep purple sloes. A tiny robin darted in front of her, chirping brightly, then landed on a tree stump as she paused to tie the lace of her boot, cocking his head sideways and looking at her with a bold, curious expression. In the distance she could hear the mournful lowing of Jimmy's cows, who'd be gathering at the field gate waiting to be taken into the barn, where they'd feast on silage and the sweet-smelling treacly food that they received each afternoon as they stood waiting to be milked. It was the same every day here, and whilst sometimes that sameness made Polly want to jump in a car and head for the bright lights of the city, today it filled her heart up and made her feel nothing but joy.

Mabel, Martha and Hugh were feeling the same joy. They zig-zagged in front of her, noses to the ground, tails wagging in interest as they followed one scent trail after another, delighted to be out of the warmth of the house where Kitty – their biggest fan – tended to love them just a little bit too hard. Polly giggled at the thought, remembering poor Hugh's face just before they left, when Kitty had squished him in such a tight embrace that his eyes had goggled slightly. When Rilla had released him – Kitty howling in fury – Hugh had shot off towards the other end of the kitchen with a determined expression, pawing at the door hopefully.

She walked up towards the beach, watching as a handful of sheep shot off on spotting her. They'd been grazing the *machair*, the grassland that edged the beach. In summer it would be dotted with rare wildflowers and home to all sorts of nesting birds who travelled to the Highlands each year, but right now it was dotted with sheep poo – which Mabel was rolling in, the expression on her face as luxurious as someone who'd been treated to a massage at a high-end spa.

'Mabel, you absolute horror,' Polly shouted, pulling off

a glove and reaching into her pocket for a dog biscuit. 'Come on, come and get this.'

Mabel, who was the podgiest of the three spaniels and on a permanent diet, sprang to her feet and rushed over, tail wagging in delight.

'You can have one now, and one when we get to the beach.'

The wind whipped her face as they made their way onto the white sand. The waves were crashing loud and foamy against the shore, and the water beyond was dark turquoise. It looked tropical, but the water was so cold that even the spaniels who loved to swim were giving it a wide berth.

Polly grabbed a piece of driftwood and threw it as far as she could. Martha galloped off after it, reaching it so quickly that by the time she was cantering back with it in her mouth the other two were still halfway there. Mabel, wise to the game, stayed put.

'Good girl, Martha.' Polly leaned down, taking the stick from an expectant Martha. A moment later Hugh gave a bark of surprise and shot off in the opposite direction. Polly turned, expecting to find him chasing one of the deer that often wandered down to the beach, but was surprised to see that it was someone else who'd decided to take a wander on this freezing cold afternoon.

As she got closer she realised it was a woman, wrapped up in a long, pale beige quilt-like coat with a pink bobble hat and a pair of matching gloves. Hugh, who loved people and food, not necessarily in that order, hurtled towards her at speed. Polly started to run, aware that he was, in his enthusiasm, very likely to cover whoever it was in slobber.

'Hello,' waved Polly.

'Hi,' said the woman.

As they reached each other, Polly realised that underneath all the layers and wrapping was Ivy. Hugh started to cover her in enthusiastic licks, sniffing hopefully at her pockets. Mabel joined him after a few moments, with the shyer Martha hovering slightly by Polly's side.

'They'll be smelling Felicity.'

Polly looked beyond Ivy, scanning the beach. 'You didn't bring her out for a walk?'

Ivy giggled 'No, she's not really a walking sort of dog. More a handbag sort, really. She'd freeze to death if I took her on a beach like this.'

'I suppose it's not really Shih Tzu weather, is it?' Polly laughed as Ivy straightened up.

'You're a long way from the village. Have you walked all this way?'

Ivy shook her head. 'I left the car at Jack's outdoor centre and followed the trail. He said it would be okay.' She frowned slightly and rubbed her nose. 'I'm not trespassing, am I?'

'Course not.'

'Phew. I just fancied a bit of a walk to clear my head and get some fresh air.'

'And now here I am, getting in the way of your peace and quiet.' Polly summoned the dogs, getting out another biscuit for each of them.

Ivy shook her head again. 'No, it's actually nice to see someone. It's lovely here but it's so empty that it's a bit weird, if that makes any sense? Probably not to you, seeing as you live here.'

'No,' Polly fell into step beside her. 'That makes perfect sense. Lots of people say it. I think you get used to it, but it doesn't mean I don't sometimes long for all the stuff that comes with city life.'

'I wondered about that. I mean you can't just pop out for a McDonald's or go and have a spa treatment.'

Polly giggled, thinking of Mabel's luxuriant rolling. 'No we can't. I mean you can, but you'd have to drive to Inverness for a burger and to be honest they're not a patch on Conor's. Did you try one?'

'Yeah they were gorgeous. Harry was sweet and let us have room service.' She looked sideways at Polly. 'You're lucky, he's really cute.'

Polly blinked hard. 'Oh, no, we're not – '

Ivy put a gloved hand to her mouth. 'Oh, sorry, I just assumed. You – well, anyway. Me and my big mouth. Ben says I spend too much time people watching and making up stories about them.'

A huge wave rose up, taking Hugh, who'd been sniffing a clump of interesting-smelling seaweed by surprise. He jumped back a little too late and then scuttled up the sand out of reach of the icy cold water, shaking himself and looking indignant.

'Making up stories sounds like a nice thing to do. Maybe you should be writing books.'

Ivy looked thoughtful. 'Funnily enough I've always wanted to. I used to write little stories when I was younger, sitting at my Grandma's table after school.'

'There's nothing stopping you.' Polly pulled her hat down over her ears, which were going numb with cold. She tugged at the zip of her coat, pulling it up so the collar settled just below her chin. She looked sideways at Ivy, who somehow managed to look chic despite being wrapped up in a series of layers, and was surprised to see her wiping away a tear.

'Sorry,' she said, rubbing her nose with a gloved finger. 'It's funny how grief hits you when you don't expect it. I think I'm fine, then it comes along and it's like someone's literally kicked me in the stomach.'

'Don't apologise.' Polly's heart went out to her. She

reached across and gave her a little squeeze on her thickly-padded arm. 'I know how it feels. It takes ages. It doesn't ever leave you, really. You just learn to live with it.'

Ivy sniffed again. In a silent agreement, they turned and headed up the beach towards the rocks which formed a shelter against the wind. Almost as soon as they reached them, the air fell still and they didn't have to shout to be heard. Ivy paused for a moment, sitting down on a smooth outcrop of rock.

'Do you mind? I mean you can go on if you like, I just – I forgot how tiring it was walking on sand.'

'In a howling gale, even more so.' Polly sat down beside her. 'My – ' she always struggled to describe Joan to outsiders, because she was so much more than the family housekeeper, not just a friend, 'Joan, who brought me up, she always says that grief is physical as well as mental. It makes you really tired.'

'It really does,' Ivy nodded with alacrity. 'I thought I was going mad when Grandma died – I slept loads, and even when I woke up I'd still be bone tired. That's partly why we came up here – not just because of the wedding, but because we both decided it was time for a break.'

The dogs circled around, still chasing scents. Martha darted off, tail in the air, trying to catch a piece of dried seaweed which was being blown by the wind. The rock was cold through Polly's jeans and she could feel her bottom going numb, but she was intrigued by Ivy's opening up to her. Elfin faced and pretty, she looked a far cry from the ultra-made-up posed images that she displayed on her social media accounts.

'It must be nice not to have to be... *on*?' She chose her words carefully, aware she didn't want to sound judgemental. 'I mean, I've watched your videos and stuff. It looks like loads of work.'

'You have?' Ivy turned to her, looking surprised. 'I'm always amazed when people say that. I kinda forget people are out there. It's the only way I can do it.'

'But you've got literally hundreds of thousands of followers.' Polly was amazed.

'I know, but I sort of forget they're real. Even when they're commenting and watching stuff, it's hard to remember there are actual people out there. Except when they're being horrible, of course. Then it makes more sense, because I feel like they've caught me out and they know I don't know what the hell I'm doing.' Ivy gave a half-laugh.

It was surprising to hear someone who seemed so media-savvy and confident talking this way. Ivy Winter was the last person Polly would have put down as suffering from imposter syndrome.

'That must be hard.' Polly reached down to pat Mabel, who'd nestled against her leg and was leaning her head on her thigh, tongue lolling after her exertions.

'It can be. Ben's really good, we have a deal that he checks all the comments before I do because some people can be really mean.'

'That's really sweet.'

'Oh, he does loads more. Basically he's the back office and does all the management stuff – we used to have someone else do it, but he ripped us off and lost a load of money so we decided we'd do it together.'

'You sound like the perfect pair.' Polly felt a pang of loneliness. She'd spent so long building up the farm shop and turning the buildings into lots of little cottage industries which made a difference to the economy of Applemore, but at the end of the day she went home to her little cottage alone, and – well, there was the family, and there was Harry, but – he was a friend. If he'd ever shown any sign of interest, maybe things would be different, but she was well and truly friend zoned, no matter what Ivy might have suggested earlier.

'He's an angel. That's why I want us to get married here – not just because it means something, getting married where Grandma and Grandpa had such happy memories, but also because now – well, he's my family. I want to make it official.'

'That's so lovely. I'm very happy for you both.' Polly looked at Ivy's red cheeks and smiled. 'You look freezing. Shall we get going?'

Together, they headed back up the beach, this time with the wind behind them.

'I'm surprised by what you said,' said Polly, after a while. 'It doesn't sound as much fun as I thought it'd be.'

'Oh, don't get me wrong, when you're invited to all the exciting things like premieres and launches of posh beauty stuff it's amazing, but it's only exciting for so long then it's a bit of a drag to have to get all dressed up, haul yourself across town or down to London.'

'I wouldn't mind swapping places for a bit. Sounds a lot more exciting than commuting across the courtyard to the farm shop and listening to the same village gossip repeated by ten different customers by lunchtime.'

'You wouldn't leave Applemore?' Ivy looked shocked.

Polly made an open-handed gesture. 'No. Yes. Maybe?'

They both laughed.

'I've worked really hard to get the farm shop going. I can't imagine just walking away. This place is home.'

Ivy nodded again. 'That's it. I feel like I've spent the last few years working so hard to build this whole thing up. But the truth is I'm done. I don't know what to do next.'

'Really? But you've got all those followers and you're famous.'

'You can't take it with you, can you?' She made a face. 'It's weird. Grandma died and after the funeral I thought I'd go back to normal and carry on the way we always had, but nine months later it's like… I've worked out that I can't. Something changed, and my heart's not in it any more.'

They trudged back up the long narrow path in single file, the wind whipping between them and making it hard to talk. By the time they reached the woods the moment had been lost, and Polly felt awkward about bringing it all up again. It was funny how sometimes you could talk to a stranger more easily than you could someone you'd known for years. The weird thing, she thought, as they parted ways with a little wave and a mutual smile, was that in doing so she'd dragged up all sorts of emotions she'd kept well hidden for longer than she could remember.

CHAPTER NINETEEN

'I HOPE those dodgy Inverness builders are doing a decent job up at Midsummer House.'

Kenny the builder rolled up the sleeves of his shirt and cracked open his third can of Diet Coke of the morning. Harry looked across at Rob, who'd arrived with a travel mug of coffee and was now sitting on an upturned barrel, legs spread, rapidly typing something onto a laptop which was covered in dust.

'You hear that?' Harry nudged him with a knee.

'What?' Rob looked up and closed the laptop. His dark hair was untidy and his expensive shirt collar was half-up, half-down, underneath a dark blue sweater, which Harry suspected had probably cost three figures.

'I said I hope they're doing a decent job.' Kenny's greying curls stood like a halo round his head, above a round face with ruddy cheeks and eyes that disappeared when he laughed, which was often.

'Oh I'm fairly sure they'll not be doing as good a job as you're doing here,' teased Rob, 'but unfortunately much as

I'd like we can't split you in half and have you doing building work in two places at once.'

'Aye,' Kenny swigged his drink. 'I'll mebbe come up in the afternoon and have a wee look for myself, see what they're up to.'

'Excellent plan.' Rob stood up. 'I suspect with Charlotte cracking the whip they won't dare put a foot out of line. I wouldn't mess with her, would you?'

Harry snorted with laughter. 'I've known her too long for that. Those poor builders have no idea that they're dealing with a force of nature.'

'Yeah, well, she wasn't wildly impressed when I told her that I couldn't see any reason why we couldn't work on the hotel and Midsummer at the same time.'

'It's unusual, I'll give you that,' said Kenny, who'd unfastened the button of his shirt and was cleaning off sawdust from underneath the base of the mitre saw. 'We're no' used to all this excitement in the village.'

'That's city high flyers for you,' Harry said, archly.

Rob gave a good-humoured grin. 'Just because we're not moving at a glacial pace, village style. You love it really.'

'Whatever,' Harry grinned and shook his head. It wasn't in his nature to hold on to things, and he'd got over his initial grouch about Rob railroading him into the wedding. He couldn't deny the fact it was a brilliant opportunity for free promotion. It just all felt like a bit of a rush job, and he wanted everything to be perfect. It was his name on the door, after all. Rob had pitched in and was happily getting his hands dirty helping with the clearing out of the old furniture, breaking it down and cramming as much as possible into the huge skip out the back. He might come from money and a glamorous life in the city, but he'd settled into Applemore and he and Charlotte were completely loved-up, which was nice to see. At least someone was. He needed to get a grip and accept that he needed to get his feelings for Polly under control, or else man up and do something about them. He grabbed the screwdriver and flipped the switch, catching each screw in a cupped hand as it was removed until the door he was working on dropped sideways, and he stopped it with his knee.

He'd been best friends with Lachlan since school. How the hell was he supposed to turn around and tell him he was in love with his youngest sister?

'Talking of city high flyers,' Rob said, breaking into his thoughts. 'We've got visitors.'

Harry looked up, and the door swayed, almost walloping him on the head.

'Ooh, careful,' said Ivy.

'Watch yourself, lassie,' warned Kenny. 'You'll need a helmet if you're coming in here.'

Harry watched Ivy glance from one man to the other, silently observing that none of them were wearing helmets. Donald, one of Kenny's apprentices, noticed and swiped his from where it had been hanging on a hook, shoving it on his head where it sat slightly off centre. Donald looked at Ivy with his jaw hanging open.

'Close your mouth man, or you'll be catching flies.' Kenny chuckled.

'Give me two secs,' said Rob, brushing down his trousers and running a dusty hand through his hair, which gave the impression he'd suddenly gone grey. 'Harry, you got a moment? I was chatting to Ivy yesterday when we popped round to the cottage to fix the shower. We've had an idea.'

'Coming.' Harry eyed Kenny, who looked at him with interest. The village of Applemore was fuelled by gossip, and Kenny's wife would get home from her job in the bank in the nearby town, avid to hear the latest news.

'If I hear anything interesting, I'll let you know,' Harry added.

'Mind you do. I'm on strict instructions.' Kenny gave him a brief salute then picked up his helmet. 'Better do my bit.'

Rob was standing outside with Ivy and Ben, who were wrapped up against the cold. The sky was bright blue and the sun shining. If it wasn't for their breath freezing in the chill and the dead plants in the hanging baskets, it could have been spring. Harry made a mental note to chuck them in the skip when they'd finished chatting about whatever it was.

'I bumped into Polly on the beach,' Ivy said, 'And it got me thinking. I'm on a bit of a hiatus from social media stuff right now, but we thought maybe we could give yours a bit of a revamp.'

Harry scratched his head. 'A revamp?'

'Brilliant idea, isn't it?' Rob beamed at him.

'We're looking to diversify a bit, maybe change things up,' explained Ben. 'We've learned a bit over the last few years. But –' he glanced at Ivy, giving her a brief smile, 'We've been thinking it might be time to put it into practice in a less public facing sort of way. We've already got the business, so it's a natural progression to sidestep into managing social media and that sort of thing for businesses, do marketing and that sort of thing.'

Ivy gathered her long hair into a bunch and twisted it over one shoulder, looking at him expectantly. 'I'm not saying your social media presence isn't good,' she added.

'No, nobody's saying that.'

Harry realised that it was his silence that was causing everyone to feel they needed to fill the space with chatter.

'Sorry, I'm a bit stunned.' He looked at Rob, wondering how on earth to telepathically communicate the question of payment. Rob looked back at him with a blank expression.

'It sounds great,' he began, 'But we're a bit – well, the last time we had our website designed it was done by someone's cousin in their office in a garage. And much as it sounds amazing we're a bit committed to the –' he nodded his head in the direction of the bar, where the building works had recommenced and there was a dull thud of something being smashed with a sledgehammer.

'Ah, no,' said Ben, realising what he was getting at. He shook his head. 'Gratis. Just as a bit of a trial run, if you like. I mean you've bent over backwards for us, and it'd be an interesting experiment to see what a difference we can make if we get some decent photos up there and maybe a bit of a before and after vibe with the building works.'

Harry felt his eyebrows lifting slightly at the thought of Kenny discovering his work being described as a *vibe*. 'That sounds – great. I mean brilliant. Seriously?'

Ivy nodded. 'I know it's a bit out of left field, but I had a really good chat with Polly on the beach yesterday and it made me really think about what mattered.'

Harry opened his mouth to ask how she was, then closed it again. 'Cool,' he said, instead.

'She's lovely,' Ivy added. 'So funny that she said she'd like to swap places with me and live in the city.' She gave a little giggle at the thought.

'She did?' Harry's eyebrows rose sky high at this.

Ivy shook her head slightly, putting two neatly manicured fingers to her lips. 'Oh, it was probably just something she said.'

Rob shot him an odd look. 'I can't see Poll going anywhere, can you?'

Harry lifted a shoulder, trying to appear casual. 'Who knows?' He turned on his heel, grasping the metal knob of the hotel door. 'Thanks, it sounds like a great idea. Rob, can I leave you to iron out the details of this one? I promised Kenny I'd help him get that stud wall up this afternoon.'

Rob lifted his chin in acknowledgement. 'Sure.'

Harry headed back inside, pausing for a moment in the reception area. The old wooden stair rail was covered with thick cloths to protect it from any accidental bumps during the renovation work, and he leaned against it, huffing out a heavy sigh. If he needed a sign, that had to be it. If Polly was interested in him, she wouldn't be day-dreaming about leaving Applemore and living in the city. Time to focus on the things he could control, like getting this place sorted, and face up to facts.

CHAPTER TWENTY

'I'M SO TIRED,' Polly said, collapsing on Joan's sofa, and removing one of the myriad of tartan cushions which decorated the place. 'I swear the entire population of the North West has been doing their shopping today. I never thought I'd say it, but if I hear another Christmas song I'm going to go bananas.'

Joan chuckled, setting down a tray on the little coffee table. 'Get this inside you and you'll feel a good bit better, I'm sure.'

Polly looked at the tray which was spread with everything she remembered from childhood teas. Joan had made a pot of her home-made cock-a-leekie soup and a loaf of crusty bread, slicing it and buttering it so thickly that Polly knew when she bit into it she'd leave toothmarks. There were chunks of Highland cheddar from the local dairy, a pot of tea with the crocheted cosy she'd had forever, and on another little plate there was a stack of the thick, round little Scotch pancakes which Joan made in batches on the griddle pan. They reminded her of winter afternoons sitting on the kitchen counter beside the Aga, watching Joan as she cooked, her dad pottering around somewhere in his book-strewn study or outside helping David with one of his inventions. She gave a happy sigh, and allowed Joan to pass her a little cushioned tea-tray, before putting a bowl of soup down in front of her.

'I feel like a little girl.'

'If you can't have a bit of fuss after a long day, there's something wrong. All you girls work far too hard if you ask me. Anyway, I need you on full power for the race night later.'

Polly groaned. 'I can't believe I've got roped in to help.'

'Well your sisters managed to duck out, and Lachlan's doing the bar, so someone had to step up.' Joan picked up the remote control. 'Shall we have a little look at my quiz programme on the television?'

Polly smiled to herself. Joan's little routines were set in stone. She privately wondered how George, who'd been widowed fifteen years before, had managed to fit himself in around them. He was off for the week visiting his daughter down in Galashiels ('rumours I'm avoiding this fundraising nonsense are completely false,' he'd told Polly with a conspiratorial wink) and so Joan was full steam ahead, along with Dolina and Greta, like some sort of terrible triple-pronged attack. They'd have the whole village rounded up and their pockets emptied before anyone knew what had happened to them.

'I've told Dolina we need a decent target for tonight. I'm not having any excuses. We're putting on a good spread, the least everyone can do is put their hands in their pockets.'

'It is Christmas,' pointed out Polly, reaching forward to take a piece of bread and biting into it with a sigh of delight.

'It is indeed, and if everyone gave us five pounds we'd

have enough to reach the total we need for the school climbing frame.' Joan tutted. 'With the hotel shut, everyone should be saving money not spending it all in the pub.'

Joan looked at her for a moment. 'Talking of the pub, you haven't mentioned Harry. How's he getting on with the renovations? I went by the other day when I was going to the shop to get some bits and pieces and there was an awful racket coming from inside. Mrs Mackay told me they're crashing and banging from morning until night.'

Polly shrugged. 'I haven't seen him. Well, I did pop by the other day but he was busy.'

He'd been a bit off, actually, but she wasn't going to admit that to Joan, because doing so would elicit a string of mother-hen questions which would make her feel even more uncomfortable than she already did. She'd popped her head around the door, calling him, and he'd given her a fleeting wave and a gruff greeting before apologising and saying he had to get back to work. Polly had retreated, feeling oddly hurt, and since then she'd seen neither hide nor hair of him.

'I expect he'll be there tonight. He better had be,' Joan added, warningly. 'I've got Murdo and the rest of the men from the village coming on the basis that they'll have an unofficial Applemore Bar for the night, albeit in a slightly less glamourous setting.'

'I don't think the bar is particularly glamorous right now,' laughed Polly, thinking of the sawdust-strewn floor and the sheets of plasterboard leaning up against the walls. 'Not from what I could see, anyway.'

'Aye, well, it'll be looking as good as new soon enough. And then you'll all be starry eyed for that Ivy Whatsit's wedding.' Joan gave a slight tut.

'She's nice, you know,' protested Polly. 'She's quite normal in fact.'

'Och,' said Joan, pursing her mouth. 'All dressed up and pouting with those goldfish lips. I've seen her Instagram pictures.'

'You're sounding alarmingly like Dolina this evening,' warned Polly, laughing. 'You've been spending too much time with her if you ask me.'

Joan's eyes widened in horror. 'Oh my,' she said, genuinely alarmed. 'Well if that's the case, I'll have to make an extra effort.'

She was true to her word. Four hours later, with the draughty memorial hall hung with every festive decoration the village committee could get their hands on and the ancient oil-fired radiators pumping as much heat as they could manage, they opened the doors to an impatient and chilly queue of villagers who'd come for the first annual race night fundraiser. The air was full of chatter as people poured in, handing their coats to Joan and Polly who were in charge of the cloakroom.

'What do you mean I've got to pay you fifty pence for my coat?' Kenny the builder, who had removed his flat cap, revealed his halo of fuzzy hair which was now standing on end. He stopped dead in the entrance, looking at Joan with an outraged expression.

'You're no' paying fifty pence for the coat, you're paying for a cloakroom ticket. We'll give you it back at the end of the night.' Joan somehow managed to prise him out of his jacket and hang it on a wooden hanger before he knew what had happened.

'This is daylight robbery,' muttered Kenny, pocketing the cloakroom ticket.

'It's for a good cause,' beamed Joan. She turned back to Murdo, who was hovering by her side.

'What's up, Murdo?'

'Greta says the oven's playing up.' Murdo gave Polly a

wink. 'It's probably keeled over in fear of having to cook her sausage rolls.'

'Don't let her hear you saying that. She's been working on them all week.' Joan shook her head, laughing. She ushered in a young couple, who wandered off unwrapping scarves from their necks and waving a greeting to another couple who were settling themselves down at one of the round tables, inspecting the plastic glasses that had been set out on the table and laughing. Polly recognised a couple of them from the times she'd stood outside school waiting to collect the twins.

'Give me two ticks and I'll sort it.' Joan hung up another couple of coats on the portable metal rail. Murdo, noticing at the same time as Polly that it wobbled slightly, reached over and tightened the bolt on the side.

'If that gives way there'll be a mighty fuss,' he chuckled as he headed back to his wife in the kitchen. 'You'll be having to give all those fifty pence pieces back as refunds. Mind and look after those coats, Polly.'

Mrs Drummond, the school head-teacher was standing at the far end of the hall, organising a couple of the teachers who were trying to get the projector to stay in place. Someone turned on a speaker and the over-excited sound of a horse-racing commentator blared into the room at full volume.

Mrs Drummond flapped a hand. 'You need to get that back to the beginning before we get organised!' she shouted, at full head-teacher volume. Polly looked over to see Mr Drummond, who was as peaceful and easy-going as his wife was strident and bossy, fiddling quickly with an open laptop on the table. He looked up for a second and she gave him a reassuring smile. Despite their differences they seemed a perfect pairing and were clearly devoted to one another. Nobody in Applemore could disagree that

Mrs Drummond had made a huge difference to the little village school, demanding every penny of government funding they were entitled to, organising constant events with the PTA to fundraise for school trips and equipment. The race night was a brand new idea, coming a couple of weeks before the school carol service which took place around the village Christmas tree. Watching as Mrs Drummond started marching around with a book of raffle tickets and a glass jar, Polly hoped that the villagers weren't going to get compassion fatigue.

There didn't seem to be much chance of that tonight. A steady stream of people came through the door, handing over their coats, many of them giving a bigger donation than the suggested pennies for the cloakroom. Festive music was playing and brightly coloured metallic tinsel and bright fairy lights hung in long swathes along the walls, lighting up the decorations which had been made by primary school children and stuck up – lightly askew – with Sellotape on the windows.

Polly rolled the first portable clothes rail to one side, bringing the next to the front. She turned to the doorway, surprised to see Ivy and Ben standing, hand in hand, looking slightly non-plussed.

'Hi,' she said, as Ben took Ivy's coat and passed it to her. She ripped off a ticket, hooking it through the coat hanger and passing the other end of the stub to him.

He shook his head as she tried to offer him change from the £2 coin he'd passed over. 'Don't worry about it, keep the change. We thought we'd come along after Charlotte and Rob said it would be an experience.'

Polly giggled. 'They're not wrong. It's definitely the best way of seeing what village life is like. You'll be rushing back to the city before you know it.'

'Hello there,' beamed a returning Joan, taking Ivy's

hand and shaking it vigorously. 'Lovely to meet you properly at last. I've heard so much about you.'

Polly gave her a wide eyed glare of warning.

'You have?' Ivy did a tiny frown of confusion.

'Oh yes,' said Joan. 'I've watched your videos on the
internet and everything.'

Polly kicked Joan on the shins.

'What?' said Joan a moment later, as Ivy and Ben made
their way across the hall to join a table where Charlotte
and Rob were standing, shrugging off their coats, smiling a
welcome.

'Nothing.' Polly giggled. 'I've never heard you using
your posh telephone voice in real life.'

'Shush, you.' Joan shook her fist. 'You said be nice. I
was being nice.'

'I said don't be like Dolina. I didn't say act weird.'

'Get away with you,' said Joan, ushering in the last of
the queue. 'Now let's get this show on the road.'

CHAPTER TWENTY-ONE

HARRY STOOD BY THE DOOR, taking in the progress they'd made. It was dark outside and the builders had long gone, but he'd worked on alone, determined to get the place ship-shape and ready for the next phase. After a couple of weeks where they seemed to do nothing but tear the place apart, with all the rubble and wood cleared away and into the skip he could see the bare bones of the bar. The tired old tartan carpet had been ripped up and the wooden floorboards were swept clean. The walls had been skimmed by Kenny's plasterer, and once they were dried out would be painted – the pots stood stacked in a corner, ready to go. They'd ripped off the old-fashioned mantelpiece, chipping off the hideous 1970s style brick surround, opening it up and replacing the mantle with a new lintel of dark-stained wood and the open fire with a wood-burner, which would mean the place would be far less dusty and need a lot less cleaning – which would be a relief to everyone. The new furniture was on order – scrubbed wooden tables and fashionably mis-matched chairs along with a couple of big squashy sofas where people could sit back and look out of the window at the little harbour. It was exactly as he'd envisioned it. Now he could allow himself a fleeting moment of imagining the place with a huge Christmas tree in the corner dotted with pin-pricks of white light and the place tastefully decorated with Beth's flowers, setting the scene for a wedding he never thought he'd be hosting, in a hotel which was only halfway through being renovated. He let out a sigh and shook his head, half-smiling. The truth was he'd never have bent over backwards to do all this if it hadn't been for Polly. She'd been the one to convince him that they could pull it all together with her usual cheerful determination. He glanced at his phone, checking the time. Talking of which, he'd better get a move on. He'd promised Lachlan that he'd help out after he'd been roped in to run the bar at the primary school fundraiser. There was a text reminding him that if he didn't show face he'd be dead meat. Harry grinned. Right now Lachlan was probably being nagged into submission by Mrs Drummond, the headmistress. Or Dolina, or Greta, or Joan. He wasn't sure which was more terrifying. A gust of wind battered the window panes, blowing off the sea, and he heard a spattering of hailstones following a moment later. It was icy cold outside. The lights dimmed for a second and he glanced up at them then shrugged to himself – probably just something to do with the power and the weather.

He switched off the lights in the bar and headed upstairs to have a quick shower and change.

Ten minutes later he pulled on a coat, turning up the collar against the wind which had picked up considerably, and jumped on his bike. If he didn't take the car at least he could have a couple of drinks and catch a lift home with someone else at the end of the night.

He could hear the race night before he saw it. Uproarious cheering and laughter carried down the hill from the memorial hall which stood on the outskirts of Applemore, where it had been built a hundred or so years before. Coming over the crest of the hill he saw the windows glowing in the darkness and cars parked all along the grass verge, which no doubt would cause a litany of complaints on the village Facebook group the next day. He parked his bike down the side of the hall beside a gorse hedge, swearing as he caught his hand on a thorn, and pushed the door open, finger in his mouth to stem the blood where he'd been pricked.

'Saved by the bell.' Lachlan shouted at him from across the room. There was a long queue of people standing by the open kitchen window hatch. Behind it he could see Polly, hair tied up in a ponytail and a festive red shirt on, carrying a tray of something from the oven. Joan and Dolina were serving cups of tea and coffee.

'Sorry, got caught up.' Harry threw his coat under the table and rolled up his sleeves as a group of already merry school parents approached the makeshift bar. 'What can I get you?'

They managed to shift a surprising amount of alcohol in the half-hour long interval. There had been a raffle in between the first two races previously, and it was pretty clear from the general atmosphere that people had been helping themselves to the alcoholic prizes on offer.

'Well there's a sight to make a man glad,' said Murdo, spotting Harry behind the bar. 'Even if it isn't the Applemore Hotel, I'll take it.'

'We don't have anything on draught,' said Harry, apologetically. 'D'you want to try some of this new bottled stuff Lachlan's been brewing? I'm almost certain it won't kill you.'

'Watch it,' said Lachlan, laughing. 'I've just sold a huge

order to a craft beer bar in Inverness, I'll have you know. I'm on the up.'

'I'm only kidding.' Harry grinned. 'How are you, anyway, Murdo?'

Murdo gave a nod. 'No' bad. I have to admit the girls have done a grand job with this race night. My horse came second in the first race and I won twenty pounds, so I'm quids in.'

'And you'll be putting it straight back into the fundraising coffers,' said Greta, who'd approached her husband from behind, making him turn and jump. Everyone laughed at Murdo's face.

'Aye, yes. Of course I will.' His eyes almost popped out of his face as Greta held her hand out flat, waiting for him to hand the money over. Murdo reached into his pocket and pulled out his wallet, removing the note reluctantly and handing to her with a mock-sorrowful expression.

'No beer for you then?' Lachlan laughed.

Murdo shook his head. 'I'm no' drinking tonight. Duty calls.'

'That'll be the takings down by half,' teased Harry, before he turned to serve the couple who were waiting by the table for a beer and a plastic glass of wine.

'Watch it laddie,' said Murdo, chuckling, a moment later. 'Or I'll not be visiting your fancy new bar when it's open.'

'I'll believe that when I see it.'

'Ladies and gents, let's get you all back in your seats please and ready for the next race,' called Mrs Drummond a while later. People were still milling about, hoping to get one more drink before the temporary bar was closed. Lachlan and Harry worked together at speed. Having been friends since childhood, they read each other well, and somehow despite

Mrs Drummond's exhortations they managed to get everyone sorted with drinks and shooed back to their tables before she gave them a telling off for holding up the proceedings.

'This is your life for the next eighteen years or so,' said Harry as Lachlan leaned back against the wall, surveying the packed hall. Mr Drummond was having some problems with the projector connection and the race they were supposed to be watching was starting and stopping as if the horses were being freeze-framed.

'What d'you mean?' Lachlan started wiping the table.

'Primary school fundraisers, family stuff, all that jazz.'

'I don't know if you've noticed,' said Lachlan, drily, 'But you don't have a wife or kids and here you are doing your bit as well. Look, even Ivy and Ben have been roped in.'

Harry followed Lachlan's gaze and saw them sitting at a table with Charlotte and Rob, along with Fi, the red-haired recently retired vet, Mel, the artist who exhibited at the gallery and the other Fiona, who worked alongside Charlotte running the holiday cottages. A moment later Mel shifted sideways and Harry caught a glimpse of Polly, who'd joined them and was laughing at something Ben and Ivy said. He dragged his eyes away, conscious of Lachlan's eyes on him and feeling like his face might give away his feelings.

'She told me she loves all this because it reminds me of her gran,' Lachlan said, giving a nod of his head in their direction.

'Who, Polly?'

Lachlan gave him an odd look. 'No, Ivy Winter. Apparently she was brought up by her and didn't have any more family, and she loves all that mother hen stuff that Dolina and the others do.'

'My god, is everyone in this village under her spell?' Harry growled.

'What are you on about?'

'Oh I dunno, everyone seems to be bending over backwards to make sure she's happy. The whole place has gone mad.'

'You're the one having a wedding in a half-renovated hotel because she wants to have it there,' said Lachlan, with a lift of his eyebrows.

'Don't I know it,' Harry groaned. 'Still, it's made everyone work at record speed, so that's something.'

Dolina bustled over to join them, her mouth pursed as usual in an expression of mild disapproval.

'I tell you what this race night would be better organised if Morag Drummond wasn't such a control freak that she had to have a finger in every pie,' she said, folding her arms over her ample bust. 'If it wasn't for the fact that half the room is pie-eyed on your beer Lachlan they'd all be complaining. I don't know why she can't get the laptop working –'

'There we are, sorry for the delay,' said the head-teacher, shooting a look in their direction as if she could tell that Dolina was chuntering away with her usual grumblings.

'Too many cooks,' said Harry out of the side of his mouth. Dolina fixed him with a beady glare then stumped back off to her table.

'I've put a tenner on number nine in this one,' said Harry, watching the screen with intent.

The commentator's voice grew louder and more frenzied as the race went on. People were banging their tables with excitement and whooping encouragement at horses who galloped across the screen, tails flying, their eyes wide as they leapt courageously over huge green fences.

'And we're coming up to the finish post and Bobby Jane's making a last dash for the lead, coming up on the inside we've got Hamburg Boy, no, Hamburg Boy is falling back and Bobby Jane is making ground…'

'Come on Hamburg,' urged Lachlan, hands fisted and leaning forward as if he was riding the horse himself.

A split second later the screen went blank and a huge groan rose in the air as Mrs Drummond's husband grabbed a black pager from his pocket and glanced at it for a moment before looking across at his wife who raised her hands in a gesture of defeat. The air was filled with a high-pitched insistent bleeping. Harry watched as Mel reached under the table and pulled an identical pager out of her bag, and pushed her chair back, pausing only to bend and give her girlfriend a kiss on the top of her head before she headed for the door, rapidly followed by Murdo and another of the school dads.

CHAPTER TWENTY-TWO

Ivy LOOKED at Polly in confusion.

'What's going on?'

'Just a moment ladies and gents, and we'll get started again,' said Mrs Drummond, smoothly. She stood at the front of the hall. Dolina had taken control of the laptop and stood poised and ready like a gundog waiting for the signal from her handler. Her hand hovered over the mouse.

'They're retained fire-fighters,' Polly explained.

Ben leaned forward in interest. Charlotte kissed Rob and headed off to the loo, taking advantage of an unexpected break in the proceedings.

'What does that mean?'

'I don't know if you've noticed that there's a building on the other side of the village, behind the row of cottages as you're driving up to Applemore House and the farm shop? Well, that's our fire station – it's run by retained fire-fighters, people from the village who work on a part-time basis for the fire service. They can't justify employing a full station full of workers, so instead people are trained and they carry a pager. When they're on duty, they have to be ready to spring into action whenever there's a call. It could be anything from a house fire to a cat up a tree, but they take it all in their stride,' Polly said, taking a sip of the wine she'd won in the tombola. It was disgusting but she gritted her teeth. She'd decided that the secret to getting through the evening with Harry on the other side of the room seemingly avoiding her eye was to anaesthetise herself. So far she'd had three plastic glasses full, and it wasn't working at all. She turned to look at Ivy, determined not to look over in his direction.

'That's amazing. They must be so brave.' Ivy squeezed Ben's hand. 'You could do that if you lived here.'

Ben looked slightly alarmed. 'I could,' he said, 'Don't think there's much call for volunteer firefighters in the city centre in Manchester, though.'

'Okay everyone, sorry for the interruption. Let's hope that tonight's call out isn't anything major, cross our fingers everyone stays safe, and get back to the important business of watching your steeds crossing over the finish line.' Mrs Drummond sounded even more hearty than usual. Polly suspected, watching as she glanced towards the door with an anxious expression, that she wouldn't be happy until her husband had returned home safe and sound.

'And that's a surprise fall for Hamburg in the final furlong,' said the commentator. Polly heard her brother give a groan of dismay and looked across without thinking, seeing Harry digging him in the ribs with a burst of laughter. He didn't look her way for even a second. She gave a sigh and turned back, gluing her eyes to the screen.

Ivy excused herself to go to the loo and Ben tipped the last of the bottle of white wine they'd bought from the bar into his glass, looking at Polly thoughtfully.

'Ivy was telling me you were thinking of making a move?'

'She did?' Polly looped a long strand of hair back behind her ear and turned to look at him. Joan wandered past with an armful of raffle prizes.

'Yeah, I mean I can see why you love it here. I mean Ivy's fallen in love with the place.'

'And you?' Polly sipped her wine.

He shrugged slightly. 'I'm a city boy through and through. She said you'd thought about making a change – well, you know if you fancy it, I've got a mate who owns a couple of little arty shops, the sort of stuff you sell. He's looking to expand. You'd be perfect for the job, if you wanted me to put in a word.'

Polly sat back in surprise. 'A whole chain,' she said, faintly.

Ben nodded enthusiastically. 'Yeah. I mean you built the farm shop up from nothing and made a go of it in the backside of – I mean the depths of beyond.'

Polly giggled. 'Fair point.'

'Why don't you give it a go? Have a chat with him at least.' He pulled his phone out of his pocket. 'I'll drop him a message just now, get him to give you a shout about a meeting.'

Polly opened her mouth and then closed it again. She'd come back to Applemore after university, lost and at a loose end. When her dad had died, she'd found a way to make a place for herself and surrounded herself with family, but since then all her siblings had paired up and were busy building their own lives. She had friends, of course, but – she glanced briefly over at Harry, who was nowhere to be seen. Lachlan was folding up the trestle table they'd used as a makeshift bar. Back home Rilla was waiting for him, with baby Kitty fast asleep in her cot. Rob and Charlotte were loved up and full of plans for the future. Beth and Jack hadn't been able to find a babysitter for the evening and were probably sitting at home, feet up in front of the fire, watching Netflix with a bottle of red on the go. She'd made a success of the farm shop, expanded into the disused buildings that surrounded it, and – well, where was there to go from there?

'What d'you think?' Ben prompted, breaking into her thoughts.

'Okay,' said Polly, with some of her old impulsiveness. 'Go for it. I can't do anything until after Christmas – the shop is manic.'

'No probs,' said Ben, tapping into his phone. He shifted as Ivy returned, making space for her and reaching out absent-mindedly to squeeze her fingers as he carried on typing a reply to whoever was on the end of his conversation.

'Sorted.' He looked up. 'Tyler sounds really excited. I've told him I'll connect the two of you and you can head down to Manchester and have lunch and a chat in the new year.'

'Just like that?' Polly was astounded.

Ben nodded. 'Just like that.'

'What's happening?' Ivy looked at the two of them with interest.

'I'll fill you in after this, babe,' said Ben, who seemed revitalised by a bit of contact with the outside world.

'Okay, darling.' Ivy seemed content to wait.

Polly rifled in her jeans pocket for the raffle tickets she'd bought earlier, thinking as she did that it was going to be interesting to see what Ivy and Ben did in the future. It was clear that they both had a head for business, but Ben was definitely far more fired up by city life than she was. Maybe another couple of weeks in Applemore would give

Ivy her fill of living miles from everything and she'd be desperate to get back to the bright lights of the city. Meanwhile – Polly gave a little shiver of excitement – *she* would need to think about what on earth to wear to a business lunch in Manchester. She took another slug of wine. Maybe this was exactly what she needed.

CHAPTER TWENTY-THREE

JOAN WAS READING out raffle numbers, pulling them out one by one from the huge glass jar where they'd been folded neatly earlier that afternoon.

'And we have a winner – blue, number sixty four,' she said, cheerfully, waving it in the air. 'Do we have a blue sixty-four?'

'That's mine!' Ivy looked down for a moment then jumped up in delight. 'I have it.'

'Congratulations,' said Joan, beaming at her as she handed over a bottle of purple bath oil which looked like it had come out of the ark.

'I swear I won that in last year's raffle,' said Fiona under her breath to Polly, as Ivy made her way back through the tables towards them. 'It's been sitting in the cupboard in the hall all year.'

Ivy returned, looking as delighted with her bargain bottle of bath oil as she would have if she'd won a weekend spa break. Fiona craned her neck forward and peered at it for a moment, then nodded.

'I think Mel probably gave it to Dolina when she came round looking for donations.'

Polly burst out laughing. A moment later she looked across at Lachlan, sensing somehow that he was trying to get her attention. Charlotte had joined him and was standing with an anxious expression on her face. She beckoned Polly over.

'Sorry, just a sec,' she said, excusing herself and squeezing her way across to her brother and sister. 'What's going on?'

Lachlan pushed his dark hair back from his face, showing brows knitted together in concern. Charlotte put a hand on her arm.

'There's a fire,' she began.

Polly felt her stomach drop, as if somehow she could sense that something was very wrong.

'The call out was to the hotel.' Lachlan finished his sister's sentence.

CHAPTER TWENTY-FOUR

POLLY DASHED out into the dark night. The wind was howling through the trees and the moon hidden beneath a bank of thick cloud. Heavy rain lashed down, soaking her shirt almost immediately.

'Come on,' said Lachlan, grabbing her by the arm and pulling her towards his Land Rover. She slammed the door and he hit the accelerator, bumping off the verge so she shot out of her seat before she had a moment to fasten her seatbelt.

As they sped into the village they could see a strange light coming from the little main street, and smoke rising in a cloud, lit orange from below. Lachlan screeched to a halt on the side street beside the little bookshop and jumped out, following Polly who'd already started running down the street towards the village fire engine which was parked outside the hotel, blue lights flashing.

'What's happening? Where's Harry?' Polly grabbed Conor, who had appeared from his little cottage along the road and was standing, drenched already, in a hoody and a pair of crocs, his arm still bandaged.

'He's inside.'

'What?' Polly felt her stomach drop to the floor like a stone.

A moment later she saw Mel, swamped in her huge safety gear, eyes visible above the black face mask that covered the bottom half of her face. Polly wanted to grab her and scream at her for answers, but knew she had to let her do her job.

The long hose had been unravelled and was leading through the door into the building. Polly stood on tiptoe trying to peer inside. Where the hell was he? How could he have been at the race night one moment and gone the next?

She curled her fingers into her fists, feeling them digging into her palms, trying to take a breath to steady herself. If something had happened to him, she'd –

'Harry!' She ran forward, seeing the familiar outline of his broad shoulders as he emerged from the side alley, carrying something in his arms.

He strode up to them and she realised it was Pickle, held firmly in his arms, soaking wet and hissing with outrage, eyes wide and teeth bared. She glared at Polly and spat with growling fury.

'That's thanks, in cat language, apparently.' Harry held her fast as she continued to squirm. 'Rescued her from the back.'

Pickle wriggled like a fish in his arms and managed to get free, jumping into the air and hurtling off, tail in the air and the hair on her back standing on end.

Polly looked at Harry for a moment, unable to find words. She turned a moment later, sensing eyes on her, and saw Charlotte, Rob, and Lachlan all looking at her. Realising with a jolt of embarrassment that they knew her far too well, she glared back at them, summoning up as much outrage as Pickle. Lachlan arched an eyebrow and looked at Charlotte, who raised both of her brows. Right then Polly could have happily thumped them both.

'I'm glad you're okay,' she said, lamely.

Harry looked at her for a moment, a crooked smile forming on his lips. His face was smudged with soot and rain was trickling down from his hair in rivulets, but he said nothing as their eyes met. For a moment, despite the industry of the firefighters and the gathering crowd of villagers, it felt as if they were the only people standing outside the hotel in the rain.

'Well,' said Charlotte, a moment later, 'I'm guessing you're going to need a bed for the night.'

'He can stay at the cottage,' said Polly, firmly.

Harry gave a fleeting nod. 'If that's okay?'

'Course.' Polly stepped back as one of the other firefighters appeared and started reeling the hose back in.

'What's the damage?' Harry wiped the rain from his face with the back of his arm.

'Not as bad as it seems. Thank goodness Mrs Mackay happened to hear the alarm, with half the village up at the hall for the race night.'

He shook his head, his voice gruff with gratitude. 'I can't thank you all enough.'

Mel had reappeared and taken off her mask, rubbing her nose for a moment and looking up at the hotel as she spoke. 'That could have been a lot worse. You've got off pretty lightly. And don't thank us. It's all part of the service,' she said, with a smile, before getting back to work.

The rain abated slightly. Polly sheltered under a borrowed umbrella which kept turning inside out in the wind, watching as the firefighters worked quickly and efficiently to clear up, get everything back into the fire engine and head back to the tiny station, chatting and laughing.

RACHAEL LUCAS

The adrenalin rush of a job had left everyone wide awake. Slowly the crowd of interested onlookers melted away. Lachlan gave Harry a brief hug before saying he'd better get back to Rilla and Kitty, and Charlotte and Rob – who looked a bit shell-shocked by the whole thing – took up Lachlan's offer of a lift back to their cottage.

'Well,' said Harry, finally, 'I guess it's just you and me.'

'What a night.'

Harry groaned. 'Not exactly part of the plan.'

Sodden strands of hair whipped across her face and she pushed them back, turning to look at him for a moment. He gazed out to sea, lost in thought for a long moment.

Polly stood beside him, silently. As the rain started falling heavily once more, Harry turned to her, jingling the keys to his car.

'Shall we?'

She nodded.

'We'll come back in the morning and see what it looks like in daylight. Not much we can do now.'

CHAPTER TWENTY-FIVE

HARRY WATCHED Polly as she slipped into the passenger seat and fastened her seat belt. He'd watched her in stolen glances from the opposite side of the hall that evening, thinking how beautiful she looked as she laughed and chatted with Ivy and Ben, her always-ready smile lighting up her face. She'd bent over backwards to make them feel welcome and include them in the evening which was typical of her, and then when she'd heard about the fire she'd dashed straight down with Lachlan and the look on her face had been... he frowned, rubbing between his eyes with two fingers.

'You okay?'

He felt a hand on his shoulder and turned to see her looking at him with concern.

'Have you got smoke in your eyes? Do you think we should get you checked out?'

He shook his head and turned the key in the ignition. 'They're fine. What I need is a drink and a shower.'

'I can do both of those.'

Unusually for Polly, the car was silent as they drove up

towards the cottage. The sound of the windscreen wipers sliding on the glass was hypnotic and he drove on auto-pilot, pulling up outside the front door and bringing the car to a halt before she seemed to shake herself and shoot out of the car rapidly, opening the door and beckoning him inside in a matter of seconds.

'Sorry, it's a bit untidy,' she said, grabbing an armful of clothes from the sofa and throwing them onto the armchair. 'Wasn't expecting guests.'

She switched on a couple of side lamps, turning off the main light so the room glowed warm and welcoming. It was comfortably untidy – the coffee table stacked with books and papers, the mantelpiece decorated with swathes of greenery and berries which looked like Beth's handi-work. In the corner baubles sparkled on a bushy Christmas tree. Polly had clearly been busy wrapping presents already – they sat underneath in colourful piles.

'I'm hardly guests.' He felt the corners of his mouth lifting in a half-smile. 'I'll get this fire going again if you sort out a drink.'

'You don't want a shower first? You're soaked.' Polly stood with a hand on the door, looking at him, her blue eyes gentle. She had a smudge of soot on her cheek.

Now they were inside in the light he realised that she was soaking wet too, the red shirt clinging to her body. He gritted his teeth and turned away, trying not to notice.

'I'm fine, honestly.'

By the time she returned a few minutes later he'd coaxed the dying embers in the fire back to life, stacking a heap of kindling and logs in a practised manner. As she sat down on the sofa the flames burst into life and he straight-ened up, feeling the heat against the sodden fabric of his jeans.

'Here. Have this, then you can jump in a shower.'

He took the solid glass, looking down at the amber liquid which promised warmth and a sense of peace after the night's drama, swirling it for a moment before taking a gulp, feeling it burn on his tongue.

'I needed that.'

Polly sat perched on the arm of the sofa, holding her drink, looking into the flames. He followed her gaze.

'I can't believe Pickle,' she said after a moment, starting to laugh. 'Her face was the perfect picture of outrage.'

'Bloody cats.' He shook his head. 'Risk your life to save them and what do you get in return?' Pushing up his sleeves he examined his shredded forearms.

'Most people end up with smoke inhalation after a fire. You've got cat scratches.'

He shook his head in amusement. 'I'll take it.'

'Compared to the alternative, I would.' Polly took another sip of whisky and made a face. 'Ugh. I always think I'll like this more than I do.'

'It's a good whisky.' He drained his glass.

'I'm sure it is.' She passed her drink to him, and he felt the softness of her fingers tracing the scratches on his arm for a moment. 'We should probably do something about those.'

He shrugged. 'A shower will do.'

'Oh,' She jumped up. 'Sorry - of course.'

'You go first.' He gestured with an arm. 'I'm fine, honestly.'

He sat watching the flames while Polly was gone, staring blankly into space. Time slipped away without him noticing and what seemed like moments later she returned, in a pair of jeans and a faded grey sweatshirt, her hair still damp and her cheeks flushed from the heat of the shower.

'Come on, I'll get you some towels.'

He followed her into the hall, standing wait as she

disappeared into the kitchen, returning and putting them into his arms.

'Not matching, I'm afraid, and they're not a patch on the posh hotel ones you use.'

'I couldn't care less.' He raised his eyes heavenward. 'When have you ever known me to stand on ceremony?'

'Never.'

'Exactly.'

The tiny bathroom had a shower which stood over the bathtub. The room was still full of steam from Polly's shower, the mirror fogged up completely so he couldn't see his reflection. He stripped off, dropping his clothes to the floor and stepping under the hot water, allowing it to pour over his face as he closed his eyes and thought for a moment. What the hell had caused the fire? Murdo had said that there would be an investigation, and tomorrow would bring loss adjusters and insurance people ready to fill in forms and pick their way through the damage. It hadn't looked too bad to his untrained eyes, but that meant nothing. He rubbed his face with both hands, groaning at the prospect of it all, and reached for the shampoo. Besides scrubbing off the reek of smoke and the layer of dirt, there was nothing more he could do right now.

CHAPTER TWENTY-SIX

'POLL?'

Five minutes later she heard a call from the bathroom and jumped up from the edge of the sofa where she'd been perched, staring into the flames.

'Hang on.'

She walked into the hall of the cottage and her heart stopped for a moment. Standing, naked but for a towel which was wrapped around his hips, Harry stood surrounded by a halo of steam in the bathroom doorway.

'We didn't really think this through.' He motioned to his bare chest.

Polly reached out, putting a hand on the doorframe to steady herself. Here was Harry, broad-shouldered and muscled from years of physical work wrestling barrels and sailing, looking at her with a rueful half smile. It was pretty much everything she'd ever day-dreamed about, only not under these circumstances. Pull yourself together, she told herself firmly.

'Give me two secs.' She lifted a finger. 'Hold that thought.'

She grabbed the keys and headed over to the farm shop, shrugging on a raincoat and slipping her feet into a pair of wellington boots. The alarm beeped briefly as she tapped in the code and then flicked on the lights, heading across to the back wall. She grabbed a t-shirt, pulling it from the hanger and tearing off the labels, and reached over to the shelf where a neatly folded pile of trekking shorts sat folded. She frowned at the sizes, not sure which to go for, and made a guess.

Two minutes later she returned. Harry was sitting on the edge of the bath, still wrapped in a towel, his hair standing up in damp spikes. He stood up, and Polly felt herself drawing in a sharp intake of breath. She'd seen him bare chested before, working with Lachlan on the forest or out messing about in boats on hot summer days, but somehow it felt quite different – more intimate, perhaps. Mutely, she handed him the clothes.

Harry shook out the t-shirt and gave a snort of laughter. 'Well, it's different.'

'Beggars can't be choosers,' she said, as he raised an eyebrow whilst examining the design. The t-shirt was dark gunmetal grey, with a minimalist line drawing of a Highland cow's head printed on the front.

'Oh, believe me, I'm grateful.' He pulled it over his head. 'Thanks.'

Polly stood for a moment, and Harry looked at her with an odd expression.

'What is it?'

He brandished the shorts. Polly put a hand to her mouth, realising that if he dropped the towel to put them on in front of her he'd be revealing – well, everything.

She felt her cheeks going pink and started backing away. 'Sorry, I didn't think.'

Harry gave her an odd look before he pushed the door

closed with a foot. She collapsed against the wall, closing her eyes.

A moment later Harry emerged, barefoot and with a teasing smile on his face. 'What d'you think?'

'Perfect.' Polly walked down the hall towards the sitting room, acutely conscious of every movement she made in a way that she'd never been before. This is Harry, she tried to tell herself, but somehow he made the little cottage seem tiny and when he collapsed on the sofa in front of the fire the space beside him seemed to shrink. She'd opened a bottle of wine and he leaned forward, pouring them both a glass and handing one to her as she sat, legs curled up underneath her, body tense.

'Cheers.' He tipped his glass towards hers so they clinked gently.

Polly shifted slightly and her foot brushed against his leg. She pulled it away as if his skin was molten lava, tucking it back and picking up a cushion which she hugged as they settled back, watching the flames.

'I'm glad you turned up,' he said, eventually. She turned to look at him, her eyes meeting his as he gazed at her steadily.

'I thought –' she faltered for a moment. 'When Lachlan said that there was a fire, and I realised you weren't there, for a moment –'

'If it had been you,' Harry said, his voice low. 'I'd have done the same.'

She looked over at the fire and glanced back, realising he was still fixing her with the same intense focus. Her heart was bumping against her ribcage as if she'd run all the way home from Applemore. As if transfixed, she reached across, tracing the scratches on his arm.

'Could have been worse,' he said, mouth twisting in a half-smile.

'Don't.' She grabbed hold of his wrist, her fingers wrapping around it. This time it was Harry who took a breath in and held it, leaning across and putting his glass down on the table where hers already sat. He turned back, long fingers wrapping over hers and a question on his face. She moved almost imperceptibly towards him and a moment later his fingers were laced in hers, the other hand caressing her cheek gently for a moment. He let his fingers trace down her neck and along the line of her collar bone, and then somehow he'd drawn her towards him, his mouth only a heartbeat from hers, and he paused for the briefest of moments. Polly reached up, curling a hand around his neck, and she felt his lips graze across hers, their softness contrasting with the roughness of the stubble of his face. He untangled his fingers from hers, sliding a hand down her back and drawing her in close, murmuring her name as he trailed kisses along her jaw and then, tangling his hand in her hair, pulled her into his arms.

CHAPTER TWENTY-SEVEN

HARRY WOKE WITH A START, blinking hard as he tried to get his bearings. An alarm was blaring – not a familiar one – and the ceiling was unfamiliar. He'd been in a sleep so heavy that waking felt like coming back to life after a century, and it took a moment for him to turn, realising with a start that jolted him awake that he was in Polly's pale cream bedroom, and that she was sitting, wrapped in a duvet, holding her phone which she'd thankfully silenced.

'Morning,' he said, and she turned around.

He caught a glimpse of the long line of her back and the curve of her waist before she wrapped the covers more tightly around herself, pushing her hair back from her face and tucking it back behind her ear. She looked up at him through lowered lashes. Harry, no stranger to the morning after the night before scenario, sized up the situation and reached over, grabbing his shorts from the top of the chest of drawers where they lay at a jaunty angle.

'I tell you what, why don't I stick these on and make us a coffee while you get dressed. I assume there's a reason why your alarm's going off at —' he peered at his own phone '- six thirty in the morning?'

'I've got a delivery at half seven,' said Polly, with a rueful expression. 'Sorry. I forgot the alarm.'

'No worries,' he said, managing to manoeuvre himself into his shorts. It was pretty clear that there wasn't going to be a repeat performance of last night. 'Chuck me over my t-shirt?'

'Here,' Polly tossed it towards him, still not quite meeting his eyes. 'I'll be two seconds.'

Harry filled the kettle and found two mugs from the dishwasher. He heard water running in the bathroom and a few moments later Polly appeared, hair brushed and dressed in her farm shop branded polo shirt and last night's jeans. She was holding a pair of red and blue striped socks.

'Nice socks,' he said, taking the milk from the fridge and pouring it into their coffee. He handed her a cup.

'Thanks.'

'I-' he began.

'About —' Polly faltered at the same moment.

'Look,' he said, taking the lead. He hitched a hip up onto the table and looked down at Polly who was cupping her mug of coffee, gazing into it as if all the answers to the worlds problems could be found there. 'I'm sorry about last night. No, I'm not sorry.' He shook his head. He was sorry about – this. Whatever was going on here.

'I think we were both a bit spooked,' said Polly, taking a sip of coffee. 'I mean you could have died.'

'Yeah,' he tipped his head in a teasing gesture, 'Cat scratches can be deadly. It's a little known fact.'

Polly giggled. He'd broken the ice. 'You are an idiot.'

'I am,' he agreed. 'Look, the last thing I want is for last

night to screw anything up between us. You're my best friend, Poll. It's probably a rite of passage, isn't it?'

'Like in When Harry met Sally?'

'Exactly like that.' Harry, who could only vaguely remember the movie, nodded.

Polly looked at him suspiciously. 'When's the last time you watched When Harry met Sally?'

'I dunno,' he shrugged, 'I saw it once, years ago.' He was pretty sure he'd watched it in Sydney with his Australian ex-girlfriend, but he wasn't about to admit to Polly that he was also pretty sure he'd dozed off before the end. If it had been a Star Wars movie, that would have been a different matter.

'Okay. Well, that's that sorted.' Polly wrinkled her nose, the way she always did when she was trying to look as if she wasn't bothered by something. Harry cursed himself for knowing her too damn well. 'The next thing we need to address is the minor detail of Ivy's wedding.'

If he'd been harbouring any last vestiges of hope that they might have been up for a repeat performance of last night, those words were as effective as an ice-cold bucket of water. He looked at Polly, his mouth falling open in horror as he realised that in the panic of the fire that had been the furthest thing from his mind.

'Well there's nothing we can do, is there? Even if the damage is minor, there's no way we can get the place ready now. We've got a week and a half.'

Polly's face gathered in a frown. 'She's going to be devastated.'

Harry gestured with his palms open. 'I wish there was something we could do.'

He watched as she took another mouthful of coffee then placed her mug back on the table.

'I better get you back to the hotel.'

It was still dark outside, and Polly's car was freezing. It couldn't have been more apposite – the atmosphere echoing the situation perfectly, in comparison to last night's warm glow of welcome and firelight.

'I can't turn up in shorts and t-shirt,' he said, as she switched on the engine.

'I tell you what, why don't we nip up to Applemore and grab some stuff from Lachlan?' Polly turned the car right instead of left outside the farm shop and started making her way towards the big house. It rose out of the darkness, the turrets etched against a pink-streaked sky as they swung onto the wide open drive, parking close to the steps that led up to the back door. A light was on upstairs, and the kitchen light glowed a welcome as they pushed open the hall door into the boot room.

'Harry!' Rilla rushed forward, pulling him into an embrace, hair sleep-mussed. She was in blue and white pyjama bottoms and an old t-shirt of Lachlan's, and Kitty was sitting in her high chair gnawing on a banana. Harry made a beeline for the warmth of the Aga.

'Thank god you're okay. I was worried sick. When Lachlan got back last night we couldn't sleep for ages thinking about what might have happened.'

Harry smiled at Kitty, who was beaming at him and waving her banana in welcome.

'I'm fine, don't worry. But a bit –' he gestured to the shorts and t-shirt he was wearing.

'Yeah, it's not really shorts weather unless you're doing some sort of Christmas in Australia thing.' Rilla laughed.

'Definitely not. I came to see if I could borrow something from Lachlan until I can get into the hotel. I've got to wait for the fire service to come back this morning and check it all out, and I suspect I'm in for the long haul with loss adjusters and goodness knows what else.'

Rilla gave Polly a quizzical look, which he suspected wasn't meant for his eyes. He pretended not to notice.

'Course you can. He's just in the shower. Let me nip up and grab something, tell him you're here. D'you want breakfast? Coffee?'

Polly glanced up at the clock. 'I've got a delivery coming.'

'I don't want to hold you up, Poll.' Rilla stood with her hand on the doorknob. 'Do you want to get off, and we'll give Harry a ride into town once we've eaten? We can always drop you off a bacon roll on the way down?'

Polly shook her head. 'It's fine, honestly. If you don't mind?' She looked over at him, brows raised in query.

'Course not. Thanks for –' he was about to say thanks for last night, but he hesitated. Surely Rilla must realise something was up – you could cut the atmosphere with a knife. He caught Polly's eye and she dropped her gaze, fiddling with her hair for a moment.

'No problem,' she said, a second later.

'I'll go and get Lachlan, shall I?' Rilla's tone was slightly too bright.

'I'll come and see how things are going later,' said Polly. She shot out of the door, leaving him standing by the Aga, surveyed by a solemn-faced Kitty.

Five minutes later, Lachlan strode into the room and tossed a pile of clothes onto the table. He eyed Harry's outfit with raised eyebrows, saying nothing, then made his way over to the fridge where he pulled out a pack of bacon and tore it open.

'Shove over,' he said, lifting the lid of the Aga and sliding the frying pan onto the hotplate. Harry watched as he peeled off the slices of bacon and arranged them on the surface of the pan. His stomach churned as Lachlan finished what he was doing and turned to look at him for a long moment, not speaking. Was he going to sock him one for going to bed with Polly?

'I –' he began to say.

'Thank God you're okay. I swear, I don't think either of us got a wink of sleep last night, did we?'

Rilla smiled. 'Not a lot. On a plus note it gave us a chance to talk about what happened.'

Harry shifted uneasily.

'I spoke to Rob last night after I got back. He didn't call you because he thought you'd be...'

'Because he thought you probably had enough on your plate,' Rilla finished Lachlan's sentence.

'Anyway we've come up with a plan. Obviously you can't very well have any sort of wedding at the hotel when you've had a massive setback like this, but we had a brainwave.'

'Who did?' Harry scratched his head. It was only just past seven in the morning and the night's event seemed to be catching up with him at last.

'Me. Rob. Well, all of us, really.' Lachlan ducked as Rilla threw a dishtowel at his head.

'It was my idea, actually,' she said, wiping Kitty down with a flannel as she spoke. 'Poor Ivy, she's had a horrible year losing her grandma. We all know how it feels to lose someone. And it was clear how much it meant to her getting married here in Applemore, so we thought we'd offer her the next best thing.'

Lachlan looked over at Rilla with a smile.

'Which is?' Harry stepped out of the way again as Lachlan shook the frying pan. The air was filling with delicious bacon smells and his stomach growled in appreciation.

'They can get married here. It wouldn't take much to make the drawing room look nice – Lachlan can cut another tree and we can decorate it, and Beth can go to town with loads of greenery and stuff.' Rilla waved her arm around to demonstrate.

'But –' Harry opened his mouth to speak.

'No arguments. What's the point of having a massive place like this if we can't open it up and make a difference when it's needed.' Lachlan's tone was final.

Harry was immensely touched. 'What can I say? You two…'

'Brown sauce or ketchup?'

Harry looked at Lachlan who was grinning. 'That's what you can say. I mean you've got to get your priorities right. And something tells me you're going to have a long day.'

Forty five minutes later, dressed and fed and feeling slightly more human, Harry was sitting beside Lachlan as he drove down into the village. Harry glanced at him sideways, half expecting his oldest friend to have a go about Polly now that they were on their own, but he didn't say a word. Humming along to the radio, he turned up the news when the sports reporter came on and grumbled about the state of his football team before pulling up outside the Applemore Hotel in the first light of morning. From the outside it looked as if nothing had gone on.

'Shall we have a look?'

'Murdo said we needed to wait for him to make sure it was safe.' Harry paused, but got the keys out of his pocket.

'Come on, we can go in the side door – let's see what the damage is.'

Lachlan followed him in. A thin shaft of early morning sunlight illuminated the bar, which looked almost completely untouched on first sight, until you looked up. Harry gazed at the ceiling, which had collapsed at the archway that led through to the restaurant.

'Well, that's not great.'

'Did I no' say you weren't to come in here until we got here?'

They both turned, hearing Murdo's voice. He was clad once again in his firefighters' kit and standing in the doorway with a couple of others standing at his heels.

Harry put his hands up. 'Mea culpa. I just wanted to know how bad it was.'

'Leave it to the professionals,' said Murdo, pointing a finger to the exit. 'Get on with you. We'll come and find you after.'

There was nothing for it but to head back up to the farm shop. Lachlan strode in ahead of a slightly reluctant Harry.

'Och that was quite the fright you were giving all of us,' said Dolina, who surprised him by rushing across from her place in the café queue and wrapping her arms around him in a hug which almost knocked all the air out of his lungs. 'I'm glad to see you in one piece. It's been all over the village Facebook group, you know. So many rumours.'

'Most of them started by you,' Harry heard Lachlan mutter under his breath, but he was laughing as he said it. Dolina, oblivious, released him from her grasp and looked at him. 'And I bet you haven't even rung your parents to let them know you're safe.'

'I wasn't even in the hotel when the fire started,' protested Harry, but he felt for his phone, pulling it out of the pocket of his jeans. 'I'll give them a ring just now. Will that make you happy?'

Dolina beamed. 'That it will. And if you sit yourself down and take the weight off your feet as well, I'll be even happier. Shoo.' She waved her hands, sending him in the direction of the table by the window.

'What the hell is everyone doing up here at this time of day?' Harry rubbed his face in confusion.

'Tom and Gavin reckoned there'd be a surfeit of gossip to be had today, so they opened up when Polly started dealing with the delivery,' Lachlan explained. He dumped his coat over the back of a chair before heading over to order coffees.

The café was surprisingly busy. A constant stream of villagers wandered in, popping over to his table to say how glad they were that he was okay and asking what the damage was to the hotel.

'Well, I bet you were glad to discover the place hadn't been burnt to the ground,' said Murdo's wife Greta, who appeared a while later with a wicker shopping basket over her arm.

'Very.' Harry noticed that Polly was standing on the other side of the shop, looking in their direction. She lifted a hand in a wave.

'I gather Polly came to the rescue with a bed for the night.'

Harry looked at Greta, who looked back at him. Was that a twinkle in her pale grey eyes?

He nodded. 'Yes, she's a good mate.'

A hint of a smile twitched at her lips. 'Mmm,' she nodded. 'Joan and I were just chatting the other day about what good friends you were. She's a nice lass.'

'She is.'

'Who is what?' Beth arrived, wrapped up warmly and looking like she was twice her normal size.

'I was just telling Harry what a good girl Polly is. It's a pity she hasn't found a nice man, mind you.'

Beth eyed Harry with a meaningful look. 'Well, maybe she will one of these days.'

'True enough.' Greta gave a nod. 'Anyway I can't stand

around chatting all day, I've only come up to pick up some sausages from the shop. After his hard work last night he deserves his favourite casserole for dinner.'

Beth raised an eyebrow. 'Because of course the last thing Greta would do is stand around chatting all day. I gather the entire village has been burnt to a cinder following a massive inferno. Or that's the rumour, anyway.'

'Am I supposed to feel bad that it was only a minor electrical fire?' Harry laughed and moved his chair so Beth could sit down beside him. She shook her head.

'Can't sit down, I've got loads of work to do up at the gardens. I've got a wedding to think about, you know.'

'Is that why you're wrapped up in about fifteen layers of fleece?'

She nodded. 'I'm trying something new with some greenery, but that means I need to go out cutting it in the woods and it's blooming freezing out there.'

Lachlan returned with coffees, followed by Rob and Charlotte who'd turned up unnoticed while they'd been chatting to Greta. A moment later Ivy and Ben appeared, pulling off scarves and gloves, pink cheeked and looking ridiculously loved-up and happy.

'The gang's all here,' said Harry, drily. 'Is this some sort of intervention, or are we having a meeting and nobody told me?'

Rob's mouth twitched in amusement. 'I'm saying nothing.' He looked at Charlotte who pulled her best angelic face.

'Did you walk here?' Beth said, taking in Ivy and Ben's flushed cheeks and pink-tipped noses.

'They did,' said Charlotte, pulling up a chair. 'We did offer them a lift,' she added, reaching over and pinching the biscuit that was sitting on the saucer beside Lachlan's coffee. She nibbled it thoughtfully.

'We said no,' said Ivy. 'Thought it would be fun to have a bit of an early morning hike. I got loads of lovely photos as well, which will look really good when we're doing some promo stuff for the hotel.'

Harry grimaced. Had they missed the news altogether?

'I mean obviously there's going to be a bit of a delay,' said Ivy, equably. 'But never mind that. Just a minor detail.'

'And the…' Harry winced as he finished his sentence. ' – the wedding?'

'It's fine.' Ben said, closing his hand over Ivy's. They looked into each other's eyes for a moment before turning back to look at everyone.

'Really?' Harry was astonished. This laid back couple, standing hand in hand, were a million miles from the people he'd met the first day they'd checked into the Applemore Hotel. Relaxed and smiling, they slipped into the chairs on the opposite side of the table, Ivy giving a little wave across the floor to Polly who was busy serving her first customers of the day.

'I've told them about Lachlan's offer.'

'We're going to go up to Applemore House after we've had a coffee and have a look around.'

'Rilla's frantically tidying as we speak,' said Lachlan, laughing.

'Oh I hope not,' said Ivy. 'I don't want to put you to any trouble.'

'It's no trouble at all,' said Lachlan. 'Honestly, it's a pleasure.'

'Thanks guys,' said Harry, feeling touched.

'Yeah,' said Rob. 'It's amazing of you to offer.'

Lachlan shrugged. 'Don't mention it. Anyway, enough with the gratitude. We've got a wedding to re-organise.'

CHAPTER TWENTY-EIGHT

'It's a castle!' Ivy turned, her mouth a perfect circle. Ben drew her close and dropped a kiss on her temple.

Rilla looked at Polly, who'd left Jenny in charge and snuck off for a quick half-hour to see Ivy's face when she saw what she was being presented with as an alternative.

'Not quite,' laughed Lachlan. 'It's the turrets, they make it look more impressive than it is.'

Polly looked up at the house she'd grown up in, seeing it through Ivy's eyes. Now the old house had been renovated, it really was quite beautiful. Tall poplars stood sentinel on either side, and a huge glass-roofed summer house had recently been rebuilt. Beth had planted all sorts of climbing plants along the sides and they gave the place an exotic look. Outside the huge wooden door hung an enormous wreath of holly and greenery, finished off with a looping bow of scarlet ribbon. Twinkling fairy lights were woven through the twin laurel bushes which sat in pots on either side of the step. The sweeping gravel drive was raked and a far cry from the weedy scrub it had been when they were growing up. In the distance, at the far end of the lawn, Polly spotted two deer grazing. She tapped Ivy gently on the arm and put a finger to her lips.

'Look.' She pointed them out.

'Oh wow,' whispered Ivy, 'They're so beautiful.'

Two seconds later there was a crash and a scrabble of eager paws as Rilla – unaware – pushed open the front door and all three spaniels hurtled out, barking with delight at the sight of the deer, and galloped off at speed down the lawn in hot pursuit.

Rilla shook her head in despair. 'Hugh, Mabel, Martha – come back!'

They stood and watched as the dogs did a circuit of the huge lawn and then – satisfied that they'd chased off the intruders – returned, wails high in the air, their chocolate-brown eyes settling on their mistress as she leaned down to pat them all.

'They're so cute,' said Ivy.

Ben shook his head, laughing. 'No, we're not taking a spaniel home. Don't get any ideas.'

'So we thought you could get married in here,' said Rilla, opening the door to the big, barely-used drawing room. In the old days, when her grandparents had lived at Applemore, they'd used it for entertaining guests – Polly had seen lots of old photographs through the years. When her dad had been alive it had ended up as the place where things that didn't have a home ended up living, and it had taken Rilla and Lachlan ages – and a skip – to clear it out before it was painted a beautiful dark green. Now there were huge squashy sofas and armchairs, along with a polished grand piano in walnut wood. Rilla had lit a fire, which gave the room a welcoming glow.

'If we move the sofas over, there's room for the registrar to conduct the ceremony by the tree – I mean the tree that'll be here,' Rilla waved her arm in the direction of an empty corner.

Ivy wiped her eye with the back of her hand.

'Are you okay?' Polly put a hand to her arm, touching her gently.

Ivy nodded. 'It's just so gorgeous and you're so lovely. I can't believe you're willing to do this.'

Rilla smiled. 'We've all had our own experience of grief, maybe that's why. I think when you know how it feels, it's easier to understand people. Does that make sense?'

Polly nodded and gave her unofficial sister-in-law a smile. Rilla had made such a difference to Lachlan and to Applemore, turning the place back into a home, helping him to fall in love with the old place again. She had a good heart.

'That makes perfect sense.' Ben gave a nod.

'And we're really lucky to have this place. We don't take it for granted.' Polly ran a hand along the old piano which had been in the family for generations.

'It's funny, I think I always thought people who lived in big houses like this were really stuck up.' Ivy wrinkled her nose. 'But you're all really normal.'

'I think if you asked most people,' said Polly, 'They'd tell you that they had misconceptions about social media influencers as well.'

Ben looked at Ivy and laughed. 'Good point. There's probably a lesson there, isn't there?'

'Definitely.' Rilla opened the door. 'Come into the kitchen, we can have a coffee and a chat. I made a lemon drizzle cake yesterday as well, if you fancy a bit?'

'I'd love some.' Ivy followed her. 'I'm ravenous after that walk.'

Polly followed them out, closing the door behind her. She popped to the bathroom and by the time she'd returned, the coffee was in the pot and everyone was sitting at

the big scrubbed oak table in the kitchen, making plans.

'We'll have a big celebration when we go back to Manchester,' explained Ivy. 'But this – we want the wedding bit to be just for us.'

'I love that you're doing it just the two of you. If I ever got married, I'd want to do exactly the same.'

Polly shot Rilla a look, eyebrows raised. 'Do I need to start shopping for a hat?'

Rilla giggled. 'No, we are happily not married, and I suspect we'll probably stay that way. It works for us.'

There was a thump from the hallway and a blast of cold air as Lachlan walked into the kitchen, covered in needles and smelling like a pine forest.

'We were just talking about your wedding,' Polly teased him. Lachlan did a double take and looked at Rilla, his brow furrowed in confusion. Rilla shook her head, still laughing.

'Have I missed a memo?' Lachlan asked, picking needles off his sweater.

'Definitely not.' Rilla leaned across, giving him a kiss. 'But we are making some plans for Ivy and Ben.'

Ben had stood up and turning, shook Lachlan vigorously by the hand. 'Thanks again. I can't tell you how much we appreciate it.'

'Don't say another word.' Lachlan returned his handshake then wandered over to the sink to wash his hands. 'Unless the word is cake, that is?'

'Funnily enough, that was next on the agenda.'

'So if there's just the two of you, do you want cake?' Polly sat up on the countertop, crossing her legs and looking at them thoughtfully.

Ivy looked at Ben. 'Well, we were hoping we might get some of those chocolate brownies instead of a proper cake,'

'Anna's brownies are amazing,' Polly agreed. 'I bet you could get her to make them into some sort of cake? It can't be that hard.'

'Don't ask Polly for catering advice,' said Lachlan, grinning. 'It's a standing joke that she's the worst cook in the family.'

'Am I ever going to live that down?' Polly groaned. She watched as Rilla pulled down an old-fashioned metal cake tin from a shelf and popped open the lid to reveal a delicious looking lemon drizzle cake, which she tipped out and started slicing thickly.

'You don't need to be able to cook when you can twist Harry round your little finger. He's an amazing chef, and he's got Conor as well.' Lachlan chuckled.

'What do you mean, twist him round my finger?' Polly felt herself going red and pulled a sheet of hair down over her face before tucking it back in place as a distraction. Rilla and Lachlan looked at her with comedy blank expressions and both shrugged in unison.

'No idea,' said Lachlan.

'Not a clue,' added Rilla.

'She won't need a chef when she's living in Manchester,' said Ben, taking a mouthful of coffee and then putting his mug down on the table.

Everyone turned to look at him for a moment, and then Rilla and Lachlan turned to look at Polly, their faces a picture of confusion.

'Manchester?'

Polly waved her hands in the air in a vague manner. 'It's nothing. Well, it might be something. I don't know.'

Ivy shot Ben a look.

'Anyway,' said Rilla, ever the peacemaker, 'shall we get back to making plans?'

Lachlan agreed.

'I'd better get back to the shop,' said Polly, glancing up at the clock. 'I've been gone for longer than I said I'd be already. Jenny's going to be having kittens, especially if it's as busy as it was yesterday.'

She said her goodbyes and headed back to the shop, where she was so flat out with work that time sped past until it was closing time before she'd realised. Cashing up the till at the end of the day she didn't hear Lachlan approaching until he was looming in the doorway.

'Hello, little sis.'

She glanced up at him and smiled. 'How's it going?'

He lifted a shoulder. 'Good. Nothing much to report. How are the takings?'

Polly looked down at the piles of coins. 'Amazing. We've done so much better this year. I think maybe having the Christmas market put the place on the map. We've had a lot more visitors coming from further afield and making an afternoon of it, having lunch with Tom and Gavin, then doing the shop and the gallery and all the rest.'

'You've built all this out of nothing, Poll. That's pretty impressive.'

She ducked her head, feeling self-conscious. Lachlan wasn't one for effusive praise.

'Anyway,' he continued, 'I suspect you know where I'm going with this?'

She made a face. 'Manchester?'

'Manchester.' He nodded. 'What the hell?'

She puffed out a long sigh. 'Ben's got a friend down there who is planning to expand. Retail stuff. It was only a conversation we had when I'd had a couple of glasses of wine at the race night.'

'And you haven't told him you're not interested?'

They both looked up and waved a brief farewell as Tom and Gavin shouted a goodbye from the door, waving as they headed back to their little cottage and Will and Fred, their little sausage dogs. Lachlan turned back to look at her, a curious expression on his face.

Polly grimaced. 'It's not – I mean, I love it here. It's just – everything's different now. You're all settled, I'm not. Sometimes I feel like I'm going to wake up one morning and realise I'm twenty years older and nothing's changed.'

'What do you mean?'

'I mean I love the shop, and I love Applemore. But maybe there's something more. I don't want to miss out.'

'Does this have anything to do with anyone in particular?'

Polly shook her head. 'Why do you ask?'

'I'm not going to get involved, Poll. But don't make the same mistake I nearly did.'

'As in –' She looked at Lachlan, who lifted both eyebrows slightly.

'Sometimes you have to make a decision to choose to be happy, and doing that means putting yourself on the line. It's always worth the risk.'

She thought of the chilly January day when he'd sped off to Paris to find Rilla and tell her he loved her. They'd cheered him on, and now – well, they couldn't be happier.

Lachlan shrugged. 'I'm not telling you what to do. I'm saying think about it.'

CHAPTER TWENTY-NINE

'CONSIDERING WHAT COULD HAVE HAPPENED, you got off pretty lightly.'

Harry, Rob and Conor were standing in the restaurant – or what was left of it. They looked up at the blackened ceiling.

'Cannae believe a fire was started by a leak. That makes no sense to me.' Conor shook his head.

'That shower in room nine. Remember it flooded the night you fell and hurt your arm? Harry picked up a piece of sodden plasterboard looked at it with dismay. 'The electrics shorted, and that's all it took. The next thing you know… whoosh. It's lucky we caught it so quickly.'

'And just as well you had a decent alarm.' Rob folded his arms and spun on his heel, surveying the room. The walls were streaked with soot and water. 'Anyway, it's only going to put us back a few weeks. We needed to rewire this part of the hotel anyway, and we've been lucky, really.'

'Imagine if it had happened after we'd renovated the rooms.' Harry grimaced at the thought.

Conor adjusted his sling. 'Well, let's be glad everyone

got out in one piece. What's happening with this wedding then? When are all the guests turning up? I was hoping she'd be inviting a load of her mates and I might get lucky.'

Rob and Harry looked at him with matching disapproving faces.

'First of all,' said Harry, shaking his head and laughing, 'They're not having guests. And if they were, I'd imagine they're hardly likely to be turning up in the hope of copping off with a stray Highlander.'

'No guests?' Conor was wide-eyed.

Harry shook his head. 'Nope, just the two of them, two witnesses – we can do that bit - and the registrar.'

'That's a bit weird, isn't it?'

'I think it's quite sweet,' said Rob. 'Not everyone wants all the showy stuff, especially if they haven't got their parents around.'

Harry glanced briefly at Conor, who clearly caught the meaning. Rob was pretty much estranged from his parents, a fact which – Applemore being Applemore – everyone was aware of.

'Whatever,' Conor dusted his imaginary lapels with his good hand. 'I'll have you know I'm a bit of a catch. I can make a mean Eggs Benedict.'

'Is that the line you use on the girls?' Rob looked at Harry and grinned. 'Maybe I should have tried that, instead of offering to order a Sausage and Egg McMuffin on Deliveroo.'

'Worked on Charlotte, didn't it?' Harry pulled out his phone, quickly checking his messages as he spoke. Nothing from Polly, he noticed, with dismay.

'Funnily enough, no, I didn't try that with her. But I got lucky anyway and somehow she's stuck with me now.'

'Looks like I'm gonna be single for a bit longer. At least

I'll have you for company.' Conor jabbed Harry in the ribs with a chuckle.

Harry winced. It wasn't the poke in the side that did for him, more the grim reality that he needed to accept nothing was going to happen with him and Polly.

The other two headed off, Rob to see how Charlotte was doing down at the Applemore Cottages office where she was dealing with a morning of admin, and Conor to catch a lift to Inverness with a friend where he was going to size up the menu of a new place that had opened by the river.

'Knock knock,' called a familiar voice half an hour later, taking advantage of a break in the clattering of Kenny and the other builders who were busy catching up now that the place had been given the okay to work on. Harry clambered over a pile of rubble and made his way over to the doorway, where Beth was standing, a twin holding each of her hands.

'Harry, guess who came to school today?' Edward grinned up at him with his gappy smile. He was holding a Christmas present, the wrapping torn off one corner, and thrust it out proudly.

'Santa Claus!' Lucy beamed. 'But Edward tried to open his present and Mummy said we're not supposed to open them until Christmas Day. Do you think that means he's on the naughty list?'

Harry looked at Beth, who rolled her eyes, laughing.

'I think you're probably okay,' he said, ruffling Edward's hair. 'What's up? Or have you just come to check out Kenny's handiwork?'

Kenny looked over and gave Beth a wave. 'How's it going?' he shouted.

'Lovely as Kenny's work is,' Beth said, 'It was you I came to see. Thought I'd pop by on the way back from the end of term carol concert to check you're okay after everything.' She waved an arm in the direction of the damage then looked into his eyes, narrowing hers slightly as she did so.

'I'm fine.' Harry pulled at the collar of his hoody. 'Lachlan and Rilla have come to the rescue, Ivy and Ben have given me a load of social media help gratis, and the insurance people reckon that this is all straightforward.'

'Everything's just great then, isn't it?' Beth said, arching an eyebrow. 'Apart from the obvious.'

He shrugged. 'Don't know what you mean.'

Beth fixed him with a look. They'd known each other forever – once upon a time people had wondered if their closeness might have led to something more, but much as he adored her and valued her friendship, that was all it ever was. The trouble was, though, that she knew him far too well. He shifted from one foot to the other.

'You know Poll's been offered an interview for a job down south?'

He took a step back, knocking his shoulder against the doorframe. 'What?'

Beth nodded. 'Manchester. Some mate of Ben's, apparently.'

A scuffle broke out between the twins, who had scampered off to sit on the wooden tables by the side of the hotel. 'He ripped my paper,' cried Lucy, indignantly.

'Did not,' muttered Edward.

Beth lifted a warning finger. 'I don't want you two fighting over presents. Father Christmas is watching, you know.'

Edward and Lucy exchanged a wide-eyed look and sat up, suddenly angelic.

'I swear I haven't had an uninterrupted conversation since the two of them were born,' Beth groaned. 'Anyway, don't shoot the messenger. I didn't know you didn't know.'

She chatted for a while longer, detailing her plans for the flowers at the wedding, but Harry didn't take in a single word.

Later that afternoon he drove up to the farm shop on the slightly spurious premise of picking up some food for dinner. There was no sign of Polly when he walked in. Jenny and a couple of the other regular workers were bustling about, serving customers and tidying up shelves, and the place was running like clockwork as ever.

'How's it going?' Gavin beckoned him over.

'Not too bad. Getting there.' Harry turned around. Almost every table at the café was full, and the air was full of chatter. 'Looks like you're raking it in. Where's Tom?'

'Out the back with Polly trying to sort something out. He needed an extra pair of hands and I said I wasn't going out there in that blooming weather. It's so cold I swear bits of me are going to freeze off if I do.'

Harry smiled. He couldn't very well hover around on the off chance that Polly returned, and even if she did right now he had literally not a clue what he'd say to her. The night they'd spent together had been amazing, and since then – despite her promise that she'd pop down and see him – he hadn't set eyes on her once. It felt very much like – despite their cheerful assurance to each other that it wouldn't change a thing – it had screwed things up royally.

'Anyway, what can I get you?' Gavin looked at him expectantly.

'Actually,' Harry made a show of taking out his phone and looking at the screen as if something vitally important had come up, 'I'm going to need to get back. I'll take a rain check. Say hi to Tom for me.'

'Will do,' said Gavin, cheerfully, with a little wave,

turning to smile at a couple who were approaching the café counter.

He crunched across the gravel, feeling despondent and reprimanding himself. Get a grip, man, he muttered. This is ridiculous.

Someone had parked their car so close to his that he had to edge in sideways and was standing, scratching his head, wondering if it was just as easy to climb in the passenger seat when he felt a tap on the shoulder. Turning, he saw Polly standing, hair twisted in two long plaits. She was pink-cheeked from the cold and her eyes looked bluer than ever, sparkling in the winter sunlight as she smiled at him.

'Hey.'

'Hi.'

'Gavin said I'd just missed you. I ran out to say hello.' She shifted slightly, crossing one long leg behind the other as she stood in the gap between the two cars.

'Well, hello to you too,' he said again. For god's sake, this was ridiculous. He was a grown adult, as tongue tied as a teenage boy faced with the girl he fancied from school.

'Sorry I haven't made it down to the hotel. It's been completely bonkers all week. And now somehow I'm helping Rilla sort the house out after hours, because she's got it into her head that she wants the place completely spotless for the wedding.'

'I should nip up and offer a hand. After all, it was supposed to be taking place at the pub. I can't just abdicate responsibility.' He'd been so flat out dealing with the admin after the fire that he'd pretty much let all thoughts of Ivy and Ben's wedding slide out of mind, letting Rob deal with whatever had to be done. He seemed more than happy to take it on. It had suited him to avoid the whole Fraser family for a bit while he worked out what the hell he was going to do – until today, when –

'Saw Beth earlier,' he said, looking at Polly and wondering if she'd say anything.

'Oh that's nice. It's the last day of term today.'

'Yeah, she had the twins. Lucy was warning Eddie he'd be on the naughty list for ripping the corner of his present.'

Polly laughed. 'The usual, then?'

'Pretty much.'

There was a long pause. A magpie hopped onto the ridge of the roof and chattered at them crossly. One for sorrow, Harry thought, giving him a vague nod in lip service to the old superstition. Normally they were comfortable in each other's company and this weird awkward silence was something neither of them seemed able to navigate.

'You'll never guess what,' said Polly, her voice slightly too bright. 'You know Ivy wanted to have a wedding just the two of them?'

'Oh yeah?' He cocked his head sideways, waiting for the news. He had a suspicion that with the change of venue to Applemore House, maybe she'd have changed her mind. The lure of showing off a place like Applemore would be almost irresistible.

'Well she's changed her mind.'

'I thought she might.' He felt oddly disappointed. It had seemed over the last weeks as if Applemore had worked its particular small-town magic. Ivy had unwound and Ben seemed far more easy-going, but in the end, he supposed, everyone reverted to type.

'Yeah, we had a really good chat about it, and she's invited anyone in the village who wants to come along.'

Harry opened his mouth and closed it again in shock. 'She's what?'

'They said that they love the way that the village has opened its arms to them and made them feel so welcome, and that she thinks her grandma would approve.'

Harry grimaced.

'What's up?'

'Well, don't I just feel like a complete heel. I was expecting her to have decided she wanted all the right people here to see and be seen.'

Polly tutted. 'You old cynic.'

'Maybe my judgement was coloured a bit,' he began, then tailed off.

'What d'you mean?'

He shook his head. Now wasn't the time to bring up the whole Manchester thing. It wasn't his place. If Polly wanted to talk about it, she'd find the right time. He jingled his car keys absentmindedly.

'Ach,' he said, giving a wave of greeting to the driver of the car who'd boxed him in, who was rushing over with an apologetic expression, 'You know what? This is one time I'm glad to be proved wrong.'

CHAPTER THIRTY

EVERYTHING MIGHT HAVE GONE wrong on the run up to the wedding, but the day itself seemed like a fairy tale. The winter cold snap had returned and the villagers of Applemore woke to a carpet of snow, deeper than any they'd seen in years.

Kirsty from the stables outside the village had lent her old fashioned carriage with her black and white pony, Puzzle, between the shafts. His bridle and the cart had been decorated with bunches of greenery and bright berries, and the seat had been covered with a white fake-fur rug. Polly rubbed Puzzle's nose as they waited for Ivy to emerge from the car which had drawn up outside the farm shop. A moment later, the door opened and Ivy – dressed in a long dark-cream dress in a thick damask silk – emerged, looking nervous and bright-eyed with excitement.

'Are you ready, love?' Murdo brushed down his black jacket and took her hand. When Kirsty had offered the carriage, he'd jumped at the chance to accompany Ivy.

'I've no daughter of my own to give away, after all, and I'd be honoured to have such a lovely young woman by my side,' he'd said. Greta had shot him a slightly narrow-eyed look after which he'd hastily added 'Of course, I've been lucky to have my lovely wife on many occasions' which had made everyone laugh.

'Ready as I'll ever be.' Ivy gave a slightly nervous giggle and stepped up onto the carriage, pulling the fluffy cardigan she was wearing around her shoulders.

'We've put a heated pad underneath the seat so hopefully that'll stop you freezing, and –' Polly passed up a fur-covered hot water bottle, 'Three hot water bottles.'

'Three?' Ivy took the first one, placing it on her knee.

'It's blooming freezing. We don't want you turning up to the house looking like an icicle.'

'Let's tuck you in,' said Murdo, solicitously. He was taking his role very seriously, and climbed up beside her, taking the reins from a slightly anxious-looking Kirsty.

'He'll be a good boy,' said Kirsty, giving Puzzle a schoolmarm-ish look, 'And I'll be following behind in the car, so if there's any trouble I'll spot it.'

'You could always drive the carriage up there and then swap places with Murdo,' said Polly, watching as Murdo – who'd insisted he didn't want a practise run – fiddled with the reins, frowning as he got the end tangled round his foot. She had a vision of him getting mixed up and the stolid, eminently sensible Puzzle shooting off at a gallop and had to suppress a giggle.

'I will be fine, thank you, Polly,' said Murdo, pulling the blanket over his knees as well. 'This thing is going to cover my kilt in white fluff, mind you.'

'Wagons roll,' said Kirsty, a few moments later. 'Polly, if you shoot up to the house and tell them we'll be about ten minutes at the most.'

Polly grabbed her bag and resisted the urge to double check that Jenny was organised and had everything under control at the shop across the courtyard. She jumped into her car and slowly overtook the horse and cart before putting her foot down and scooting up the drive towards Applemore House.

It had taken almost superhuman effort to keep the villagers of Applemore from spilling the beans. Rob and Lachlan had put their heads together and decided that if they were going to do a wedding at Applemore, they were going to do it in style.

Polly pulled up in the driveway, where cars were already lined up. The band were back, playing a jazzy version of "Jingle Bells Rock", and snow covered the wide expanse of lawn that stretched out in front of the house. They'd worked hard to reassemble the wooden market stalls, setting up a marshmallow melt and a hot chocolate factory, complete with huge vats of chocolate and bowls overflowing with chocolate chips to sprinkle on top of piles of cloud-like whipped cream.

Rob had pulled some strings with an event planner friend, and an old-fashioned helter-skelter and coconut shy had arrived the day before and been assembled as the snow fell. Polly had strung the glowing fairy lights from long poles between the stalls to give the place the air of an old-fashioned Christmas fair.

'All this for some lassie that isn't even from the village,' Dolina had tutted, the lone voice of disapproval.

'Sometimes it's nice to do something kind for the sake of it,' Joan had said, heading into the house with a still-warm tray of her delicious pancakes. 'And look at everyone. Do they not look like they're having a good time?'

Ben was standing chatting in the doorway of Applemore House with Jack, who had Lucy in his arms. Ivy's little dog Felicity was running in excited circles, yapping shrilly, a red velvet ribbon tied in a bow at her neck.

The old house looked beautiful – Polly and Charlotte had strung lights everywhere, and the big pine trees were laden with snow that had fallen overnight.

Polly looked around. She hadn't seen any sign of Harry, and was trying to pretend to herself that she didn't mind. She'd spent every spare second working on making Ivy's wedding lovely, and looking around she had to admit that they'd done an amazing job. It looked like something from a movie set – the irony was that the only people who'd see it were the villagers, Ivy and Ben. Everyone had agreed that they'd keep it off social media – even Gavin and Tom, who were champing at the bit to show off to their friends back in Wales, had grudgingly promised that they wouldn't breathe a word.

Lachlan had ushered the registrar inside, making her feel welcome and showing her into the drawing room. Polly could see them standing by the fire chatting. Joan dashed after one of the twins, who fell over into the snow with a howl of dismay.

'Let's get you dried off, little one,' she said, picking Edward up and wrapping him in a warm hug.

And then everyone heard the clip-clop of hooves and rushed to the door to gather and watch as Ivy and Murdo arrived.

'You should all be inside,' chuntered Dolina, who was standing there as well.

'And miss this?' Gavin waved an arm at the sight of black and white Puzzle trotting around the long poplar lined drive and pricking his ears in delight as he realised that there was a whole gathering of people waiting, some of whom *must* have a carrot or a mint in their pocket as a treat for him. He put on a last spurt, increasing speed, making Ivy burst into giggles and Murdo grab for the reins in alarm.

'Steady, there,' said Murdo, but Puzzle stopped of his own accord and the cart jolted slightly, sending both of them lurching forward with another burst of laughter.

'Arriving in style,' Ivy said, lifting the blanket off her knees.

'Inside, you lot,' said Joan, beckoning everyone. 'Let Ivy have her entrance.'

Ivy walked into the drawing room looking breathtakingly pretty. Her hair was pinned in a half-up style which trailed in loose waves down her back. Beth had created pretty combs of winter greenery and berries which were tucked into twists of honey-gold curls. The dress she'd ordered had arrived and been taken in by Greta, who'd nipped in the waist so it emphasised Ivy's petite size and showed off her curvaceous figure.

Ben looked at his wife to be and Polly felt a sting of regret. Would anyone ever look at her that way? She turned to look at the door. Where the hell was Harry?

'Ladies and gentlemen,' began the registrar.

'This is amazing,' Ben said, afterwards. They stood in the doorway, hand in hand, looking out at the magical scene spread before them on the lawn. 'We had no idea. I thought when you said you'd let us use the house, that was amazing enough.'

Lachlan shrugged. 'I think we all decided to run with the idea. Sorry if you were wanting it to be super low key.'

Rilla slipped in beside him, and Polly watched as she laced her fingers through his hands. 'You don't mind, do you?' She looked at Ivy, her face gathered in a sweet expression of concern.

Ivy shook her head. 'It's magical. I came here to find a connection with the past, and we've made our future.'

Outside people were standing in the snow, wrapped up in coats over fancy outfits, cupping hot chocolate and listening to the band play as they chatted and laughed. Children were squealing with delight as they whirled down the helter-skelter, shouting as they tried to hit the coconuts and win a prize at the coconut shy. Beth and Jack stole a kiss as they watched the twins – dressed in padded snow suits now – rolling about and playing on the bank by the edge of the lawn. The spaniels and Jack's terrier Archie were chasing each other through the snow, barking with excitement. Even little Felicity shot off, as white as the snow itself, and threw herself with excitement into the gang of dogs as if she too had embraced Highland village life. Through the window of the drawing room, Polly could see Charlotte and Rob embracing by the fire. It was every-thing she loved about Applemore, and her heart ached so much that she thought it might break in two. She turned away, feeling tears prickling at her eyes, making an excuse about checking in case Joan needed any help in the kitchen.

She headed along the narrow darkness of the hall, suddenly overcome with tiredness and emotion. They'd worked so hard to turn a disaster into something wonderful for Ivy and the one person she wanted to see was –

'Watch out,' said the familiar voice as she crashed into the solid wall of a suited chest. She looked up into eyes which crinkled with amusement.

'Where the hell have you been?'

'It's lovely to see you, too.' Harry had taken hold of her wrists and stepped back, looking her up and down. 'You look amazing.'

Polly felt her heart hammering in her chest. 'You weren't at the wedding?'

Harry shook his head. 'I was on my way when the loss adjuster called. They needed to sort through some details on the phone and I got stuck outside for ages. By the time I got off, the whole thing had kicked off and I didn't want to be that person who turns up halfway through and makes it all about them.'

'I thought you'd just decided not to bother.'

'And miss all this?' Harry raised his eyebrows, a smile curving on his lips. 'I don't know how you did it, but you've done it again. Charlotte told me you basically made all this happen.'

Polly shook her head. 'Rob got the helter-skelter, and Rilla did the drawing room and –'

Harry let go of one of her wrists, lifting a finger to her lips. 'Hush. You are amazing, Polly Fraser. You make things happen, and you make other people's lives wonderful.'

Polly felt the tear that had been threatening to spill over trickling down her cheek.

'What's the matter?'

She shook her head. 'It's nothing.'

Harry looked at her, a muscle flickering in his cheek. 'I wanted you to know I'd heard about the job offer.'

She took a step back, frowning. 'What about it?'

'Manchester. Ben's mate. It's great.' He was talking in a strangely staccato tone, which was most unlike him.

'Oh, that.'

'Yeah. That.' Harry lifted an eyebrow slightly.

'I –'

He cocked his head. 'You.'

Polly let out a sigh. 'I don't want to go to bloody Manchester.'

'That's a bloody relief.' Harry grinned.

'What?' He still hadn't let go of her wrist. She looked down at it for a moment, then back up at his face, which was looking down at her with an expression of such gentleness and –

'Harry, what is it?'

'The film.'

'What film?'

'When Harry met Sally. "When you realise you want to spend the rest of your life with somebody, you want the rest of your life to start as soon as possible". I hadn't ever seen the end, I fell asleep. So I watched it last night, and realised I don't care if I make an idiot of myself. I love you.'

'You do?'

'I do.' Harry drew her closer. 'And if you want to go to Manchester, we'll make it work. Hell, I'll move to Manchester if you want. I don't care. You spend your whole life making things good for other people, so if that's what it takes to make you happy, I'll do it.'

Polly shook her head in astonishment. 'I don't want to move to Manchester.'

'You don't?'

She shook her head again, more vigorously this time. 'I don't.'

'What *do* you want?'

Polly answered the question, but not with words. She curled her hand around his neck and tipped her mouth up to meet his as he kissed her, pulling her body close, not caring who might notice, until they pulled apart, breathless and both half-laughing.

'You,' she said, simply. 'That's what I want.'

.   .   .

'I should think so too,' said a voice from the other end of the hall as someone flicked the light on. There was a flurry of whispering and a second later it was followed by a roar of laughter and a round of applause from behind the kitchen door. 'Get a room you two, will you. We've got a wedding to celebrate.'

EPILOGUE

ONE YEAR LATER

IT WAS Christmas morning at the Applemore Hotel. The bar was garlanded with evergreens and hung with gold and silver stars. In the background, classic Christmas tunes were playing. There was a hum of industry from the kitchen, from which the most delicious smells were emitting as Conor and his helpers got to work, preparing the festive lunch which would be served in the restaurant in a couple of hours. Breakfast had long been cleared away, giving a brief lull in the proceedings.

Polly peered over Harry's shoulder as he smoothed out the pages of the Press and Journal newspaper from Christmas Eve. There was a huge photograph of Harry, Rob, and Conor the chef, standing in the doorway of Lochinver House, which was being redeveloped at great speed now the planning permission had finally been approved. Rob had bought the country estate, and the old Scottish Baronial style house was going to be turned into a high-end destination restaurant with rooms.

'That's doesn't even look like Rob.'

'He hates having his photo taken, you know what he's like.' Harry gave a snort of amusement.

'You'd think he was being tortured, not following his dream.' Polly giggled at the expression on her brother-in-law's face. 'Mind you he had the same look on his face in all their wedding photos and he was deliriously happy then.'

She cast her mind back thinking of the glorious day in June when Rob and Charlotte had surprised them all. She'd come a long way from the control freak uber-organised Charlotte of the past, tricking the family into turning up at Midsummer House for a wedding under the apple tree, which only Beth – who'd prepared a beautiful bouquet – had known about. It had been a rare weekend when the house - now officially open as a holiday respite for families - wasn't busy. It had been quite a year for weddings, starting with Ivy and Ben - now happily settled back in Manchester with a burgeoning social media marketing business, and then Joan and George, who'd tied the knot in the little Applemore church, with what seemed like everyone in the village there to celebrate.

'On our wedding day,' Harry said, lacing his fingers through hers and turning so they were facing each other, 'I solemnly promise not to look like that in the photographs.'

'Are we having a wedding day?' Polly went along with the joke.

Harry shrugged, his eyes twinkling with amusement. 'Possibly. Unless I get a better offer.'

'You won't get a better offer. I'm the whole package.'

They'd had this same conversation a million times over the last few months, all the time making plans, safe in the knowledge that both of them knew they'd found happiness right on their own doorstep.

'You are.' Harry drew her close as he spoke. He gently

tangled a hand in the back of her hair, so her face lifted to meet his as he found her mouth. She felt the roughness of his stubble grazing her skin and -

'What's happening here?' With a bang of the door Murdo interrupted them, clearing his throat with an over-exaggerated cough.

'Murdo, your timing is impeccable as always.' Harry pulled away, shaking his head.

Polly smiled to herself. She didn't mind sharing Harry with the village - she knew that at the end of the day, when the hotel closed its doors and the last of the regulars had wandered off into the night, he'd be hers.

'You said the bar would be open for drinks at midday on Christmas Day,' said Murdo, looking pointedly up at the clock on the wall. It was hung with fairy lights - Polly's work - and very clearly stated it was a minute past twelve.

'And here we are.' Harry grinned at Murdo, whilst raising his eyes heavenward. 'You've made it in before the pre-Christmas-dinner rush. Pint of the usual?'

'Aye, thank you. I've left Greta at the house with her mother and her sister. Might as well pour her a gin and tonic, because I suspect from the bickering I heard over the turkey she'll be joining me in a moment.'

'Family harmony at Christmas?' Harry chuckled as he started pulling a pint of beer.

'Something like that. I swear next year we're going in a cruise to the Caribbean and skipping the whole shebang.'

'And miss all this?' Polly nodded her head in the direction of the window, and together they watched as one by one the villagers trooped into the Applemore Hotel bar, where the a log fire was glowing in the grate and a huge tree from Lachlan's wood stood sparkling in the corner, filling the place with a scent of pine. She reached out a hand and took the glass of Mimosa which Phoebe - who'd appeared from the bar cellar - handed her, and said thank you.

'Aye, well, you've got a point.' Murdo shrugged, shifting over as Ben, one of the artists from the gallery, leant across to kiss Polly on the cheek and wish her a merry Christmas.

'When are you off to England?'

Ben pulled off his thick gloves and placed them on the bar along with his hat, shifting them over to peer at the photograph in the newspaper article.

'I'm driving down to get my daughter tomorrow. Is this the new place Harry and Rob are opening?'

Polly nodded. 'Now the hotel is renovated and the seafood shack is up and running, we're onto the next project.'

'You, Harry and Rob make a good team.' Ben caught Harry's eye and nodded when he pointed to a glass and his usual beer.

'Charlotte, too.'

The four of them had worked hard all year - with the farm shop up and running, it had seemed natural for Polly to get involved in the plans for Lochinver. She'd been hired officially as a consultant, and was working more and more from the sleek new office at the hotel where Rob and Harry were close to hand. There was so much to do that the days of feeling that she'd outgrown Applemore were long gone. Now the future was full of promise and excitement. It turned out that the missing ingredient had been right here all along - she looked up, sensing Harry's eyes on her, and smiled as he gave her a wink before turning back to serve Rob and Charlotte, who'd just arrived and were unwrapping scarves and shrugging off their coats, their noses pink with cold.

'You look quite at home there,' said Rob, who spotted the newspaper and folded it in half, laughing. 'Can we shove this on the fire? I saw it yesterday and Charlotte hasn't stopped teasing me about the photograph.'

'I won't tell if you do.' Polly grinned. 'Are you going up to Applemore after this?'

Rob nodded. 'Lachlan's making a buffet for everyone. Charlotte spoke to Beth earlier and apparently nobody got any sleep last night so all the parents are going to be like the living dead.'

'Hopefully they'll have recovered by tomorrow when we have our second Christmas.' Polly took a sip of the mimosa. She wasn't planning on drinking anything much - they had a busy day at the hotel and she'd offered to help, which meant that there was the bar, then Christmas lunches, and then clearing up afterwards to get through. Tomorrow the whole family were having Christmas dinner and grown-up present opening a day late, to allow for the fact they had to work.

'Poll?' Harry's voice broke into her thoughts. She looked up to see him standing by the edge of the bar, giving a brief nod in the direction of the door. 'Can you give me a hand with this thing?'

'Of course.' She put the drink down and followed him out, through the little group of villagers standing by the bar chatting.

Harry reached out a hand, pulling her gently out of the door so they stood looking out at the little harbour, and the street strung with Christmas lights. The sky was a misty blue, and frost still lingered in the shade. Their breath clouded in the air.

'What did you need a hand with?' Polly looked confused.

Harry shook his head, a smile playing on his lips and his eyes twinkling in amusement.

'Nothing.' He pulled her close. 'Just wanted to tell you I love you.'

'In the middle of everything?' Polly laughed. 'Your staff will start protesting if you start sneaking off –'

'And to give you the kiss that Murdo interrupted.' He lifted her chin gently so his eyes met hers.

A moment later, slightly breathless but laughing, he took a step back. 'That's better.'

Polly shook her head. 'You are ridiculous, Harry Robertson.'

'I am,' he agreed, taking her hand, 'But I'm yours.'

And with that they headed back inside, to the bar packed with the villagers, the promise of a Christmas holiday full of family and love, and a future full of plans.

ACKNOWLEDGMENTS

Huge thanks as always go first of all to you the reader - because this has been such a fun year of writing the stories of the four Fraser siblings, and seeing everyone fall in love with Applemore has been absolutely amazing. Reader support also saw Midsummer House become one of five finalists in the Kindle Storyteller Award this year which was a lovely surprise!

Thanks in particular to Sue and Fiona who run the Heidi Swain book group on Facebook for all their cheering of my stories, and to Heidi for being such a generous and lovely supporter of other authors. We are lucky to share an agent in Amanda Preston, who also gets an enormous cheer for all the hard work she and everyone at LBA does to sell my books to lots of different countries around the world.

A shout out and thank you to our friends Ricki and Lisa Brown who run The Mended Drum in Huby, near York. I shamelessly stole their burger ideas when I was writing Conor's pub lunch ideas, so if you read them and felt hungry, you know where to go for the real thing (which is even better than you could imagine...) and for the warmest welcome you could hope for.

Thanks and huge love to my friends (you all know who you are) who keep me sane when I'm writing. Well, sane-ish. And to my friends who wonder if I've fallen off the end of the earth when I'm writing and don't mind, huge love to you, too.

Thanks to the dogs and the children, without whom I'd probably be able to write ten books a year but life would be a lot less interesting. (I'd be a lot richer and less covered in dog hair, though, so... watch your step you lot.)

And to James - thank you, darling, for everything.

Printed in Great Britain
by Amazon

17814521R00148